Bedding the Burglar

'Turn your engine off and give me the keys, ma'am,' Griff said curtly, accepting the dark-haired beauty's picture ID. He was taking no chances on her running, especially if he found half of what he expected to on her.

She smiled coyly as she extended her wrists, palm up. 'Am I under arrest, sir?'

On the mainland there was action like this to be had all the time: pretty women with cop fetishes looking for a little nice and consensual police brutality. Yeah, this one would take it hard and deep and she'd shimmy out of that dress plenty fast to avoid getting herself a citation if the officer was anything but buck ugly.

The waft of sweet, womanly perfume nearly knocked him on his behind. 'Just stay put, ma'am.'

It was more than a little difficult to walk back to the Jeep. Hopefully she hadn't seen his erection, the little wench.

Bedding the Burglar
Gabrielle Marcola

BLACK LACE

Black Lace books contain sexual fantasies.
In real life, always practise safe sex.

First published in 2004 by
Black Lace
Thames Wharf Studios
Rainville Road
London W6 9HA

Design by Smith & Gilmour, London
Printed and bound by Mackays of Chatham PLC

ISBN 0 352 33911 X

1

It was the oldest cliché in the world: the attractive single white female luxuriating in the Jacuzzi at her beachfront home, bubbles cradling in her pert breasts, a glass of Pinot Noir nestled in her plum-frosted fingertips, scented candle on the marble counter, moonlight streaming through the open door to the balcony as she listened to the collapse of wave after silvery wave against the pure white Florida shoreline.

Except, in this case, the bather, one Magdalene Marie Quinton – known as Maggie to everyone – happened to detest warm baths and overpriced wine, not to mention scented candles. For that matter, she didn't even own the house or the Jacuzzi.

This cozy little scene was her interfering and over-bearing older sister Diane's idea – yet another in an endless series of vain attempts on the woman's part to awaken her little sister to the more sensual side of life. Maggie, as always, was oblivious to Diane's efforts. As an architect, she'd been hired to develop a multimillion-dollar resort community on remote and unsullied Osprey Island for the house's absentee owner, Cal Heeter. The project would be one of the largest ever attempted in the Florida panhandle and, by the time she was done, she'd be collecting enough in commissions and fees to build a house like this all her own.

Then she could have two Jacuzzis if she wanted and a balcony to boot. Not that she'd use them. As far as she was concerned, they could be filled in with dirt and used as terrariums, although she might go out on the balcony now and again just to look at the stars. The important thing would be to own the place. To have achieved it as a personal objective, and, of course, to have it as an investment.

Such austere notions made Diane cringe. In her opinion, Maggie's entire existence was one missed opportunity for a good time after another. It wasn't that Diane didn't like money; it was just that she didn't like to think about it or work for it.

'The world needs people like me, dear,' dark-haired Diane was fond of telling her redheaded baby sister. 'We make money look good. We give it style. Wealth would be ever so embarrassing without us.'

You could be sure, if things were reversed and a billionaire developer like Calvin Heeter Jr had given Diane a gorgeous house like this to stay in while he sailed the Caribbean in his yacht for a month, she'd have made the most of it. Maggie hardly noticed a thing about the split-level ultra-modern beach house, except the bottom line on her adding machine and the seemingly endless series of scratched-out lines on her blueprints as she sat at the kitchen table, day after day, trying to make it all fit on the oil baron's budget: four golf courses, three high-rise hotels and a shopping mall as well as a selection of four-star restaurants, all on a shoestring.

And then there was the fieldwork: scouting out sites on the island as well as overseeing the early phases of construction on Resort Tower One.

'This is my baby,' the thirty-nine-year-old son of a Texas cattle rancher had told her, stretching his porcelain-white hand out over the sprawling, palm-tree-infested vista that had been named by *Regional Geographic* magazine two years running as one of the most unsullied nature spots in North America. 'I'm turning her over to you. Bring her to life, Miss Quinton, let her suck on the imagination teat a while, and then, when I come back, we'll make sweet love to it.'

The snub-nosed, balding Cal was always talking like that, in sexual imagery, and frankly she wasn't always thrilled with the way he looked at her. As a result, she'd been doubly sure to keep everything between them beyond reproach. Some of her competitors from the larger architectural firms in Chicago had grumbled that the curvaceous five-feet-four redhead had used spread legs and not a spreadsheet to get the contract. In truth, her competitors were a bunch of jealous old farts and they could go stuff themselves. Maggie's firm was lean and mean and they'd submitted the best preliminary designs, making use of the latest in 3D graphics software.

The loudmouthed, pompous Texan might want to sleep with her, but what he was going to get was the best value for his money and nothing more. In short, an ergonomically designed, architecturally sound and aesthetically pleasing twenty-first-century environmental marvel. And Heeter knew that, too, as evidenced by the fact that he was giving her exclusive use of his million-dollar beach house to command the whole enterprise while he took his little sightseeing trip around the islands.

Maggie didn't need a billboard to recognise this as the opportunity of a lifetime, which is why she'd dropped everything, leaving her office in the capable hands of Reid and Tanya, her trusted assistants and compadres for life. One for all and all for one: that was the motto at Dream Designs, Inc. In fact, if they played their cards right, she thought, as she toasted the luscious half moon with her Venetian crystal glass, there would be beach houses for everyone when all the ribbons were finally cut.

The wine warmed her belly, raising it nearly to the temperature of the gently surging waters around her. Maybe this little Jacuzzi idea wasn't so bad after all. It was fun to think she was living it up while back home in Shy Town the streets were covered in ice and snow, forcing all the pretty boys to cover themselves in parkas and obnoxious winter hats. Down here was skin galore, with nearly every male a scrumptious fantasy feast, half naked, tanned and ready for love. Unfortunately, Maggie was having to use her imagination more than she wished because, unlike at the nearby beach resorts, the island of Osprey was a closed community of hicks, instinctively suspicious of outsiders.

Heeter in particular was anathema for his plans to convert their ancient home into a thriving vacation site for Yankee tourists. Police Chief John 'Griff' Grifford, a stern, fatherly sort just shy of fifty with silver-black hair, had warned her to watch her step and to be respectful of island sensibilities. Whatever that meant. Frankly, she thought the man was a hunk, with his blue eyes and cleft chin and that very solid body under his khakis. His one and only officer, the much younger Mike Cosgrove, was a looker, too, with his brush-cut hair and cute little moustache. Definitely an athlete of some kind.

Leaning back, Maggie let her hand stray down to her left nipple, already peaked. Mike Cosgrove was six feet tall, not an ounce of fat on him, and she would dearly like to strip that tan uniform and badge off him and throw him down on the nearest flat surface. Preferably a bed, though the beach would do fine in a pinch. Maggie's taut, well-exercised belly quivered in anticipation as her naughty finger strayed lower. Something

4

about this hot water and this soft, sexy atmosphere was making her need a man – or at least the dream of one.

Tweaking her swollen nipples one after the other, she won from herself a moan. Would a man like Cosgrove ever give her the time of day, sexually speaking? After a week here she'd learned that the dreamy young cop was unattached, though he kept company with a hot little blonde, a stripper at a club called Diamond Pete's. Katy Sue was every guy's fantasy, and she also happened to be married, though she didn't act it. One time Maggie had seen Cosgrove kissing her, the girl's slim, barely dressed body sandwiched between his muscles and the rear door of his squad car. There was no doubt from the look of it that he was going to get lucky. Probably in the back seat or maybe back at the station.

Maggie would definitely give him a go, showing him what a city girl could do with her mouth, tits and pussy. She wouldn't say no to that police chief, either. He might be as old as her father, but he was far from over the hill. Spreading her legs, Maggie worked her fingers into her tingling, waterlogged opening. Chief John Grifford could fill a hole like this, she was sure of it. The buzz down at the island's only restaurant, Barnacle Bill's Seaside Diner, was that Griff had split with his wife some years ago and hadn't been with anyone else since, except a crazy witch-woman on the far side of the island named Star Shine, who supposedly danced naked, tits swinging under the light of the full moon.

You had to love these rural people and their colourful ways. Her thoroughly urbanised and proper sister Di would freak out if she ever came down here from Chicago – though she would certainly enjoy the male scenery. There were the local construction hunks working on the tower, and a sprinkling of college boys too, early spring breakers renting some of the big new beach houses nearby. Maggie had seen three of them yesterday on a speedboat, a fourth in tow on water skis. They gave her war whoops and hollers, which at the age of thirty-one she found damned encouraging, not to mention flattering. They were even waving handfuls of those cheap coloured glass beads at her, which, according to Tanya Moore, her twenty-three-year-old ambassador to the Youth Culture of America, was a very direct invitation for a desirable girl to bare her breasts, often for the benefit of a digital or video camera.

'Oh yeah, that's a compliment,' pixie blonde Tanya had enthused over the phone when Maggie had called in this morning to trade her newest adventures for the latest reports on the dozen or so other projects Dream Designs was engaged in at the moment. 'Trust me.'

'I'm sure it is,' she'd retorted. 'But you'll forgive me if I'm a bit leery of winding up topless on the Internet.'

'Might help business, though,' had piped up her twenty-seven-year-old junior architect and general wise-ass back-up man, Reid Fuller.

And wouldn't that just thrill mommy and daddy, too, not to mention her self-appointed though horribly unqualified guardian of morals, the ever-vigilant Diane, who had got more mileage out of her six years of seniority than any big sister in history.

Then again, maybe that was just the sort of reason she needed for doing something so outrageous: just to shake things up a bit in the house on fashionable Lake Shore Drive that the elder Quintons called home.

Settling back, Maggie worked on conjuring the scene. The boat-load of hunks steaming past, flashing their sunlit beads, taunting her till she finally gives in, untying the back of her sky-blue string bikini, revealing her not too large, not too small set of hooters. But, unlike the rest of the girls who strutted their stuff for the flashing cameras, Maggie wouldn't just be teasing. She'd be offering herself, letting them know as she cupped herself, pushing her bouncy globes up and out, that she was ready for action, ready to put her money where her nipples were, so to speak.

They'd circle round a couple of times, checking her out, deciding if she was going to be worth their while. Feeling like a total tramp, she'd continue advertising, sliding her hands down her torso, letting her fingers slip into the front of her bikini bottoms and then turning for them, bending over low so they'd see the ass that came with the package.

She'd be competing against all the little nineteen- and twenty-year-olds with their gravity-defying bodies, but in the end she'd hold her own and those college jocks would come steaming towards her over all the others. She'd be afraid for a moment as they pulled ashore calling her bluff, but the looks on their faces would be too big a turn-on to resist. Not to mention the swells in their swimming trunks. Big young college cocks, barely constrained. The group of horny boys would want her quickly and without fuss or muss. She'd be more than accommodating, welcoming the hungry hands on her body. Eager young hands, the hands of well-endowed studs, mauling the breasts they'd so enjoyed viewing at long distance. Rubbing and caressing her stomach, tugging apart the ties of her tiny bikini pants, exposing her cunt and ass.

Touching herself expertly, Maggie pictured them now, slipping off their shorts, vying for the right to be first, pushing and shoving good-naturedly, giving her a view of their lean, fat-free bodies in action. Smooth, muscled torsos, protruding pecs and large, tasty nipples. She's so wet, and so ready. She tells them there's room for all, no waiting. Down she goes, onto all fours, so she can take them on, two at a time. One dick in front, plunged between her lips, while another is accommodated with laughable ease down the channel of her slick sex. They go at her like this all afternoon, shooting themselves off, switching places, using her with general abandon. Pure libido with no limits.

Happily, she lets them do anything, showing them all the things their coed girlfriends would be too timid to try, like anal intercourse. Allowing them the pleasure of blasting one's load between a woman's squeezed-together breasts. They could even jerk off all over her body, standing over her while she writhed at their feet, fucking herself like an animal, not caring what anyone thought, as long as she was getting herself off and they were being turned on watching her – her and no one else. Not the girlfriends, not the pinups or video queens, just little old Maggie to pump their loads onto. The come would spray down on her like a hot, sticky rain, in her hair and all over her face, down her neck, on her chest and stomach and even in her eyebrows.

Maggie had all she needed now to finish her Jacuzzi fantasy. One finger jammed deep in her hole, another flicking across her nearly drowned clitoris. All those boys. All those spurting cocks. Just a moment more and she'd be over the edge.

Or so she thought.

The banging noise could not have come at a worse time. Freezing mid-stroke, her concentration blown, she cursed Rosco for whatever feline trouble he had gotten himself into this time. How did animals know when humans were having sex, anyway? Because they sure never missed a chance to ruin it.

Letting out a cry of exasperation, she called out to her bevy of imaginary studs. 'Come back,' she cried, trying to stop them taking off again in their imaginary boat over the imaginary ocean without offering so much as an imaginary goodbye. 'Don't leave me like this.'

'Men,' muttered Magdalene Marie Quinton, extricating herself from paradise and stepping onto the cold hard tiles of reality.

She really did wish her goofball cat would get the hang of this place. As it was, the neurotic angora was forever under her feet or else trying to hide in whatever cramped spaces it could squeeze its bloated body into. Maybe she should have left Rosco with Tanya and her brood of strays, but Cal had been insistent she bring her feline buddy along so she'd feel as comfortable as possible. This in itself was a testimony to how much he valued her work. Of course, the oil baron had also made her sign a binding agreement rendering her liable for all damage from cat claws, cat hair or any other havoc a feline might create.

'You're killing me, Rosco,' she quipped en route to the master bedroom via the living room. 'Do you have any idea how long it takes to dream up a good gangbang?'

Maggie's monologue was cut short by the sight on the other side of the door. It wasn't a cat making the noise, but a much larger, far more dangerous creature: a handsome hunk of a man wearing nothing but a pair of dark-blue Speedos.

He had his back to her and was looking casually through Calvin Heeter's jewellery box, oblivious. A pole lamp was beside him, on the floor. Not a very careful intruder, she thought. All in all, quite a sight: wet, like herself, broad-shouldered and defined but not overly muscled, his long sandy-brown hair hanging mane like down his sinewy neck.

Maggie was still frozen there, her busy mind processing the various options for fight or flight, when the burglar turned to face her. She nearly swooned. The guy was like a refugee out of her Jacuzzi fantasy, his eyes the deepest green she'd ever seen, almost jade, piercing like a hawk's, his features finely chiselled and covered with a three-day growth of beard, baby-soft, nearly the colour of spun gold. For several heartbeats they simply stared at one another till finally the intruder broke the silence.

'No one's supposed to be here.' He creased his forehead. The note of irritation in his voice seemed to Maggie somewhat bold, under the circumstances.

'Sorry to burst your break-in bubble,' she replied, spitting out the Bs like machine-gun bullets. 'But, as you can plainly see, I *am* here, which means you have exactly thirty seconds to get the hell out of my house before I call the police.'

The bare-chested Greek god in Speedos cocked his head. 'Your house?' His voice was pure drawl, sexy as hell. 'What are you, then? Heeter's not married, so that would make you either his girlfriend or his whore. Which is it?'

Maggie grabbed a small stone Buddha off the shelf by the armoire and brandished it with malevolent intent. 'I'm neither, you sick son of a bitch. Consider your thirty seconds expired.'

'I don't mean any offence,' he explained soberly, as if he had some honour worth preserving in her eyes. 'I simply attempted to draw the logical conclusion, given your remarks and your, shall we say, lack of attire.'

Maggie looked down, realising for the first time that she was stark naked. 'Don't you dare look at me,' she cried. She dropped the Buddha onto the plush dusty-rose carpet in a vain attempt to cover her still-aroused privates.

'It's a little late for that, ma'am,' pointed out the lazily drawling robber with the ill-disguised ten-inch erection. 'Although, if it's any consolation, I've taken a vow of celibacy.'

This guy was unbelievable. Did he really think he could get away with this just because he was cute and eminently beddable?

'No, it's not a consolation, you asshole,' she fumed. 'You've just broken into my house, drooled over my naked flesh and insulted me, all in the space of five minutes.'

'Who said I was drooling?'

'Excuse me?' Maggie adjusted her hands, one arm across her bosom, the other over her crotch.

'You're assuming that I find you attractive.'

She arched her eyebrows, indicating his crotch, the swollen cock and balls blatantly outlined under the absurdly tight Lycra. 'Well, if you don't, Tarzan, you're sure doing a pretty good imitation.'

Good grief, Maggie thought. Why am I doing this? My heart's going ninety miles an hour, this guy could kill me any moment now and I'm trying to score bitch points.

'Adrenalin is stimulatory in males,' he said flatly. 'It's completely asexual. Besides, you're changing the subject. We need to discuss our situation and how to resolve it.'

Maggie shook out her shock of damp copper curls with as much insolence as humanly possible. '*Our* situation? What, do we have a relationship now? Why don't we just go on one of those stupid talk shows? They could call the segment "Lady Hostages and the Psychos Who Kill Them".'

'You know I wouldn't hurt you,' he said with sudden, melting sincerity. 'You're not really afraid of me, and you're not even angry with me for being here.'

'Angry? Of course not,' she snorted sarcastically, trying to keep herself from falling at his feet. 'I'm thrilled. How many women get to be burgled and psychoanalysed all in one night? And pray tell, Doctor Freud, just how did you come to such brilliant conclusions?'

'Because you haven't tried to run. Nor have you tried to attack me.'

He was right and she hated that. This combination of brawn, country charm and Oxford intellect was not only unprecedented, it was also downright fatal.

'Why bother?' she retorted. 'You're obviously bigger and faster than me.'

'You could use that cane over there –' he inclined his head to the old-fashioned umbrella stand close to the door '– if you really wanted to stop me.'

Again, he had a point. Maggie scowled, treating him to her patented laser-beam stare, the one Di had insisted was capable of penetrating lead at twenty paces. 'What exactly are you insinuating, buster? You think I get off on strange men popping up in my bedroom half-naked in the middle of the night?'

She winced slightly at her choice of words. That hadn't come out right, had it?

The burglar smiled slantedly, clearly amused. 'To use your own words: if you weren't, then you were doing a pretty good imitation when you saw me.'

Her nipples! They'd been hard as rocks and still were. He could probably smell the heat between her legs, too. Well, she hoped he was enjoying himself, because it would be a long time till he got this close to a woman again. With any luck, he'd be rotting behind bars in the next half-hour.

'Look,' she said, doing her best imitation of the naïve, distressed damsel wooed by the charm of her captor. 'If you go now, I'll agree not to call the cops. You look like a decent guy, down on his luck. I can even give you a few bucks to tide you over, till you get where you're going.'

'Oh, really?' He put his hands on his lean hips, the neon eyes and dimples lighting up as if he was enjoying this. 'And may I ask the motive for this sudden act of generosity?'

Maggie licked her lips. 'I'm a softie for desperate, on-the-edge types. Ask my sister if you don't believe me.'

The burglar put his hands together, slapping them several times slowly in simulated applause. 'Bravo. Fine performance. Of course, we both know the minute I'm out of sight you'll be on the phone blabbing your little red head off.'

'I won't,' she lied. 'You have my word.'

'Spoken under duress.' He shook his head. 'It has no meaning.'

Maggie snorted. Who was this guy? He looked like a surf bum and talked like a Harvard professor with a twang.

'For the record,' he told her now, 'I am not a thief. My cause is just. Lady Liberty is at my back.'

'Yeah, you're a regular Robin Hood. Now, would you mind telling me what you intend doing with me?'

He thought for a minute, the shimmering emerald eyes busily flashing. 'I believe I will have to tie you up,' he informed her, not cracking a smile.

'You can't be serious.'

'In fact I am. Do you have any rope?'

Maggie laughed without humour. 'You actually expect me to provide rope for you to tie me with? What kind of burglar doesn't even come properly equipped?'

13

'The kind that isn't expecting any naked nymphs to be cavorting about while he's trying to work, that's what kind.'

'I'm not a nymph,' she shot back. 'And I was certainly not cavorting.'

He was standing there, just looking at her, not leering but examining. Tranquil, almost possessive, as if he had every right in the world to be here. For some reason the idea made Maggie feel hot and weak all over.

'Why are you staring at me like that?' she demanded.

'Like what?'

'Like you're going to ask me on a date or something.'

'Do you want me to?'

'When hell freezes over.' She turned up her nose. 'There's rope in the garage. I'm sorry, but we're fresh out of gags.'

'That won't be necessary. No one will hear you if you scream.' He took her hand, escorting her out through the living room. The contact made her pulse race. His grip was strong and capable and almost gentle. Why do I always meet men at the absolute wrong time and place? she lamented. A guy like this would have drawn her like a moth to fire at a club any night of the week. Of course, it was her propensity for choosing complicated, troubled men like this that had led her to focus on her career and not her love life in the first place.

Heeter kept plenty of rope for his boat in the carport. Finding the burglar a sufficiently long coil of it, Maggie allowed him to lead her back inside to the kitchen.

'This looks like as good a place as any.' He held out one of the high-backed stools at the breakfast island for her to sit on.

'Haven't you forgotten something?'

He blinked.

'I'm naked,' she said acidly, peeved at having to remind him. 'If you don't mind, I'd rather not be found by Sheriff Andy and Deputy Barney in my birthday suit.'

He cocked his head. 'Sheriff who?'

'Andy.' She glared in disbelief. 'You know, from the old Andy Griffith show on TV? That's what this place reminds me of: Mayberry, if it were an island.'

'Hmm.' He nodded, grasping the reference with all the hip aplomb of a Martian trade delegate. 'I'm afraid I don't watch much television.'

Maggie rolled her eyes. 'Just let me get something to wear, OK?'

Why she chose nothing but the floral silk robe on the bathroom door and a pair of pink panties, she didn't know. The robe was sheer and short and not at all decent. She should be getting jeans, a sweatshirt – as much clothing as she could find. But she didn't want that, didn't want her body hidden from the man. Didn't want to lose her chance at . . . what, exactly?

Sitting up on the padded stool she found her crotch at the same level as his. Close up, she could smell the sea on him and the sand and the sun. She suspected he'd been outside for some time, though he wasn't sour or dirty. It was as if the island had showered him in the natural fragrances of the coloured flowers she'd seen everywhere around her, and the lush green plants.

'You'll need to sit back,' he told her.

Was it her imagination or had his voice softened, becoming just a tiny bit more intimate?

Maggie complied, putting her spine against the back of the stool. The fabric of the seat tickled her barely covered buttocks and crotch. Shivers ran up the back of her calves, where the metal of the stool legs pressed against her flesh. As many times as she'd sat here this week eating her grapefruit and yogurt, she'd never imagined it feeling like this.

'Tell me if it's too tight.'

The first coil of rope cinched Maggie's stomach, just above her belly button. 'It's fine,' she whispered as he drew it firmly round her arms, pinning them to her sides.

He worked quickly but carefully, drawing loop after loop, each coil imprisoning her flesh that much more. At the same time, he was unleashing her sexual heat. The more closely restrained she felt above, the freer and more exposed she felt below the waist. It was as if each coiled cinch was squeezing her open, causing her to moisten between her legs just a tiny bit more. Such a strange combination, to have this man over her with so much power, putting her into harsh bondage and yet seemingly so concerned and protective of her at the same time.

She listened to his breathing as he worked, his mouth close to her ears, his heart by her chest. And those hands – the little touches of his fingers, grazing the skin through the silk robe, sending tiny jolts of electricity straight to her core.

'You're sure it's not too tight?' he asked again, leaning in too close, mouth-to-mouth, electric sparks arcing between question and answer.

'No,' she replied, her lips meeting his.

Maggie hadn't intended the kiss, but here she was, her mouth opening, her tongue fencing with his. Releasing a moan that spilled between his lips, she tried to reach for him. It was a supreme frustration not to be able to touch him, or even to be able to position herself to be touched. On the other hand, there was a whole new thrill in being helpless before him, utterly vulnerable to any touching he might wish to do. Straining at the ropes, pushing herself towards him like the booty she'd become, she gave him licence, encouraging him the only way she knew how. He took her breasts first, running his fingertips over the silk that barely constrained the eager nipples. The way he'd tied her above and below the bosom, she was sticking out that much more, the captive mounds almost begging him to strip the halves of the robe open and gain unbridled access.

It didn't take long for him to catch the hint. Maggie threw back her head as he sank his teeth into the throbbing nubs of her nipples. It was wrong for him to take her this way and they both knew it – wrong on so many levels, and yet it was happening, skin-to-skin, male to female, the very tumult of their encounter only heating things further. Talk about ready: wantonly, shamelessly she spread her legs as best she could, taunting him to take his tethered prize, acting like the very whore he'd accused her of being.

Maggie's submission hung in the air, her ripeness for exploitation, but there was no cruelty in his answering touch. In the end, he was as tender as he was hungry for love. Her lonely, petulant burglar, as frightened of her as she was of him – and just as horny.

She shuddered as his palms slid over her belly. Impossible! She was close to orgasm already, without even being touched there. Sucking in her breath, she rippled her stomach, undulating, inviting, teasing him lower.

He was holding himself back, sampling her neck, savouring and anticipating a handful of muff. Maggie's fists clenched as she tugged at the bonds on her arms, wishing she could somehow topple herself back so he could climb on top of her, or else push him forwards so he could spear her from above.

Yes, under the waistband of her panties, that was where she wanted his hand. He knew where to go with his crawling fingers. All men would, if they knew enough to follow their instincts. Could he smell her? How could he miss it? Oh, God, he was going straight for the clit. That mother-fucking, totally-below-the-belt bastard, he was going to make her come – tied up, the victim of a complete stranger, a felon. Unbelievable: she was going to have to share her most intimate sexual self with him, a part of her that few of her lovers had ever reached, and it was going to be in a kitchen, not even her own.

In a last-ditch effort, Maggie tried to hold to a scrap of her pride. What kind of woman could be manipulated like this? What kind of female took pleasure from such treatment? It was beyond shame. There was no resisting, though. Not now, not after all this.

'More,' she screamed. 'More, you fucking bastard!'

The burglar froze, his attention diverted by the sudden sound of approaching sirens.

'No,' she moaned, her release still hanging in the balance. 'Damn it, no!'

The rest was a blur. By the time Maggie cleared her head enough to focus on her surroundings, the burglar was gone. A few moments later, the others came. Mayberry's finest.

Chief Grifford took one look at her, covered her blatantly exposed, heaving breasts with the dining-room tablecloth and frowned. 'Search the house,' he told Officer Cosgrove. 'Inside and out.'

Cosgrove was off in a flash.

'Are you hurt?' he asked discreetly, reaching for a knife in his belt to cut the rope. If he was noticing her flushed cheeks, the odour of her sopping wet panties, he was keeping it to himself.

Maggie shook her head, unable to speak. Thighs clamped tightly together, she was trying to hold it all in, to keep it together in front of the no-nonsense lawman. Would it be considered against the chief's 'island sensibilities' right now if she asked him or Cosgrove to lay her over Heeter's genuine pirate sea chest in the living room and fuck the daylights out of her? Or maybe both of them at once, like in her Jacuzzi fantasy.

'Can you tell me what happened, or do you need a few minutes?'

'A few minutes,' she said hastily, wanting to give her mysterious would-be lover as much of a head start as possible. 'If you please.'

Run fast, she thought as the police chief finished pulling away the severed ropes. Don't let them catch you. Not tonight.

2

Ketch was not going to make it. Somehow, the Fates had conspired against him, decreeing that his noble quest should go down in failure, a shooting ball of flames, to be exposed to the ridicule of his enemies, chief among them the Great Thief and Dream Smasher, Calvin Heeter.

First of all, there had been a female in the house, a naked dryad to seduce and weaken his purpose. Next, he'd been betrayed to the authorities, the peace officers of the island somehow having been summoned, unbeknownst to themselves, to prevent his great act of justice. And finally – and this was the greatest blow of all – his one means of escape, the appropriated Sea Doo that had conveyed him to Osprey from the mainland, was no longer functioning. Sabotaged, in fact, with the ghastly insertion of sugar into the fuel tank.

By all the gods, who would do such a thing?

He needn't ask the question, of course. There was only one person who would sink so low and he could only pray that she was miles and miles away – across another solar system, preferably.

Running down the beach was no simple matter with the raging hard-on he had acquired in his dealings with the dryad. She was a redhead, with fiery gold-brown eyes and sweet aureoles, perfectly centred by nipples of the most delicious taste and texture. She had come to him unclothed and sweetly fragranced, the juices of her own desires already loosed. Who else but the dark trickster-god Pan would impose such a torture upon him? And she was no fool, either, this red-haired female. She spoke with the tongue of Athena and, whenever he saw her lips move, he felt irresistibly drawn to touch, to possess. What else could a man do, confronted with the finely fleeced copper-red pelt, that blatantly available slit so exquisitely nestled between white, white thighs and flaring hips?

It had taken all his restraint not to fuck her, thereby compromising his mission entirely. Tying her had been for her benefit as well as his. If not for the protection of the rope, sealing her body to the chair, he'd have had her on the floor, tasting her charms, filling her with cock, ranging over her breasts with his ravenous mouth. As it was, even with the awkward containment of the ropes, he hadn't been able to keep his hands off her, hadn't been able to resist feeling those curves, one piece of her flesh leading inevitably to another till he was doing all the dirty things she obviously wanted.

Who was she, anyway? Surely not the man's girl-friend. It would be too cruel a joke for such a lithe creature to be allowed to fall into the possession of the Tyrannical Waster of Air known as Calvin Leroy Heeter, Junior. She was a flower of beauty, a petal of desire, a breath of freshest springtime. Was she a relative, then? An unfortunate niece? Or some sort of serving wench?

More importantly, to Ketch's way of thinking, had she been discovered in a compromised state after his hasty departure? He'd done things to her anatomy, rather unwittingly, and after he left there wouldn't have been much time for her to calm down before the police arrived.

That last image bothered him somewhat, thinking of her being found like that. It didn't matter that she was a stranger to him. Ketch was an upholder of gentlemanly principles. He did not use and titillate women for his own enjoyment. Actually, he'd sworn off the gender entirely, thanks to a certain Supremely Traitorous Madwoman, who, the more he thought about it, was probably behind both the vandalism of his Sea Doo and the untimely arrival of the law.

Her name was Stella Sawgrass and she was the sweetest, most deadly mix of shanty Irish and Seminole Indian the world had ever seen. For the likes of her, a man risks his very reality, like Odysseus facing the sirens, and he will go down happily, babbling in mind-numbing madness.

Curse this hard-on, anyhow! Arms pumping, legs striding, you would think the blood would be diverted, but he still wanted her, the dryad, and he was still furious at the other one, the dark-haired witch-woman Stella, whose taste was firewater to a man's soul. Perhaps the danger heightened things, just as he'd bluffed to the redhead. The police had arrived quickly behind him and they were bound to start searching the beach-front any minute now, bearing down with vehicles, boats and perhaps even a helicopter from the mainland, depending on how slow a night it was crimewise.

His only hope was to make the three miles back to the bridge on foot and somehow convey himself across, either on top or underneath. It was a long shot at best. The only alternative was swimming the Gulf with its various nasty, teeth-filled predators.

Ketch shielded his eyes from the sudden burst of headlights in his face. Was it the cops? No. It was just an ordinary civilian van. Or was it?

'Climb in,' called Stella, leaning out of the passenger window, her impossibly long black hair fluttering like the wings of a thousand moon bats, clamouring to return to their celestial home.

'Go to hell,' Ketch pronounced, clinging to his last scraps of dignity. 'I'd sooner crawl into a nest of scorpions.'

'We could arrange that,' she offered, as though it were a serious proposal. 'Or maybe just a little spanking, hmm? You know you like it when I skin down your pants and paddle your tight little behind. We could pick up some boys on the mainland to help.'

'Stella, if it isn't too much trouble, I am attempting to escape a felony.'

'I know.' She nodded matter-of-factly. 'I'm the one who called the cops.'

'*Et tu, Brute*,' he muttered, his suspicions confirmed.

'Ooh, I love it when you talk French.' She pushed open the passenger door of the bizarrely painted VW microbus. 'Hop in and we'll check out your baguette.'

'It's not French, Stella, it's Latin, and I'm not getting in there. Or have you forgotten how the last time we were together you drugged me, stole my money, sold all my worldly goods at the flea market and left me for dead at the Turkey Lake Service Plaza off the Turnpike?'

'We did have a little tiff,' she agreed, making the biggest understatement since Napoleon had called Waterloo a minor setback. 'But that was four months ago.'

Ketch saw the headlights coming down the beach. A single police cruiser with a side-mounted searchlight. It was some distance away, driving very slowly, stopping every ten feet or so, but it would be here quickly enough. 'Goodnight, Stella. I wish I could say it was a pleasure.'

'You really better accept my help,' she advised. 'I called the State Patrol as well. You're going to need wheels.'

Ketch climbed onto the torn leatherette seat, cursing

the woman's name in every language he could think of. 'Here.' He held out his wrists. 'Why don't you take a razor blade to them and finish the job once and for all instead of bleeding me drop by drop?'

'Just remember who's here for you in a pinch,' she reminded him, putting the van in reverse and depressing the accelerator to the floor.

Ketch held on for dear life, barely avoiding an untimely union with the windshield. 'It doesn't count if you create the disaster in the first place, Stella, and, for Zeus's sake, watch where you're driving. You're going to get us killed.'

'You see, that's your problem.' She turned her gaunt, lightly boned yet maddeningly beautiful face towards him, ignoring that she was propelling them backwards at fifty miles an hour. 'You're always looking to blame others for your troubles. Whose fault is it you broke into the house of the richest man on the island?'

'And why, pray tell, did I do that, Stella?' He craned his neck for potential obstacles. Of all the possible times to get into a debate over the long, tragic story of how this woman had cruelly cast off his most prized possession, allowing it to come into Heeter's hands, this had to be the worst.

Which of course meant Stella would not be able to resist. Slamming on the brakes, sending the bus shimmying sideways into a near roll-over ending in a dead stop, she readied herself to take up the topic more intensely.

Could he do anything but laugh at this point?

'Great camouflage job, Stel.' He noted the deep gouges in the wet sand a hundred feet in front of them. 'We're leaving a trail a two-year-old could follow. But, hey, that cop will be here in a minute, anyway, so what does it matter?'

'I don't want to argue.' She waved her blacker-than-black nails like a witch over a cauldron. 'Not on the night of our reunion.'

He reached over to shift the stopped vehicle back into drive. 'Hades forbid. Just drive, woman. The sooner I'm back on the mainland and away from you the better.'

She pushed him off with surprising strength, as always a mass of adrenalin. 'Don't invoke your foolish deities in this vehicle,' she warned. 'I'm the driver, and that's that.'

Ketch knew better than to argue. His best shot was to let her cool off. Sure enough, she let thirty seconds or so pass, then turned the van round, beating a hasty retreat from danger.

'Here!' He pointed, seeing an exit off the beach onto the main road. 'That will take us back to the bridge.'

'I don't want to go back to the bridge yet,' she announced, pulling into an empty space in the parking lot of Huggable Harry's Gulfview Inn instead. 'I want to fuck first.'

'What!?'

'A makeup fuck,' she explained, crawling across in her dangling, beaded vest and skintight black jeans. 'And don't get all pious on me – I can see you have a load all ready to shoot. It's OK, honey, the redhead was a real looker. I forgive you for trying to pop her cork.'

Ketch forgot fighting her off for the moment. 'You watched us?'

Stella rotated his seat to the middle, sank to her knees between his legs and grabbed hold of the waistband of the Speedos. 'Yep. Tell me that doesn't turn you on, knowing I saw the whole thing, you and that little paleface slut, playing cowboys and Indians. What would you have done if the cops didn't show, huh, baby? She wanted it bad, wanted it hard and fast while she was all tied up and helpless. No guilt, no responsibility, just an anonymous fuck at the mercy of a big handsome stud.'

Stella had his cock out and was slurping vigorously, as if she'd just been bitten by a cobra and the antidote she needed to stay alive was inside the end of that long fleshy tube. There was no denying it: no one could give head like Stella Sawgrass. The way she sucked was the way she lived life, with total abandon, no forethought and a complete and utter immersion in the irrational. It was as if the cock had a life of its own and she was making love to it, biting and chewing and playing.

'We can't do this,' he croaked with his last shards of reason. 'The cops are going to be all over this place in a minute, Stella.'

'The more the merrier.' Stella relaxed her mouth, swallowing most of the length of him in one smooth motion, the fan of her hair covering him like a second skin.

'You're asking for it,' he groaned, sounding more like a man hit by a stray arrow than a participant in a lovemaking act. 'You crazy bitch.'

'Don't say it with your talking.' She released him, allowing the cool air to torture his wet, throbbing organ. 'Say it with your fucking.'

Stella's smile represented pure and total victory as he gave in to the urge to grasp the nearest handful of hair, dark and twisting as the River Styx. It was, of course, all according to her plans. All along she'd known what he would say, what he'd do and how it would all end.

'Get in back,' he told her, his voice lowered to that pitch and tone they both knew so well. 'And take off your clothes.'

Her breathing was quick, her eyes bright. In their lovemaking they were switches, taking turns calling the shots. This was going to be his. 'How do you want me, Ketch?'

'All fours, facing away.'

Stella pursed her lips. 'You're angry this time, aren't you? Really angry?'

She was getting off on this idea, just as she was over the knowledge that she was completely and utterly fucking up his life. Again.

'I'm gonna spank your ass,' he declared.

'Paddle's under the seat.'

As if he didn't know that. 'Just strip, Stella, and get down on the floor like the little witch you are.'

Stella was more than happy to crawl onto the mattress in the back, her tail wagging like a cat's. It was an aphrodisiac, that ass, and the mouth and pussy too. If only she didn't speak with that mouth, if only she wasn't his mortal enemy outside of bed.

'I called the cops on you,' she reminded him, skinning down her jeans and black lace thong.

'Just assume the position, Stella, and can the chatter.'

She was a tiny, slender woman and kneeling like this, on all fours, she could almost fool you into thinking she was vulnerable. A lesser man might fear he was taking advantage of the invitation to redden those hindquarters and afterwards plunder them in a full-on frenzy, oblivious of the normal rules of courtesy that require the man to hold back till his partner is satisfied.

The truth was that Stella Sawgrass took care of herself, orchestrating her orgasms, her little stage dramas and whatever else she needed in life. About the only thing you could really do to piss her off and end the game was tell her you loved her, which had been his mistake four months ago.

'What the fuck, Stella, this isn't a paddle.' Ketch held up the slim black riding crop that had taken the place of the more innocuous punishment device.

'Oh? Maybe somebody switched them when I took the van into the shop last week.'

Ketch's dick was straining. If he didn't get some pussy fast, he was going to be redecorating the red-curtained interior of the microbus in contemporary spunk. 'Cut the crap, Stella, this is a real whip.'

'And this is a real ass,' she said wiggling. 'You do the math.'

Ketch gritted his teeth. OK, so he was tempted to whip her. But he also wanted to screw her in whatever orifice he could get to first. 'You don't need a whipping, Stella, you need a good hard fucking.'

'Do it, then.' Stella lowered her head to the surface of the mattress, using her tiny hands to pull the hair away from her back and ass. 'You're cleared for take-off, cowboy. Show me just how much of a little bitch I am. And make it count, because, once the cops get here, this is as close to a woman as you'll be getting in a long, long time.'

Was there no limit to this woman's gall? She must have really wanted him all fired up to fuck her, that's all he could figure. 'I'm going to take you in the ass, Stella, so you better be ready.'

She wriggled it in his face. 'What if I'm not?' she taunted.

He grabbed her hips firmly to keep her in place, making use of his tensile hand and arm strength, acquired through a year and a half of working tyres on the pit crew of Bobby Joe Sutherland's Nascar team, not to mention six months on the professional rodeo circuit and a stint in the Marines.

'Tighter,' she urged. 'I need you to hold me tighter.'

Thinking of tightness made him think of ropes and that made him think of the red-haired nymph who was so hard to put out of his mind. That first touch, and the others besides, was unlike anything he'd ever experienced. What a paradox the copper-haired woman was – so strong and sassy, hard as a sea turtle, but underneath he'd felt her softness, like the bedding of a pearl, yielding herself up to his advances with total trust and total abandon. He could have done anything to her, anything at all, and she'd have met him all the way, he was sure of it. Never had he wanted so badly to stick his dick into a woman.

'You're a fucking moron, Ketch. That's why I left you,' Stella goaded, sensing his retreat into fantasy. 'You live in your head. You don't have a practical bone in your body. Look at the mess you got yourself into. Breaking and entering over a stupid fucking –'

'Don't say it!'

Stella cried out as he plunged himself home, silencing her with his long overdue anal manoeuvrings. After scooping some of her pussy juice, he lathered his shaft so he could get deeper – all the way, if possible. True to character, Stella had a female demon tattooed on her ass, inked onto the inner left cheek, and it was going to be his distinct pleasure to smother the image completely with his pelvis.

Stella cursed him, the vituperatives alternating with taunting challenges to go at her even more fervently.

'You're a big man now, aren't you? Screwing helpless little Stella into submission. Bet you wish you could have screwed that little red-thatched whore back at Heeter's house, too, don't you? She'd have crawled to you in a hurry for a taste of this, huh? Spread it mighty quick, yes, sir. Then again, she's probably waiting for some fraternity cock or her well-hung boyfriend back in Chicago.'

'Stella, shut the hell up,' he grunted, wondering if the woman really did have a boyfriend. 'Oh yeah. Oh yeah. I'm coming,' he rasped. 'Come with me.'

Stella was beyond arguing or holding back. Her ass surrendered, her pussy at the total mercy of her own prying fingers, she had little choice but to respond in kind. The first wave hit her just as he exploded himself. Pushing their sexes against one another, they shared the heat, the sweet, dark intimacy that can come only from conflict. Their curses were an unholy mix, his from the bits and snatches of classical Greek he'd picked up while casting nets with a poet-turned-fisherman on Corfu and hers in the Gaelic of her mother mixed with the Seminole of her father. All of it stewed together as they continued the bonding, sailing, diving, negotiating, rocking, pushing, scratching-till-the-itch-dies experience that is the shared human orgasm.

'Baby, you're the best,' Stella assured him, sidling up to him where he'd collapsed on his back. 'You know I couldn't live without you.'

'Thanks.' He rubbed the back of her head as she covered his heaving chest in tiny, darting kisses. 'Maybe that will score me some points with the parole board.'

'If not, I could always fuck them all for you.'

'I don't doubt you could.'

'I'm dying of thirst, how about you?'

Reluctantly he let her up so she could go to the oversized toolbox in which she kept her wine. After unscrewing a bottle of something red, she filled two paper cups, allowing him first choice. Randomly, he selected the one on the left.

'You first,' he said warily.

'Down the hatch.' She smiled sweetly.

Waiting to see if she'd keel over, he took a gulp of his own. It was a cheap Chianti, and it burned with every swallow. 'Not bad.' He held out his glass for more.

Midway through the second cup he began to feel dizzy.

Son of a bitch. She'd done it again. Drugged him. But how? The two cups were the same. He'd seen her pour them out identically and drink from the one he'd rejected.

Leaning over his prone body, her hair burying his face like a rain forest, she answered the question that would no longer come out of his paralysed lips. 'I had to put it on the rims of the cups,' she explained. 'It's an extract, you find it in the Glades. Gets absorbed real quick through the lips – unless, of course, you happen to be wearing heavy-duty lip-gloss. You know, the kiss-proof kind?'

He watched her blow him a black-lipped kiss, two Stellas in his doubled vision, twice the agony, twice the pain. What a fool he was to think she couldn't slip another mickey past him. As a Seminole medicine woman she knew things about the Florida swamps no white person would ever know. It was said the cure to every illness was in those mysterious old black waters. And every kind of poison, too.

He was trying to tell her something back, but the words weren't coming out right. She stroked his fore-head. 'I know, baby,' she soothed. 'I'm doing it again, acting like the most heartless bitch you could possibly imagine, right? If it makes you feel any better, honey, I never lied to you any of those times I said you were the best lover I've ever had. Which is all the more reason why I have to do what I'm doing now.'

Even as Ketch was passing out, he was distinctly

aware of a question trying to form on his lips. Not about Stella – who was really quite frightfully predictable in her own sadistic way – but about the other one. The woman in the house. He'd touched and kissed her – only for an instant, but there was something there, an undeniable connection. In a very real way, they'd been about as intimate as two human beings could be. And yet he didn't even know her name.

Who are you, he wondered, and why did you come into my life at such a bizarre time and in such an impossible place?

'*Adieu*,' mouthed the traitorous black lips, his final sight of the night. 'And that, my fair prince, I *know* is French.'

3

Maggie leaned over the balcony, taking a life-saving drag from her fifth post-break-in cigarette in two hours. It was a low-tar gleaned from a stray pack she'd found in the kitchen drawer while rummaging for spatulas to make Spanish omelettes. Chief Grifford had recommended she go to a hotel for the rest of the night, but she hadn't wanted to leave the place.

Not that she had any interest in consuming any of the omelettes. What she wanted was to smoke. She'd been off nicotine for a month, at the urging of Dr Luckenko, the only male in the world other than her customers whose opinion she gave a damn about at this point in her life. A refugee from the old eastern bloc, Vladimir Luchenko had cared for her since she was three and still called her his little *latke*. There were things, of course, that one didn't tell kindly old Dr Luchenko. Her encounter with last night's intruder was going to be one of them.

'You sure you don't want an omelette?' she called over her shoulder to the young cop inside, who was bent over the coffee table dusting for fingerprints. 'They'll just go to waste.'

'No, thank you, ma'am,' he replied in his sexy, twangy Floridian baritone.

It all seemed surreal now, she thought as she regarded him, her hair tied back, her body freshly dressed in shorts, sports bra and a warm sweatshirt to shield her from the predawn chill. As if maybe she'd dreamed the whole thing up after consuming a particularly spicy batch of her favourite homemade salsa. There was no denying the reality of that officer and his bag of black fingerprint powder, though. Heavenly as Officer Cosgrove might be with his broad shoulders, moustache and doubled-over short sleeves, he was anything but a figment of her imagination.

How exactly had it happened? That's what Maggie wanted to know. No man had ever brought her to the brink of orgasm like that, so quickly and effortlessly. Lord knows, there were men who'd spent hundreds of dollars to wine and dine her and hadn't engendered half the response from her sex that this one had with a few dollars' worth of rope. Was she really that much of a danger freak or was she just a closet bondage enthusiast?

She'd never experimented much in that arena, except with Kurt, a mercurial rower on her college crew team with a passion for handcuffs, especially in public places. At one point he and a couple of his friends had even sponsored a sort of bondage scavenger hunt in which they were required to produce photos of their chained girlfriends in various locations, preferably in the act of being had. Her favourite picture showed her giving head to Kurt on the college quadrangle at midnight under the disapproving bronze eyes of Doctor Hiram MacGruder, the school's founder, her kneeling body clad in nothing but bra, panties and cuffs as Kurt grinned like a fiend into the camera lens. She called that particular scene her combo Victoria's Secret/Smith and Wesson look.

More than the bondage, it had been the risk of being caught that had excited her. Was that what last night was about as well? If so, why was she still thinking of the mysterious stranger now that the moment of danger had passed? And why had she been sneaking off to the bathroom every ten minutes to masturbate thinking about him, ever since the chief had released her from her confinement?

Maggie peered out at the stunning view for inspiration. The distant, sleepy blue waters of the Gulf of Mexico, just now being awakened by the first rays of golden sunlight, seemed to offer little help, though – other than to say, with their rhythmic, timeless undulations, 'Welcome to the latest chapter of your perpetually screwed-up love life, Magdalene Quinton.'

Talk about a potentially unique triangle: her, the burglar and his upcoming chain-gang buddies. The hardest part about the whole thing, aside from the embarrassment of having been found by the flinty police chief looking like a tied-up tart, was knowing that she'd given the islanders more ammunition for their battle against Heeter and his development campaign. It was no secret a lot of the people on the Island of Osprey had no use for Calvin Heeter, Jr, his hotels or anyone associated with them. They were in the minority but they were quite vocal and, as far as they were concerned, it would have been preferable to open a sewage plant, two pig-processing plants and a functioning colony of hell than to have voted Heeter his zoning rights.

For the chief's part, he'd made it clear he was after the truth of what had happened last night and nothing else. Not surprisingly, he was looking for a crime within a crime or some kind of alternative explanation for what, at face value, made no sense: a young woman, seemingly unhurt, detained by a robber who takes nothing from the house or from her. Telling him she couldn't remember what he looked like was pretty suspicious, too, given how close up they'd obviously gotten to each other.

'It was dark. I could only see part of him,' she'd insisted, risking what she was half afraid could end up as some kind of obstruction of justice charge. It was all right, wasn't it, to tell a little white lie? Anyhow, she was the one who'd been wronged, so, if she didn't want the man caught, that was her business.

'And which part of him was that, exactly, Miss Quinton?' He'd pinned her with dissecting eyes.

For all his laidback ways, hokey Boy Scout shorts and lazy Florida accent, he might as well have been a cop back home in the Windy City. It must be a universal thing with these guys, that cool, cynical demeanour. Not to mention his ability to push her buttons like a clock radio. In less than fifteen minutes of questioning, he'd reduced her to a deep crimson.

'Just be available,' he'd concluded, handing her a copy of his report. 'We'll be looking into this by and by.'

He'd taken off at that point, leaving the younger officer behind to finish collecting evidence. She was thankful Officer Cosgrove hadn't said a word to her so far other than to ask if he could have a glass of water. She needed the peace and quiet now, and the time to think. Bad bondage jokes aside, it was more than a little alarming how she'd let herself respond to this man, this potentially dangerous invader. Magdalene Quinton was no naïve country girl: she was a born-and-bred Chicagoan, raised to take care of herself and to see instantly through the ulterior motives of even the nicest-seeming people. In fact, as her divorce attorney father Richard was always telling her, there was nothing more suspicious in the world than a person with no discernible self-interests. Or as potentially dangerous.

'Everybody's after something, Mags, or at least they should be. The sooner you figure that out, the sooner you can play ball with them,' the dapper, silver-haired Richard Quinton was apt to point out whenever some problem in her life tripped off this particular prerecorded lecture, one of hundreds in his databanks. 'And remember, if you're not playing to win, you're playing to lose.'

She could have lost everything last night. Over and over in her mind she'd replayed the scene, looking for missed escape attempts, or at least how she could have handled the thing with a modicum of common sense instead of letting herself be led around – to put it bluntly – by her pussy.

But that kiss: how could she deny there was something to it, something that only seemed to confirm what she saw, or thought she saw, in his eyes from the moment she'd laid eyes on him? I'm safe, he was telegraphing. I'm a Christmas toy dropped down your chimney early for being such a good girl and getting all your projects in under budget this year. I'll make all your dreams come true, or at least save you a night's worth of battery power on the old dildo.

Maggie turned her eyes to the beach, already busy with the activities of its early-morning inhabitants – a lone sand crane and a pair of scuttling fiddler crabs, which at the moment were crawling over a dune-buggy track left over from the previous night's search. The authorities had been up and down this whole stretch of waterfront. Maggie could only hope he'd gotten away. He didn't deserve prison, whatever his problem was. Therapy, yes, some sort of impulse-control medication, probably, but not the harshness of life behind steel bars. Besides, why waste a body like that on a bunch of male inmates?

His was the kind of body made for a woman to love and adore. To see him was to want to touch him, to kiss him all over, licking off the sweat and the salt, purifying and cleansing him for lovemaking. What would it be like if they had had more time? What would they have done with a bed? The very thought made her wet and wanton. Would her mystery man have tied her down on the mattress? Would he have shoved a gag in her mouth, told her to be quiet and spread her legs so he could pump her like a madman, or would he have gone at her all tender and gentle? Would he have blown her mind or disappointed in the end, like all the other pretty boys?

No, this man from the sea didn't seem like the rest and, though the ropes were off her body, the press of him was still on her skin. Her mind. And maybe even her heart.

God, she'd never even gotten his name. Not that criminals gave them out as a rule. She wondered if he knew hers. Or if he really liked what he saw when she was nude. Licking her lips, Maggie slid her fingers under the waistbands of her shorts and panties. Rubbing her finger over her clit, she felt the familiar heavy flow of juices. She was going to come, right out here in the open, the beach below her and the cop behind her, and there was no power in the universe to stop her.

'Oh, yeah,' she rasped, sucking on her lower lip, the salt breeze catching her hair. 'Oh, yes, motherfucking yes . . .'

Maggie had almost forgotten she had a cell phone till she heard it chirping in her purse on the chaise behind her. The sound was like a burglar alarm, forcing her to pull her hands guiltily out of her clothing. What did she think she was doing? That cop could have come out here at any time and caught her, not to mention any people watching on the beach.

Checking the caller ID, she expected to see her office number or maybe Tanya's cell.

Oh, God, it was Di. Why did her big sister always have radar for stuff like this? Time and again, at the first sign of trouble, she'd be there to bail Maggie out, whether Maggie wanted it or not. Well, this time, she was going to stay cool and not reveal a thing out of the ordinary.

'Well, well, Di, you're up awfully early,' she began, opting to take the offensive with her recently divorced, playing-the-field-again sibling. 'Or didn't you actually go to sleep last night?'

'As a matter of fact, Mags, I went to bed by eleven, alone, thank you very much, and I was sound asleep when your new law-enforcement friend gave me a wake-up call.'

Maggie felt the entire island dropping out from under her. All of a sudden her denied orgasm was the least of her worries. 'A cop called you?'

'Some police chief. Sounded like he was from a place called Hairspray. Let me tell you, Mags, if that lawman of yours looks half as good as he sounds on the phone, honey, I'm going to confess to this robbery myself. Seriously, though, are you all right, kiddo?'

'It's Osprey, and I'm fine. I wasn't hurt,' she said a bit curtly. 'In fact, it really wasn't anything at all. Hey, can I call you back? I have another call coming in.'

Di turned big sister in a hurry. 'The hell you do. And don't try to blow me off, either. I'm coming down there, and that's final. Be at the airport by one in ... Tallahassee, is it? Gracious, Magdalene, where do they get these names from? Anyhow I'm already in the cab to O'Hare, so you can't talk me out of it. *Ciao!*'

Maggie stood there in a fog holding the phone for several moments, long enough for the helpful young

Cosgrove to ask if she was all right, calling her 'ma'am' again, which made her feel that much more out of sorts, not to mention antique. Was she that much older than the twenty-something cop? The burglar might have been a few years younger than her too, though it was hard to tell, on account of his rugged, weathered features. If he was her junior, it hadn't put him off any. An erect dick stuffed into Speedos wasn't capable of lying about such things.

It had taken all her willpower to keep eye contact when first she'd seen him. What if she hadn't, though? What if she'd given in right off the bat, kneeling before him, taking the naughty robber's hard, hot penis from his pants and putting it inside her hungry mouth, sucking some discipline into him? Or dragged *him* off by the hand to be tied up instead of her? Only Maggie would be smarter about it, tying him down onto her bed, buck naked, so she could ride that monster prick till dawn.

'I'm fine.' She forced a smile, practising for her sister's arrival. 'Just nerves, that's all.'

'Maybe you should lie down for a while, ma'am.'

'No, thank you. Actually I have to go and pick up my sister at the airport in Tallahassee.'

'I'll lock up when I'm done.' He nodded gravely. 'Ma'am.'

With her pasted smile in place, armed with nothing more than her purse, she headed out front to the rental car, a sensible compact she'd insisted on using rather than the pair of expensive sports cars in Heeter's garage to which she had been given the keys. Frankly, she found such vehicles an ostentatious waste as well as environmentally unfriendly.

It was only once she'd made it to the bridge that she realised she was shaking like a leaf. Maybe she wasn't thinking so clearly after all because, at the rate she was going, she would end up at the airport about five hours too early. Grimly she calculated the number of orgasms that would amount to in the terminal bathroom, her ears assaulted by the endless drone of announcements and injunctions not to accept any bags from strangers.

Looking on the bright side, though, if she were taken hostage and tied up there, it would be in some nice impersonal way, done by international terrorists without green eyes, dimpled chins or wickedly kissable lips.

God, what was she going to tell Diane? Anything, she decided, running over in her mind all the cell phone calls she was going to need to make to cancel all her appointments for the day. As long as it wasn't the truth.

Officer Mike Cosgrove was down on one knee on the plush carpet, his thumb in front of his face helping him to draw an invisible straight line from the sliding glass door to the edge of the balcony. It was the third time he'd checked the angle of the burglar's probable entry for his report, and it wouldn't be the last. Police work was all about details, Chief Grifford had taught him. Inches, millimetres, bullet calibre size and, those most elusive of marks, human fingerprints.

He'd been dusting all over the house looking for them, and it was pretty much an unholy mess of black powder right now. But the chief had said not to leave a stone unturned. This was Mike's first solo assignment finishing off a crime scene, and he wasn't going to blow it. Three rolls of film were already in the evidence bag, along with a full cassette tape on which he'd described his runthrough of the house. So far, his theory was that there was a gang of them, maybe three or four. Probably off-islanders. Punks from Marston or one of the other trailer-trash towns over the bridge. At twenty-four,

Mike knew his way around the world. Which is why he wore the uniform and why he'd be chief himself one day.

Making his way to the bedroom next, he checked out all of the girl's shoes. The chief had wanted him to look for sand or tar on them, as if maybe he thought she'd been somewhere she wasn't supposed to be. He sure was a suspicious old cuss, but he knew his stuff. Mike squatted down and ran his finger over the tiny collection of pumps and sandals. He pictured the pert redhead wearing them. She was a real go-getter and the way they'd found her tied up sure hadn't left much to the imagination.

She hadn't said so, but Mike suspected she'd been gangbanged. Why else would she act so weird and then just run off claiming she had to go to the airport? She probably didn't even have a sister and, besides, what else could they think, finding her nude and restrained, clear evidence on her body of some kind of sexual activity? When Mike had asked the chief about sending her to the hospital for a semen swipe, though, the man had been tighter-lipped than a clam.

'Just let the thing play itself out, son. It'll fall into place. These things always do.'

Didn't make much sense to him, but the chief had left him in charge to finish with the evidence-gathering and that's all that mattered right now. He'd lifted dozens of prints and taken his photos and now he just had to attend to a few more all-important details.

The cell phone startled him for a moment, nearly causing him to lose his train of thought. He checked the number. Shit. It was Katy Sue, his sometime lover and wife of Jake Tregan, the mechanic down at the auto shop.

'Katy, I told you to stop calling me when I'm working. What? No, I can't screw around with you in the back of the patrol car right now. The chief's got me on a big case over at the Heeter place.'

Aw shit, now she knew where he was.

'Katy Sue, you listen carefully. You are not coming over here, do you understand me? I swear to God, I'll arrest you for interfering in a –'

She'd already hung up. Mike ran down to the carport to intercept her. She only lived a mile away and he could bet a year's pay she wouldn't listen to him about staying away. His intent was to send her straight home but, when the shapely blonde pulled up in Jake's beat-up red pickup, he felt his resolve weaken instantly. There was no denying what a fine-looking woman she was, waltzing over to him in her cut-offs, backless halter top and flip-flops, long yellow hair, fine as silk, trailing down her back.

'Hi, baby,' she crooned, throwing herself into his arms. 'How's my handsome detective?'

'I ain't yours.' He tried to push her off. 'And I ain't a detective, neither.'

'Sure you are.' Katy Sue put his hands on her pert ass cheeks. 'You discover new things on me all the time.'

He gave her a kiss, just one to shut her up. 'Now go find Jake. I got work to do.'

'Jake's a bore,' she said pouting. 'All he cares about is engines. I want to stay with you. Why don't you show me your work?' Her finger traced a line round the edge of his badge. 'I'm a real quick learner.'

The girl had one flip-flop off and was running her shapely leg up along the inside of his. Unlike the chief, Mike always wore long pants, but he was sure feeling the fire on his skin nonetheless.

'You wouldn't understand. It's too complicated.'

She grabbed his crotch. 'Try me.'

He yanked her arm away. 'For one thing we do fingerprints. Which is what'll happen to you if I have to arrest you for assaulting an officer.'

'Would you cuff me, too?' She nibbled his neck.

Visions of the curvy stripper locked in steel, buck naked, filled his mind, cramming out everything else, including the chief's carefully laid-out instructions. The only thing Cosgrove was going to be capable of at this rate was shoving his rock-hard dick deep inside one of her wet and willing orifices. In a last-ditch effort to regain control, he tried to refocus the conversation on something less sexy.

Turning her about, he moved her gently but firmly through the door into the bottom level of the house. 'All right, girl, I believe I will teach you something after all. You see all this black powder in here?' He showed her his handiwork in the living room. 'That's how we get fingerprints.'

She surveyed the fine layer of soot, black as coal, covering the surface of the glass-top table, the white leather couch with matching recliners, the macramé pillows, the shag rug and even the white marble statues. 'Ooh, Cos, honey, look at the mess you made. You're gonna get in big trouble for this.'

'No, I ain't.' He slapped her perfect buttocks, drawing a high-pitched squeal. 'I told you, this dust is how we get prints. Watch.'

He spilled a little of the powder from the bag, spreading it over the top of one of the architecture books left on the coffee table. 'See that?' He showed her the concentric circles on the card he'd pressed down onto it after having brushed the powder smooth. 'That's the fingerprint of somebody who touched the book. There was moisture on his hand, and that registers in the powder.'

Katy Sue looked impressed. 'Is that from the burglar?'

Mike was trying to concentrate on something other than the way the girl's flat belly was rising and falling just below her perky, braless breasts. Jake was a fool to let her run around like this, though the rumour was he had plenty of action on the side himself. As for letting his hot little wife take her clothes off at the club every night, the money was too good for any man in these parts to resist. 'Hopefully,' he said, nodding. 'More than likely, though, it belongs to the owner of the place. Or the woman who's been staying here.'

'Really?' Katy Sue cocked her head now, the way she always did when she was thinking of something really kinky. The last time she'd gotten that look they'd had sex at the top of the water tower over in Tarvall Springs. 'So why don't we try it out, then? On these.'

She untied the string at the top of her halter, letting it fall to bare her luscious globes.

'Katy, put those away. Save 'em for the customers at Diamond Pete's.'

'I won't put 'em away till you check for prints. Come on, Mikey, put your hands all over them like they're your property, then dust me for the prints.'

'Girl, you're crazy. You know how much hot water I could get into?'

'Who's gonna know? It already looks like hell in here.'

It was true; there'd been an unfortunate spill or two on the rug, but still.

'Forget it. It wouldn't work, anyway. Human skin is too porous – that means it ain't smooth enough to take prints.'

'Prove it.'

He offered no resistance as she put his hands right where she wanted them. Lord, but she felt good. Supple, firm and resilient.

'Come on,' she breathed. 'Mark me good. I'm your property, remember?'

Mike squeezed just hard enough to make her wince. Katy Sue liked it rough sometimes and it turned her on a lot that he was a cop, licensed to use force.

'Mmm, that's it. Rub them around good, baby. Make some real hard prints.'

'If I rub, it'll mess the prints up. I have to hold them in one place.'

Dad gum it, what was he saying? Now he was actually playing into her nonsense. Katy Sue's brand of loving sure felt right, though, and there was no denying how hot she got when they were doing something totally nasty that might get them caught.

'Then we'll make some new ones.' She began to fiddle at his belt. 'Where'd you put that powder? The dirty, filthy black stuff?'

He had images of rolling on the floor with her, covered in black powder, screwing like bunnies.

'We can't do that in here. Not on the carpet.'

'On the balcony, then.'

'Damn it, Katy Sue.' He tried to thrust her back. 'What if that Yankee woman comes back? Or the chief?'

'Then he can help.' Katy Sue stood on bare tiptoes, suctioning herself to his mouth. Taking advantage of his momentary weakness, she took his hands and slid them behind her under the waistband of the obscene little cut-offs, which had somehow come undone. Next thing he knew, he was clutching naked ass cheeks, wriggling and willing.

'See?' she breathed. 'Now you can make prints back there, too.'

He let himself be led by the hand like a little boy out to the tiled balcony, although his cock was feeling pretty grown up. At the moment it was fighting like a drowning man to get out of his uniform khakis. More than anything he wanted Katy Sue's wicked little mouth on him. But, knowing her, they'd have to see her game through to the end before he'd get any oral pleasuring.

'Got the powder?' She began unbuttoning his shirt.

He did and for a moment he felt that little flash of disgrace, knowing he was dishonouring the khakis of the venerable law-enforcement department of the town and island of Osprey. Luckily feelings like this never lasted more than a few seconds.

'Baby, you know how fucking hot you are?' Katy pulled off his shirt and T-shirt so she could run her hot-pink, acrylic, totally non-functional nails down his thick, fleece-covered torso. Actually, he did know, because the girls had been chasing him since high school. Staying fit was something Mike took great pride in. For his whole twenty-four years he'd surfed and fished and hunted weekly and never eaten an ounce of useless fat or sugar when he could avoid it.

'Totally fucking gorgeous,' she continued, bending to suck one of his already peaked nipples. 'And you've been lifting weights again, haven't you?'

Mike puffed out his chest a little further, giving her easier access. If he lived to be a hundred, he'd never let his body go, because that's how you drove little 'gator girls like Katy Sue crazy.

'I got me one of those workout machines,' he said proudly. 'The same one Chuck Norris uses.'

'Mmm.' She turned her attention to his other nipple,

taking a long lick across his pec to get there. 'He's a cop, too. In Texas, I think.'

'That's just a TV show, Katy Sue. In real life, he does karate.'

'Ka-what?' She skinned down her shorts and tiny purple thong revealing a hairless crotch and lovely little sex lips, pierced by gold rings. A moment later the halter was on the ground, too.

'Never mind.' All of a sudden he wasn't thinking about Chuck Norris or what would happen to them if someone walked in right now. 'The time for talking is done.'

She wouldn't let him touch her. 'You'll mess the prints,' she said, slapping his hands away from her tanned, one-hundred-per-cent-lean body with the sculpted belly, perky tits and long legs – the very same body that drove them all wild at Diamond Pete's All-American Girl Emporium, just over the bridge on the mainland.

He watched in helpless awe as the kinky little woman lowered herself to the tile at his feet. If only he could get her away from Jake and into his bed fulltime, he could die a happy man.

'Dust me,' she said throatily, hands over her head, legs spread nice and wide to reveal her glistening love canal.

Mike massaged his crotch for just a moment, thinking of how all the men wanted and couldn't touch her at the club. She was a walking erection factory, with that little butterfly tattoo on her calf, the coil of ivy inked on her lower back, just above her ass, and the tiny swan on her left tit that appeared to swim across her breast when she was on top, fucking the daylights out of him.

'Do it,' she demanded, with all the confidence of a woman used to getting what she wants.

It was true, too. The competition was fierce, and

Mike knew he had to work for it, to keep her interested. It was a fine line between losing the best sex of his life and potentially flushing his career down the crapper. For some reason, he kept thinking he could get away with keeping both. It was a lot to put on his inherited Irish luck but, so far, things had held together.

Kneeling beside her, he opened the bag, angling it just enough to let some of the contents spill, a tiny shower of soot over the domes of her well-tanned tits. Katy Sue, who spent an average of ten hours a week on a tanning bed despite living in the Sunshine State, licked her lips. 'Ooh, that is dirty, isn't it? Is it hard to get off?'

'When it's moist, it gets greasy and real sticky,' he said. He took out the whisk brush from the kit, using it to spread the substance over her bosom and down the valley that led to her quivering drum of a belly. With each little twist and slide of the fine horsehair device, she drew another soft little sigh.

'I think it is getting moist, especially here.' She checked, her glued-on nails exploring greedily between her glistening uncovered labia. 'I'm a bad girl,' she taunted. 'I'm gonna make a big mess.'

Mike was beyond reason, beyond figuring what the hell he'd do afterwards to clean it all up.

'Don't touch that,' he said sternly, pulling her hands away from her sex. 'That's evidence.'

It was time to employ the tools of the trade. The stripper's eyes got wide and grateful as he slapped the gleaming metal bracelets on her slim wrists.

'Hands over your head,' he ordered. 'And keep those legs apart. Real wide.'

'Yes, sir.' She smiled, her lips deadly as a water moccasin, her eyes bright as sin.

Mike poured the entire bag into Katy's pussy. He was

in charge now and she was going to lie there and take it.

'Who else has been down here?' he asked, reviving another little game of theirs, making like he'd arrested her for prostitution.

'No one, sir, I swear.'

He brushed her pussy back and forth with the horse-hair whisk. 'How much they pay for this little hole these days?'

'Nothing.' She shook her head innocently. 'I ain't no hooker, Mr Officer, sir.'

'Ah hah.' He probed with the bone handle of the brush, just grazing her clit. 'So you admit to giving it away.'

Katy Sue arched her back. Eyes closed, she offered herself. 'Only to you, sir. You know I'm yours.'

He dabbed her cheeks with the charcoaled brush. 'Liar. Now open that mouth. I need to do some deep cavity searching.'

Katy obeyed, her palms up and helpless, her body at his mercy. Heart racing, breathing heavily, he stood over her, feet on either side of her athletic hips, making her watch every move as he undressed. There was no denying how she made him feel, like he was the toughest, most important cop in the world.

'You'd shoot somebody, wouldn't you?' she whispered as he undid his thick black gun belt, unclipping the holster and laying the whole thing down next to her slithering body. 'Just to save my life.'

'Any day of the week, baby.' His cock nearly leaped out as he unzipped his trousers. 'I'd kill an army for you.'

'Can I move?' she asked softly as he went to work on his pants, shoes and socks.

'No.' He told her the words she wanted to hear. 'You're my prisoner. You'll lie there just like I told you.'

The naked Mike Cosgrove went for her mouth first. Big and oval ... please-sir-may-I-have-some-more big, like an X-rated Oliver Twist. Katy Sue took his dick deep, making no objections as he knelt over her pretty, high-boned face, pushing himself expertly and with authority into the smooth, silky opening. Katy Sue loved his cock, loved it for breakfast, lunch and dinner. Especially if it was at the wrong place and the wrong time.

'Oh yeah,' he moaned, enjoying the fruits of his labour, their most creative session of foreplay to date. 'That's it, baby.'

Katy Sue doubled her efforts, liking the praise. She liked to be liked, liked to tease, but even more she liked to satisfy and be satisfied in return. And that meant he'd have to get to work in a hurry.

Shit. How was he going to lick pussy with her like this? He'd have black gunk between his teeth for a month. There was the baton in the squad car he sometimes fucked her with, but how would he get there and back in the state he was in? No, his finger would have to do, propped up with a really good story to get her off while he continued to enjoy her sucking skills.

'Listen up, Katy Sue. If I tell you something classified, some real police business, will you promise to keep it to yourself?'

She nodded, giving an affirmative 'Mmmph'. She was hooked, just as he knew she would be.

'Last night, a gang of thieves broke into this house.' Without taking out his cock, he reached his hand behind him, finding by instinct her already swollen clitoris. 'There was this woman here, real sexy, a little redhead with a fine body, like yours. She had to be the guy's mistress who lives here. He's away right now, on his boat, and the chief can't reach him. Why he left this fine little piece behind, I don't know. His loss. So this gang finds her, right? She pleads and begs them not to hurt her, and they tell her they won't, so long as she cooperates. There's four of them, bikers, big mean bastards, and they tell her she's gonna have to service them all. They give her thirty seconds to get her clothes off and crawl over to them on her hands and knees.'

Katy was making noises and he pulled himself out knowing she needed to talk back.

'Did she do it?' Katy caught her breath, using her left hand to move his masturbating fingers a smidgin to the left and deeper inside her.

'She had no choice.' He sat down beside her. 'They all had big nasty knives.'

'Have you seen her? Is she really, really pretty? Even more than me?'

'Almost, but not quite,' he said, soothing her ego. 'One look at her nude body and they're all raging hard, though, ready to do her on the spot.'

'Did they?'

'No. They tell her, if she obeys them, she'll enjoy it, but she has to be their slave and do everything they tell her.'

Katy began to buck, her soot-covered, greasy, tanned, tattooed body rocking like a motorcyclist's fantasy. 'And did she obey them?'

'She has no choice. On her hands and knees, naked like a little slut, she crawls to them. It makes her wet, too, even though she doesn't want to be. She can't help it and, when they tell her to kiss their big black boots, that makes her hot, too.'

'She must have been a little whore.'

'Reckon so.'

'Keep going.'

'The leader is this guy Monk, big as a house, and —'

'How do you know his name?' she interrupted.

'We got his boot prints off the rug,' he said with a straight face. 'We matched them up against the central files. They got records there of the boots they all wear.'

'Interpol, right?'

'Yep,' he agreed, confirming a lie he'd used on an earlier case. Katy Sue might be naïve, but she was anything but stupid. God help him if she ever figured out that the international police data banks didn't know Florida bikers from Florida Marlins. 'So, anyway, this Monk takes out his prick and tells her to start sucking. Him first and then all the others. They line up in a row, right on that rug in there, and she has to take them all in her mouth.'

'Did they come that way?'

'No. They save that for her pussy. She's still on all fours, right? That's the perfect way to take a woman, from behind, like she's a bitch. One by one, they go into her, making her stay still so they can pump her deep.'

'Did it hurt her real bad?'

'No.' He worked at her clit as he kept spinning his yarn. 'She was turned on by the whole thing.'

'I would be, too,' she said huskily, though Mike knew there was a hell of a big difference between fantasy and reality. 'I'd come for all of them, because I'd know I had to or they'd punish me.'

'She knew that, too. And, after each man filled her with his load, he went round to the front of her, making her take him by mouth till he was hard all over again.

'Oh, yeah,' Katy agreed, as if she had the foggiest idea of what it was like to be assaulted by criminal bikers. 'That's how they do it in those gangs. You have to serve them in every hole. Even in your ass.'

'Yep,' he agreed, taking her hint. 'They took her ass, too. Monk was first, then the others.'

'Oh, baby.' She was shuddering, wide-eyed, her chained wrists jingling above her splayed, fine-spun yellow hair. 'I'm there.'

Mike let her come on his hand while he stroked himself with the other. He couldn't wait any longer and, before she'd fully subsided, the delectable Katy Sue found herself impaled by the rugged policeman.

'Oh, God, fuck me, baby . . . honey . . . sweetheart.' She wrapped her legs round his ass, digging her heels like spurs. 'Fuck me hard.' Using her cuffed hands, she embraced his thickly sinewed neck. Now they were one, together for the ride.

'You little bitch,' he said, grinning darkly. 'You totally hot little bitch.'

Katy was popping like those little firecrackers the kids throw down on the asphalt every Fourth of July. Each vibration, he knew from experience, was an orgasm. The girl was unique that way, as far as he knew. Get her primed right, set the mood and take the time to stroke her real good and she'd come a dozen or more times in a row.

'Uh huh, baby,' she confirmed, her voice coming in broken gasps. 'I'm your hot bitch. Your nasty little cunt you need to cuff and keep in line.'

Mike grunted like it was the end of the world. His insides were pouring out. He was flooding her, his hot white milk shooting in wave after wave. He just couldn't get enough of this girl; he was crazy out of his mind for her. Truly, he didn't have her in chains, but she had him.

'See?' she rasped, nibbling at his earlobe as he collapsed on top of her, his body spent, exhausted, drained and neutralised. 'I told you you'd find something out to help your investigation, being with me.'

Actually, she'd said no such thing.

'What's that, Katy Sue?' he said, humouring her.

'There didn't have to be four guys to take on that girl, not if she was willing herself. It could have been one, just like you did with me.'

Cosgrove thought about it for a minute.

Son of a bitch. What if she was right?

4

Diane Quinton should have been thinking about her sister. Given what poor little Maggie had just been through, trying to make a love connection – or, in this case, a lust connection – for herself on the flight down to Florida should have been the last thing on her mind.

The thing was, the guy was just so damned cute. And so tall. And rugged looking, with those smouldering kind of amber eyes and that long brown hair insolently tied back in a ponytail, like a young Antonio Banderas. How could her heart help but skip a beat or two – or her loins heat up a few degrees? And technically, if you thought about it, what difference would it make to Magdalene how Diane spent her time en route? Wouldn't she be of more help to her sister relaxed, sated . . . and fucked?

Anyway, Maggie hadn't been hurt in the ordeal and she'd made it quite clear she didn't want Diane there at all, which meant she'd catch hell when she got there, so why not have a little fun now?

She licked her lips in anticipation as her mark took off his camel-hair sports coat to reveal a long, lean torso deliciously covered in a button-down silk shirt, dark blue. He'd left several buttons undone, enough to reveal a tuft of fine chest hair, deep auburn, just right for running one's tongue over. Best of all, she noted, as he turned his firm ass in her direction to stow the jacket in the overhead storage bin, he was alone.

'Is this seat taken?' Di approached boldly, bypassing the two intervening rows of the sparsely populated aircraft.

He turned to face her, filling her nostrils with the deep scent of cinnamon and java.

'Not speak English,' he proclaimed in a rich European accent, smooth as silk. Their bodies were only a few inches apart.

'You –' she pointed first at his chest then at her own, feeling like Jane to his Tarzan, or maybe Eve to Adam – '– and me ... together ... sit.' What she wouldn't give to know the word for 'fuck' in whatever language it was he did speak.

He looked at her, puzzled, pinching his adorable eyebrows and wrinkling his lips ever so slightly. Diane made a sort of curtseying motion and that seemed to do the trick.

'Ah.' He treated her to a dazzling smile that lit his whole face. 'Sitting down.' The young Banderas ushered her past him to take the window seat, which was fine by her, because she was going to need all the cover she could get once they got flying and she started in on a few manoeuvres of her own. Pointedly adjusting the hem of her short dress, Diane settled herself strategically into the comfy leather first-class seat.

Predictably, the young man's eyes were glued to her long, stocking-clad legs. Just shy of thirty-six years old, Diane was thankful to be the sort of woman who managed to look her best no matter what the occasion. Whether it be a last-minute cocktail party invitation or an emergency trip to the godawful swamps of Florida, she was always prepared with a can of hairspray and a little black dress. One never knew, after all, when one might meet one's future husband. In her case, it would be number three or four, depending on whether you chose to recognise the marriage laws of the principality of San Castillo.

'Me –' she rested her fingers suggestively on her well-displayed cleavage '– Diane'.

Di's insides melted as he took her French-manicured fingertips in his and put them to his lips. 'Gregor Andel. Is pleasure.'

'Oh no,' she purred, wondering what those deep red lips of his might feel like on various other parts of her anatomy. 'The pleasure is all mine.' At least it would be if she had her way.

Diane took her hand back for the obligatory departure speeches. The little blonde flight attendant made no mention of Diane's switching seats, though she did seem a trifle disappointed at the competition for Gregor's attention. Di gave her a potent warning stare, tigress to tigress, as the barely legal hussy practically threw herself in the man's lap to offer him a glass of champagne.

Gregor himself – no older than twenty-five, if she had to guess – seemed unmoved by the girl's age-old tits-in-the-face routine. Just to reinforce her own position, though, Di made a point of putting the young man's long, delicate hand on her nylon-clad thigh. She hadn't bargained on the instant heat, and the need that would come with it. She wanted his hands elsewhere, and hers on him. And she wanted them both without clothes, too. This was the frustrating part of in-flight trysts. You couldn't really get down to brass tacks as you could in a proper bed. Then again, there was the ever-present zing of sex in a very public place to render even a ho-hum encounter something quite out of this world.

Gregor leaned towards her, whispering something. His breath was hot on her neck, creating an instant itch that flew down the surface of her skin. Diane couldn't make out a word of it, which she took as an excellent excuse to make up her own translation. Opting for free association with her own thoughts at the moment, she interpreted the man's remark as a request for her to take off her stockings and panties.

It might not be what he wanted, but it was certainly what she wanted, which meant at least one of them would be happy in the process. The plane was making its ascent as she tugged at the nylon. She kicked off her pumps and skinned the material down quickly and expertly. Her bare skin tingled. There was something about exposing herself in public like this that never lost its thrill. The blonde hussy was just a few rows up; they were completely exposed, and could be caught at any minute.

Gregor muttered something else, something that ended in a very cute and sexy rendering of her name, 'Dee – ahn.' Oh, God, he was massaging her breast, trying to find the nipple through the material of her dress. There'd be no missing it, as much as it was swelling in anticipation of being tweaked and teased. She had to lean forwards to pull the stockings over her feet. Showing that the ways of love needed no transla-tion, he took full advantage of her position to slip a hand down her bodice and beneath her black lace bra.

She let out a little gasp. His touch was firm and commanding. Clearly Gregor was letting her know that, while she might have started this little game between them, he was now assuming the role of the dominant male. He continued to knead her naked orb as she lifted her buttocks to pull down the panties over her hips. They were moist and fragrant, highly indicative of her deep arousal.

Gregor had a new phrase for her as she pulled the tiny garment over her bare feet. It was only when he repeated the words and held out his hand that she understood. Her young would-be lover wanted her to turn over her underwear to him. Presumably for safekeeping.

Diane felt a deep, hot wave of sexual need as she put the tiny panties in his palm. The symbolism wasn't lost on her. She'd surrendered possession of her most intimate garment, leaving herself naked and vulnerable under her dress. With a grin on his face devilish enough to make even the blasé multiple divorcée blush, he dangled them on one finger.

Diane looked to see if the stewardess was watching the flying of the colours. Did Gregor want the little yellow-haired Fly Me bitch in on his impending conquest? No, he had a different plan in mind. Repeating her name as if she were the only woman in the world ever to have borne it, Gregor put the moist, feminine fabric to his lips. Her pussy spasmed as he kissed then inhaled, slowly, decisively, the proud and noble nostrils flaring like a lion's. For his *coup de grâce*, he folded them neatly and put them in the pocket of his black jeans, right beside his huge, rock-hard cock.

Diane licked her lips in anticipation. She'd had enough of this one-sided game. Skilfully, employing small but wilful fingertips, she unzipped him, desperate to get at his concealed manhood. Gregor moved quickly to help. They were beyond caring who saw them now. She wanted her hands on him, and her mouth, too. He wore silk boxers and she practically tore at the fastenings to free him. For her diligence, she was rewarded with a full, thickly veined nine-inch pole, tall and straight, uncircumcised.

'Oh, what I wouldn't give to have you by my nightstand every night,' she whispered hotly, addressing the man's endowment.

Gregor tossed an airline blanket over her head as she dived to taste him, though it really wasn't going to accomplish much by way of disguising their blatant violation of airline policy. At least they weren't terrorists; the airline people ought to be happy about that. Ordinarily, Diane liked to tease and sample a man, but she was hungry and horny and she wanted him as far back in her throat as she could get him. Just like she wanted – and got – his fingertips under her dress and between her splayed, swollen sex lips. Unabashedly, she humped his hand as she gave him what she was fairly sure was the blowjob of his young life.

His fingers were fairly skilful and she managed without too much trouble to get him to rub right over her clit, just where she needed it. Diane came just as the flight attendant walked up to chastise them. It was a guttural climax, down and dirty, her fluids gushing over the young man's fingers as she bucked on the seat, shamelessly squeezing and releasing her spasming pussy muscles. One, two, three aftershocks and she was back on earth – ten or twenty thousand feet above it, at least. Now to get this splendid specimen of masculinity erupting his white-hot lava.

'Sir, ma'am, I'm going to have to ask you to refrain from whatever it is you think you're doing,' said the young woman pointedly.

'Gregor Andel. Is pleasure,' said Gregor to the attendant, obviously understanding nothing of what she was saying. Diane paused to giggle in mid-suck at the double entendre. Such an irrepressible lad; Gregor would probably have been happy with a threesome, the fastidious blonde's breasts popped in his gorgeous mouth one by one like rich, dreamy treats, followed by her pale, clearly underused snatch. Meanwhile, Di would ride this hard cock into the sunset, all the way to the landing strip, bucking up and down, tearing her nails at his skin, nibbling at his nipples, licking the sweat from his chest.

'This will be reported,' said the blonde, beating a hasty retreat.

If she was hoping to garner attention, she'd failed miserably. Gregor was too busy moaning, low and deep in his throat, as he readied himself for orgasm. He was like a baby, totally at her mercy. Di sat up just a little, wrapping her fingers round him, her head still completely concealed by the blanket. She was not about to take his come in her mouth, but she would masturbate him to climax, right here, as close as possible to Blondie. Better yet, why not let the girl do it herself?

Diane came up for air. The attendant was several rows down front and fading, her pert posterior shaking with proper indignation. These young people really did need to loosen up, she thought, feeling like a randy old grandma.

'Pardon me,' she called innocently. 'Miss?'

The woman returned, looking as professional as possible. It had been cruel of them to torment her by masturbating each other right under her nose and Diane intended to make up for it right now.

'I wonder if you'd come a little closer, miss.'

'Yes?' she replied warily, taking the smallest possible step.

'It's Lee Ann,' Diane read off her name badge, placed just below the collar of her open uniform blouse. 'Isn't it?'

The attendant nodded. 'Is there something I can do for you, ma'am?'

'Not something.' She shook her head. 'Someone.'

Lee Ann's eyebrows rose in disbelief. Had the unruly, sex-crazed passenger in seat 7B really just inclined her head to the blanket-covered lump in the lap of the young man sitting next to her? The lump that obviously covered the penis she had been deep-throating just a few minutes ago? Why yes, she had.

'Ma'am, I am going to have to call for the air marshal.'

'And waste a perfectly good hard-on?' Diane snatched the blanket away. Poor Lee Ann looked as if she might faint. Gregor, loving the attention he was getting from the two attractive women, just grinned, shrugging his shoulders.

'Ma'am, please.' She grabbed at the blanket, trying to cover him up again. 'This is against regulations.'

Diane stroked him, long and slow. 'You should taste him,' she suggested. 'Or give him your panties – that seems to speak volumes in his language.'

Lee Ann was weakening, her natural sense of duty conflicting with her even more natural desires as a woman. Diane thrilled at the conflict on her face. She loved to see the bad girl winning out over the good. It was just like with Maggie, when her hellion side took over her do-good daddy's girl side and all reason was lost.

Personally, Diane liked to keep in the middle, not fooling herself with pretensions of sainthood that would only backfire later on.

'It looks to me like a nearly empty flight,' said Diane, playing devil's advocate.

Lee Ann licked her lips. Her eyes held transparent visions of herself, bent over the food service cart or shoved against the wall of the food prep area, Gregor's cock plundering her thirsty hole. 'I'll lose my job,' she said.

Gregor weighed in now, reaching up to touch Lee Ann's skirt-clad leg, just below the hem. She seemed powerless to prevent him running his hands up between her thighs. 'Please,' she said, her chest rising and falling with noticeable rapidity. 'Don't.'

The young man laughed, releasing her. Lee Ann's obvious relief was mixed with frustration as well. A part of her had wanted him to force the matter.

'*Vrohsh.*' He pointed, indicating she should return to work. The callous tone seemed to unnerve Lee Ann more than the wild sex acts she'd witnessed.

Lips trembling, her eyes moist like a puppy's, the rejected flight attendant did as she was told. Gregor seemed to lose interest in sex after this. Brushing off Di's well-meaning attempts to finish him off, he zipped himself back up, reclined his seat and went to sleep. Di watched his erection fade in his jeans. She hadn't the gumption to ask for her underwear back.

This appeared to be the end of the matter, but just as the 'fasten seat belt' sign went on, indicating that they were coming in for a landing, Lee Ann came by with an unusual offering. Pretending to check his seat belt, she leaned forwards, pressing something white into his hand.

Diane felt a fresh stab of sexual heat. It was the flight attendant's underwear. The look in Lee Ann's eyes confirmed what the gesture was saying. She was his for the taking, as soon as the plane landed.

Diane sighed with satisfaction. Yet again, she had performed the service of sexual matchmaker. And all while ensuring her own erotic fulfilment. Talk about job satisfaction. Now if only she could get her sister hooked up with a halfway decent man, one who would love her normally and stick around afterwards for at least as long as the average marriage, her life's work would be completed.

Of course Maggie was a Quinton and Quinton women

had a long history of being led by their libidos. She herself had made some pretty sorry choices in her time. The only difference was that Diane went for men with money, while Maggie looked for men who'd spend hers. The woman was like a magnet for hard-luck cases. In fact, judging by the odd tone in Maggie's voice, Diane had an uneasy feeling there was more to this burglar story than she was letting on.

Would she put it past Magdalene to get involved with a hardened criminal? If he was good-looking, no. And there'd been no mistaking the emotional, defensive timbre of her voice on the phone. If Maggie didn't want her coming down here, that meant only one thing. Baby sister was in love.

'Please remain in your seats until the airplane comes to a complete stop,' droned the captain.

Stealing a last kiss from Gregor, Diane composed herself. In a few moments she would be out of this delightfully air-conditioned cabin and into the steaming swamps of the rural south. 'Luis Varell, don't fail me now.' She gave the hollow of her neck a final spray with her favorite perfume. Hopefully it was strong enough to cover swamp gas, or whatever else might emanate from the earth in a place with a name as bizarre as Tallahassee.

Ketch awoke inland, on the ground, sand on his tongue, a beetle tickling the underside of his nose. Instinctively, he tried rising to his feet, but plopped right back down. Looking up he saw Stella's legs and others besides. Men's legs.

'Easy, cowboy,' she advised. 'You're gonna be a little woozy still.'

Ketch called her a choice name, one neither classical nor noble in nature. A man reached down and pulled him up to his knees. He had arms like tree trunks, with round, smooth biceps and there was another fellow on the other side just as strong and just as nude. They had large, thick cocks and full, heavy ball sacks. It didn't take a psychic to figure out what Stella had in mind.

'I don't have time for games,' he told her. 'I'm on a mission.'

Stella was standing in front of him holding the whip she'd wanted him to use on her last night. She wore only her long black boots and a thick black collar round her neck, set with silver studs. 'So am I.' She smiled serenely, indicating for the men to hold his arms out straight so as to fully expose his breasts and crotch. 'And you're my subject.'

Technically, subjects went with experiments and not missions, but Ketch was in no position to argue. Stella intended to play with him, making him the star of one of her bizarre, orgiastic gay scenarios. The woman's theory, as tenable as anything else in her distorted world, was that all men required to be taken, on a regular basis, and used as lust objects by other men, as a way of keeping them in balance. The fact that Ketch became incredibly aroused during these sessions only reinforced her beliefs.

'You do want to make me happy, don't you, sweetheart?' Stella approached him, brushing the hairs of her sweet bush for a few maddening seconds over his mouth, making him moan.

'Yes,' he croaked.

'And you want to be happy, too, right?' She grabbed the back of his head, thrusting her pelvis onto his face.

He nodded, furiously, unravelled as always by Stella's pussy logic.

'Lick my boots,' she commanded.

The naked gigolos released him, allowing Ketch to

fall forwards onto the ground in front of the shiny, feminine leather boots. Stella's games drove him mad, but he'd never yet been able to resist them. Who knew where she came up with these ideas: hiring pretty boys and then carting them all out here in the middle of nowhere to play games far better left to sleazy motel rooms or not played at all.

'Take your time, honey,' urged Stella, tapping his bare back with the whip. 'We're not going anywhere in a hurry.'

That's where she was wrong. Ketch had work to do. He had to get to back to Heeter's house and look for another opportunity to get back his belonging. In the meantime, he needed to find out more about the woman. His fire-haired, imprisoned princess. The beauty locked in the tower.

'You're not concentrating,' she complained.

The slash of the whip brought him back to reality. 'Ow, Stella!' He shared his painful revelation. 'That really hurts!'

'Does it? You mean like the pain you caused me by cheating on me with that little red-haired whore you tied up last night? I pretended not to let it bother me, but I know how you wanted her. You even thought of her while you were with me, I know you did.'

By all the gods and goddesses, she was getting to him all over again. Quite against his will, he felt his untouched dick pulse as he kissed and sucked the feet of his mistress – the woman wielding, at least for the moment, total power over him.

It had been her divine mystique that had first attracted him, a year and a half ago when she found him sleeping under a palm tree, homeless in Key West. He'd never forget the look on the woman's face, the way her eyes shone as she introduced herself. To this day she insisted she'd put a hex on him the day he was born, the only remedy to which was to give himself to her unconditionally.

'Tell us what you want, slave boy,' she said, prodding him. 'Tell us what you need.'

Ketch cringed. She was going to make him say the words.

'We're waiting.' She struck humiliatingly at his exposed ass.

Ketch felt the awaited release, the sense of total freedom from responsibility that always came at a certain point in his games with Stella. It wasn't a bad feeling at all. Subjugated, out in the open, totally exposed, at the mercy of those standing over him.

'I need cocks, mistress.' The confession rolled all too easily off his lips.

'Where, slave boy?' asked the fifty-year-old woman who didn't look a day past thirty-five.

'In my mouth ... in my ass.' He felt the tiny hole pucker in response. No doubt he'd be getting his wish and quite soon.

'On all fours,' ordered the long-haired, wrinkle-free Stella, like a raven-haired version of the timeless Venus De Milo. 'Prepare to be taken.'

Ketch assumed the position. It had been months since Stella had made him perform this way. That last time he'd sucked the cocks of a trio of bikers after they'd both gotten too drunk to know the danger they were in.

'I want you to look at him at all times when he's in your mouth.'

He stiffened as she ran the leather lightly over his buttocks; a teasing but stark reminder that, when she assumed the dominant role in their games, she could subject him to pleasure or pain at her least whim.

The blond in front of him was a magnificent specimen. He was maybe thirty, with the body of an accomplished weight-lifter. Muscles seemed to ooze from other muscles. He had a ribbed stomach, the proverbial six-pack, and below that a tuft of yellow hair, a perfect match to the curly hair on his head. Even finer hairs graced his thighs, inviting the eye and tongue both.

'Lick him,' said Stella, freeing him of all culpability for acts that much of society had yet to condone. 'Rub your face on his balls and lick.'

The strong, heady scent of masculinity permeated his nostrils, a keen mix of sweat and testosterone. Was this what it felt like to be a female? Revelling in male power even as it overwhelms you? Ketch was rewarded with a low-pitched groan as he ran his cheeks along the side of the man's enormous cock. He felt his own balls tighten in submissive anticipation as he considered that this proud spear of flesh would soon be fully inside his mouth, receiving its due worship.

Meanwhile, from behind, the other male was positioning himself. This one had dark hair, short and straight. He was stockier, with a thicker penis. No doubt Stella had chosen him to do the anal work for this very reason. She liked to see her lover impaled, the fuller the better.

Once inserted, the male sex organ could give great pleasure, especially as it pressed his sensitive prostate. Stella reported Ketch was never thicker, nor did he ever come harder than when he was being sucked or masturbated while being used this way.

'You shouldn't ever run away from me,' Stella said, as the first man took Ketch's face in his hands.

Ketch opened wide, allowing the hot, smooth dick entrance between his lips. Immediately, he applied a suctioning motion, drawing the man deeper. Stella liked to see him this way, being mouth-fucked as she put it.

'All the way,' she ordered, smacking the ass of the blond, inducing him to push himself to the back of Ketch's throat. Ketch was good this way. He never gagged. Nor did he ever balk at being taken from behind, even without lubricant.

'Why do you make things difficult?' Stella asked as the second man aimed the nose of his cock into Ketch's nether opening. 'You ran away before I could make things right, before I could get back what was taken from you.'

He couldn't provide much of an answer, except to be as pleasing as possible. Ketch knew how hot these scenes made her and that was the biggest turn-on of all. Much as he hated to admit it, Ketch's life, at least his sex life, revolved around pleasuring this dark-haired siren. The fact that danger, and even pain, added to her thrills was his problem, not hers.

Obediently, he bobbed his head up and down on the blond man's glistening rod. The man's muscular body was shaking, which meant he'd be coming soon. It was up to Stella whether he'd swallow the man's come or take it on his face. Sometimes she liked Ketch to have the two loads inside him, in front and back. Other times she liked to jump in herself, taking one or more of the cocks in hand and jerking it to orgasm all over Ketch's body.

He'd never before thought of this as perverted, but then again he couldn't imagine his red-haired beauty doing things like this. She was a lady. He could picture her, those fiery red tresses flowing in the sea breeze as she stood on the parapet of a castle, in a long, velvet gown, contemplating noble things like the nature of love. He'd bet anything she was still a virgin, though she had the body of a stripper. Tying her up had only made her more desirable, more soft and pliant. What a wildcat she would be for the right man, for her true lord. That man alone would tame and conquer her, bringing out the full depths of her sensuality even as he left his mark on her. Indelibly. It would be no mean feat, either, given her quick wit and sharp tongue.

The anal intruder was grunting, trying to make more room for himself. Ketch's own untouched penis was red-hot and swollen enough to burst. If he didn't get some relief soon he was going to spill his own load right here on the sand.

'That's enough, boys.'

The hired hands – or cocks – withdrew on command. Ketch had to admire their discipline. He could only imagine how much Stella was paying them. Not that she cared, given her multi million-dollar trust fund left by her rich uncle, a citrus grower. Of course, she couldn't live in a nice mansion and grow fat like other millionaires; she had to be a beatnik. Jacqueline Kerouac with handcuffs.

'On your back, Ketch. Time to beg.'

He collapsed to the sand and turned himself over. They were in a clearing, away from the small overgrown palm trees, which gave him just enough room to manoeuvre. The three of them loomed above him with imperial menace. He knew what was coming next; it was just a matter of his setting the wheels in motion.

'We're waiting, Ketch.' Stella had her hands on her hips.

'Please,' he said, repeating the formula. 'I beg you to come on me. Come all over my unworthy body.'

Stella didn't often end their play sessions this way, only when she was pissed off at him, or if she wanted to teach him a lesson in dependency. He knew better than to try and satisfy himself with his hand, even as the two men busied themselves masturbating over his prostrate form. If and when he came was up to Stella, not him.

The blond came first, squirting himself all over Ketch's chest and neck. The come was hot and thick and Ketch was more than a little tempted to scoop it up with his hands and slurp it down. But this, too, was Stella's decision.

The dark-haired man had a little more trouble. He made noises, almost painful, his hand flying over the thick shaft at speeds high enough to kindle sparks for a fire. At long last he began to quiver, tensing his neck muscles. Going into a kind of standing crouch, taking careful aim, he managed to splash himself quite efficiently over Ketch's face. His load was copious, providing a splotchy coating over Ketch's cheeks, eyelids and nose.

Seeing her lover soiled this way was more than Stella could stand. Snarling like the she-beast she was, she fell on top of him, swallowing his cock whole with her greedy, gaping pussy. At once her muscles began to contract, the fever of long-delayed orgasm building from deep within.

Ketch's eyes lit up. He emitted a tiny sound, almost a death rattle, as he yielded to the inevitable. They were going to come. Together. Like fire and ice, totally wrong for one another, but still destined to live out their mutual sexual fate.

'Stella,' he moaned. 'Jeezus.'

She clamped his throat with sharp teeth, his own personal vampire. What the two gigolos made of all this, he hadn't a clue. Clutching at her wild mane of hair, Ketch pulled her up for a kiss. Lip to lip. Her eyes were white-hot. She'd bite him, but he didn't care. He'd fight back, or give in. Sweat dissolved between them, wetting the sand, already clumped with sex juice and male semen.

'I win again.' She grinned.

'I hate you,' he pronounced, flipping her onto her back. 'Stella Sawgrass.'

Her look was triumphal as he pummelled her loins, pistoning himself, his whole body a fulcrum at the single point of her bliss. And his.

'That's it,' she taunted. 'Do it to me, you spineless bastard.'

One more time he screamed out her name, looking heavenwards as he released the pent-up tensions and joys and humiliations. He was in Hades with this woman, or rather because of her. And he did not know how to get free. She was an itch that created itself then begged to be scratched. A story that built and built but had no ending.

'Get up, Ketch. We're finished here.'

Her voice came from far away. Dimly, he tried to rediscover his body, the earth beneath him. Stella was already on her feet, her mood darker now than it had been in a long, long time.

'You don't deserve me,' she said. 'And you'll never get your necklace back, either. No matter how many times you break into Heeter's house to look.'

Why not? Did she know something about the amulet he didn't? The wily bitch.

Some time later, when he'd recovered himself, long since abandoned, he found several hundred-dollar bills crumpled in the sand next to a fresh set of clothes she'd left for him. It was only then he remembered his plight.

Ketch Walker was a fugitive.

5

The sign read 'Welcome to Osprey Island, population 847', but Diane Quinton was quite sure she had ended up in the Twilight Zone. Having awoken just this morning safely, if not wealthily, ensconced in civilisation, she now found herself stranded in a tropical wilderness. It was like being in one of those old movies, except in place of cannibals there were men in grimy T-shirts emblazoned with Confederate flags, leaning against palm trees and chewing tobacco.

Could this really be the same Florida that had Miami in it and the Keys and Disney World?

'Maggie, please tell me this is just some bad excuse for a theme park on the way to our real destination.'

Diane waited as her sister negotiated yet another hairpin curve in the two-lane, sand-infested excuse for a road that constituted Osprey's main thoroughfare. The Florida Turnpike, lined with palm trees and tollbooths manned by buck-teethed men and women with necks redder than a freshly spanked bottom, was bad enough, but this – this was completely beyond imagination. That so-called bridge back there hadn't even seemed fit for mule much less automobiles.

'Sorry, sis, this is as good as it gets,' she replied at last. 'Uh oh. Hang on, Di. Road-block.' Maggie thrust her sneaker-clad foot down on the brakes, forcing Diane to brace herself on the dashboard of the embarrassingly small rental car her sister had insisted on using to pick her up.

'Road-block? What are you talking about?'

'Look down,' said Maggie, hands tapping the wheel in time to a country and western song on the radio.

Diane watched in disbelief as a large creature, green and scaly, slithered in front of them.

'Is that an . . .'

'Alligator.' Maggie completed her question as though this were a perfectly normal and acceptable event.

Di gripped the edges of the seat with the remnants of her manicured nails and pulled her feet up off the floor. 'You can't be serious. Alligators are supposed to be hand-bags and boots, not jaywalking on roads willy-nilly.'

Maggie looked at her and laughed. 'Don't be a baby, Di. They can't eat through car metal. You hungry yet?'

'A little,' Diane said, though she knew she'd live to regret it.

'Cool. I know a great place all the locals go.'

'I can hardly wait.'

As soon as the alligator had finished taking its sweet time playing *National Geographic* with them, Maggie drove on. Diane watched warily as they pulled into an ancient parking lot beside a weather-beaten corrugated steel shack with a sign declaring 'Good Eats at Barnacle Bill's Eatery'.

'I hope Bill's cooking skills are better than his gram-mar,' Diane quipped.

'Are you kidding? Bill makes the best grouper sand-wich on the island.'

'I'll bet the *steak au poivre* is to die for, too.'

'Stop being such a snob. Try opening your horizons a little,' her sister chided.

'There's opening one's horizon –' she opened her door and stepped gingerly onto the dusty gravel '– and then there's going completely off the deep end. There aren't going to be any more lizards out here, are there?'

'Nah. Bill snaps 'em up pretty fast. Especially on Tuesdays.'

'Dare I ask what's so special about Tuesdays?'

Maggie held open the battered screen door painted in red, white and blue. 'You don't want to know, Di. Trust me.'

The décor was a disaster area, with broken-down ceiling fans, patched-together wall panelling and a collection of decorations consisting of three horrifically mummified fish, a dozen or so battered licence plates and a driftwood statue that vaguely resembled the scarecrow from *The Wizard of Oz*. A middle-aged woman in a grey T-shirt and jeans led them to a square table in the corner.

'Do you have a wine list?' Di enquired as the waitress handed out a pair of grease-stained menus.

'Two drafts,' Maggie translated as her phone went off. 'And one appetiser platter.' She took the call, something about ducts in an office on the South Side of Chicago. She gathered it was from Tanya, her assistant.

Diane took the opportunity to scan her surroundings, the pair of men in racing caps sipping beers and the old woman in the far corner, vacant-eyed and whistling through what looked to be the only tooth in her head. A giant stuffed swordfish graced one of the walls, along with various yellowed newspaper clippings vaunting past achievements in auto racing.

'So?' Di asked when she'd hung up. 'Are you going to tell me what happened already? So far you've been more secretive than a fashion designer protecting a new line.'

Maggie wasn't making eye-contact, which wasn't a good sign. 'I told you on the phone, it's no big deal. You really didn't need to come.'

'Bull puckey,' Di countered. 'Spill it, sis, or I'll be

forced to tell everyone on this wretched island your nickname as a child.'

'You wouldn't dare.'

'Try me.'

The beers arrived and Maggie promptly drained half of hers in a single gulp. The ensuing moustache was endearing, though not entirely glamorous. 'If you must know,' she said, as she licked it off, 'it wasn't exactly a regular robbery.'

'Like anything around here could be regular.'

Down went the second half of baby sister's beer. This could mean only one thing. Man trouble.

Maggie took a deep breath and let loose. 'I shouldn't even tell you this, Diane. I swore to myself I wouldn't, because I know you, and I'll only end up being sorry if I do ... tell you, that is.'

'But you're going to anyway, dear, because you always do.'

Lord, but these beers looked repulsive. Where was the bottle? And why was it so pale and warm? There was no way she was going to stomach something that looked more like a racing car driver's backwash than a potable beverage.

A cigarette. Diane needed a cigarette. Pulling the slim, initialled silver case from her black purse – a perfect match to her black off-the-shoulder Sansone original – she prepared herself for a small dose of sanity in an otherwise insane world.

'Um, sis.'

'Yes, Magdalene?'

She had a sheepish look on her face. 'This is a no-smoking state.'

Di blinked. She had to be kidding. 'The entire state? What do they do if there's a forest fire? Arrest all the trees?'

'It's just in the restaurants. It's a health thing.'

Diane looked longingly at her wonderful, half-filled pack, each stick offering the promise of a few minutes' respite from this Panhandle Purgatory. 'You must really, really hate me,' she sighed dramatically. 'It's revenge for the time I cut all your dolls' hair short and used daddy's shoe polish to turn them punk, isn't it?'

'Stop trying to make me feel guilty, Diane. Lest we forget, you invited yourself down here to help me.'

Di thought she saw something in her sister's eye just then, a tell-tale glimmer. 'Look at me, Magdalene.'

Maggie averted her gaze. 'No, and you can't make me.'

'Now,' she repeated sternly, employing a voice that was sounding every year more like their mother's.

Maggie relented. Arms crossed, she offered a pouting glare, like a spoiled child. There was no hiding what was contained in those moist green depths, though, and it was hardly something juvenile.

'Son of a gun. You fucked that burglar, didn't you?'

Maggie hissed for her sister to be quiet; of course she hadn't done such a thing and did she want the whole world to know her business?

Diane leaned back, satisfied with herself. Her initial guess had come pretty damn close to a bullseye. 'OK, so you didn't fuck him, but you wanted to,' she decided.

'Absolutely not.'

'You're lying. Your nose is wrinkling the way it always does when you're not telling the truth.'

Maggie put her hand over her face to hide the evidence. 'I don't know what you're talking about, but, if you must know, something did happen last night. I was assaulted.'

Now that was a surprise. Nothing so far had given any indication of that, either in Maggie's account or the cop's phone call. 'I wish you'd have told me, Mags. That changes everything.'

'Well, it wasn't like an *assault* assault.' She started immediately back-pedalling. 'More like an almost assault.' Her nose was doing the samba.

'He tried to force himself on you?' Diane decided to go along for the ride. 'Sexually?'

'Sexually ... yes.' Maggie's eyes had that faraway look, more like a woman stung with the bite of infatuation than a near-rape victim.

'The police chief said he tied you up,' Di prompted. 'The man caught you right out of the bath.'

'I was naked,' confirmed her sister. 'He ... he made me fetch the rope. He said he wouldn't hurt me, as long as I did what he told me.'

'He could have done anything he wanted to you at that point.'

'Anything, it's true,' she said raspily. 'But he didn't. He was kind. He even let me put on some clothes before wrapping me up in the ropes.' Maggie was breathing more heavily. 'I chose a very sheer robe and a pair of panties. Nothing else.'

Diane could see the excitement in her eyes. She knew this part of her sister well. The danger-loving part behind the practical good-girl exterior. This was the part that had panted after that motorcycle hoodlum Joey Connelly all through high school, only to lose her virginity to him the night of her eighteenth birthday on the grease-stained floor of his uncle's mechanic's shop.

'That was a bold move, baby sister. You didn't leave much to the imagination, did you?'

'I don't know why I did it,' she replied. 'I only know I needed to be as bare for him as possible. More naked than naked, if that makes any sense. When I sat down for him and he started wrapping me in that rope, I just lost it. Honestly, it did more to my insides than most of the full-fledged fucks I've ever had. He could have made me come that way, just by tying me. If he'd wanted.'

'But he didn't want that?'

'No, I don't think so. At least I'm not sure. He seemed so sad, almost tragic. But he was all man. I could see how hard he was and I knew I was making him that way. That fact alone made me want to surrender to him completely. It was like he'd earned the right somehow, the right to have me and do whatever he wanted with me. Not by going through the regular channels, calling me and dating me and begging for my attention, but by virtue of just showing up, strong and macho, ready to take whatever he felt like – from Heeter's house and from me. Crazy, I know, but that's just how my mind was running at the time.'

'Women don't have to think logically when their pussies are involved, dear. Isn't that the excuse men have used for years with their dicks? Do tell me more, though. Exactly how much of the merchandise did your dream burglar sample?'

Maggie licked her lips, which seemed to Diane to have become very dry indeed. 'My breasts and my nipples. He chewed on them through my thin little robe. Till they were very swollen and very tight.'

'What about below the belt, did he get that far?'

'He went between my legs,' she confirmed.

'Did you fight him at this point?' It was a potentially loaded question, but it had to be asked.

Maggie's face flushed. 'No,' she confessed, her voice a hot whisper. 'I just sat there and . . . opened for him. I parted my legs to give him better access and then I began to moan. Di, it was like he'd known me all my adult life. He knew just where to go in my pussy, just how to stroke my clit to send me into orbit. With that tight, constrictive feeling of the ropes against my hot skin, I was ready to promise him anything. I'd have offered to have the man's babies if he'd asked. It was like I belonged to him, like I was made to give him pleasure through my own ability to come.'

Diane pressed her own moistening thighs together. She knew such feelings all too well. As she'd said already, she was a Quinton woman, cursed with the overactive sex gene. Few if any men had ever been able to keep up with them. Hartsley, Diane's last husband, had died trying – literally. The circumstances of the man's cardiac arrest, not to mention the position he'd been frozen into when rigor mortis had set in, were the scandal of his three grown children. They'd had their revenge when the old man's will was read. Predating his marriage to Diane, it left all of his worldly goods to them, with the exception of the small townhouse she now occupied.

C'est la guerre. Thanks to the generosity of an earlier dead husband, Roderick the real estate developer, she had enough to squeak by, though never quite enough to buy all the fun she wanted. Often she had to get creative, as she had on the flight down from O'Hare with Gregor Andel.

Was the young man enjoying his delectable little flight attendant by now? She doubted they would make it as far as a motel room. After debriefing from her flight, Lee Ann had no doubt found herself taken, hard and fast, over the counter of an airline restroom, or maybe over the trunk of a rental car. She was a pretty little thing; she'd make a tight fit for Gregor's wonderfully large dick, in any of her orifices. Lord, what a specimen the man would make naked, on top of her or mounting her from behind. If only Diane had had a little more time with him herself.

The waitress returned with a ceramic platter piled high with odd-shaped pieces of meat, covered in thick, fried batter. Di identified the 'O' shapes as most likely being onion rings and the tailed ones as shrimp. The rest were too nondescript for her to hazard a guess.

'So the police sirens chased him away,' Di concluded, vowing never to put anything in her mouth prepared by Bill the Beetle, or whatever his name was.

'Yes. I don't know what would have happened if he'd stayed.'

Diane had a pretty good idea, though she left the words unspoken. 'And so the cops found you like that,' she said, bringing the whole thing full circle. 'Still tied up.'

Maggie ran her hands through the mass of tangled curls, the exact opposite of Diane's terminally straight hair. 'I know, isn't it awful, Di? There were two of them. This one young guy was pretty discreet, but the older one, the chief, he acted like I had some kind of disease.'

'What do you expect, sis? He found you trussed up like the cover of a bondage magazine spouting some story about an intruder who miraculously managed to steal nothing but your modesty. What was he supposed to think? The thing I can't figure out, though, is what brought them over there if you didn't call them.'

Maggie cocked her head. 'I don't know. I hadn't thought of that. Maybe a neighbour down the beach reported seeing a strange man, or else some passing car saw the burglar coming in my window? Around here everyone knows everyone else's business.'

Diane speared a long thin strip of battered meat with her fork, more out of scientific curiosity than any gustatory intentions. 'Magdalene, please tell me this is chicken.'

'Uh huh.'

'Your nose is wiggling again, Mags.'

'If you must know, it's alligator. Left over from the Tuesday blue-plate special.'

'Charming. And the little round things?' She rolled a battered ball to her sister's side of the plate.

'Fried okra.'

'Fried *Oprah*? As in the talk-show host?

'No, okra's a green vegetable. They eat it a lot in the South. Oh, God, Di, it's him.'

'Him who?'

'That cop from last night.' She grabbed her sister's arm. 'The one who didn't like me. Chief Grifford.'

'Mmm,' Diane crooned, scanning the scrumptious-looking khaki-unformed man standing at the counter. 'So that's what goes with the voice I heard. You didn't tell me they gave steroids to their Boy Scouts down here. Or is it something in the water?'

'We've got to get out of here, sis.'

'Get out? Don't be silly, Mags. Finally I find something edible on this island and now you're telling me you aren't going to introduce me?'

'Are you kidding?' she whispered fiercely, trying to keep her head down to the level of her plate of fried alligator. 'What exactly would you like me to say? "Oh, hi, remember me? I'm the sexed-up crazy girl you found tied to a chair last night, and by the way this is my sister, who just flew down from Chicago and she has the hots for you"?'

Maggie's attempt at irony was lost on her dark-haired sibling. 'No, you can't tell him I'm your sister. Then he won't screw me because he'll think I'm some kind of accessory to the crime.'

'An accessory? But I haven't done anything wrong.'

'That's your loss. Personally I'd let him arrest me and throw away the key.'

Diane watched the black-and-silver-haired police chief walk to a booth in the corner, her eyes glued shamelessly to the cop's tight ass. There was no denying that the man filled out a uniform to a tee – from the badge-emblazoned khaki shirt to the well-filled shorts that would have done honour to even the most endowed of overnight express men.

'Oh, yeah, Mags, he is definitely doable,' Diane declared throatily as the six-foot, eagle-eyed peace officer hunkered down into the leatherette seat. The two waitresses were already cat-fighting for territory.

'Well, you can't,' said Maggie, a little petulantly. 'He's the enemy. We can't forget that.'

'And who exactly is "we"? You and I, or you and your little rebel without a clue?'

'Us. You and me. We're in this together.'

'Oh, so now we're all sisterly and confidential, huh? When it suits your convenience. Tell me honestly, sibling dearest, if your masked marvel were to drop in on us right now and offer to tie you to the nearest bed, how many seconds would it take you to ditch me?'

Maggie's eyes shifted guiltily.

'Just as I thought. Now, how about if you start helping me out here by telling me all about this island, since it looks like I'm going to be here a while. For starters, you can spill the beans on Captain Scrumptious over there.'

'He's not married, if that's what you mean. They say he sees a woman, off and on, some kind of wild witch who lives on the far side of the island. Her and a lot of cats, and some magic potions, too, depending on who you talk to on the subject. Beyond that, he doesn't date, he doesn't go to pick-up bars and he doesn't lie on the beach in a thong. Guess that doesn't leave you much to work with.'

'Maybe not.' Diane was pursing her lips. She felt that wicked glow in her tummy, the one that had landed them both in all that hot water, that time at their cousin Bobby's wedding reception, with a pair of very gorgeous twin waiters. 'But then again, he does have to pull over speeders, now, doesn't he?'

'You can't be serious. What about that dentist you were dating?'

'His drill bits weren't up to par. Nor was his bank account.'

'Whatever, Di. Right now, I just want to go home, peel off everything and bake in the sun for about two hours straight. Doesn't that sound heavenly?'

'Actually I was hoping you'd take me somewhere so I can rent a very fast car.'

Maggie narrowed her eyes. 'You're really going to do this, aren't you? You're really going after that cop, even when you know he's off limits.'

'I plead the fifth ... preferably gin.'

Maggie shook her head. 'Unbelievable. I'd be better off talking to Mom. At least she would have given me a shoulder to cry on.'

It was intended as a stab, but Di was pretty impregnable these days.

'Really? And exactly what parallel universe are you speaking of? Or have you managed to entirely redesign your Quinton family history the way you do islands and forests? When was the last time either one of our parents was there for us? Diaper changes? Whoops, I forgot, we had nannies for that.'

Maggie sighed, obviously regretting comparing the two women. 'Sorry, Di, that was a cheap shot. I don't know what's gotten into me.'

'Which is why I'm going to show you how to have some fun down here. I mean, look around – there's got to be some advantage to slumming it in Dixie. Trust me, I'll get your mind off this robbery nonsense. You just gotta give me my space when I need it. And a nice fast car. Deal?'

Maggie laughed in spite of herself. 'We're really not a normal family, are we?'

'Perish the thought.' Di shivered.

'Just go home with me for a couple of hours first, please? There's no way I can concentrate enough to go out to the construction site today and I can't bear to be in that house alone right now. We can lie out on the deck. It'll be cool.'

'Two hours,' she agreed. 'After that all bets are off.'

'They don't make odds for you any more, Diane. Not even in Vegas.'

'My dear, I resemble that remark,' she crooned in her best Mae West.

'Come on.' Maggie tossed a twenty-dollar bill on the table to cover the backwash beer and greasy 'gator meat. 'Let's get out of here while he's got his nose buried in that menu.'

They slipped out of the diner unseen. By the time their toes hit the sand-covered parking lot, they were laughing, arm in arm, like schoolgirls again.

'Katy Sue, you in there?'

'It's Jake,' she whispered to the big cop on top of her, busily fucking her on the guest bed in Heeter's house.

'Oh, Jeezus,' croaked Mike, his cock deeply buried in

her freshly scrubbed pussy for a second round. 'He must have seen the truck out front. Damn it, I knew you should have parked it around back.'

'Wouldn't have mattered.' Katy grabbed at him. 'I told him where I'd be.'

'You did what?'

'I didn't want him to be suspicious, so I told him I was helping you on a case.'

She squeezed her pussy muscles, holding him in place. Seducing Cos all over again after they'd cleaned up from the fingerprint mess was a real stroke of genius on her part. Especially since she'd now have the added fun of maybe getting caught. A lot of women called her a slut and a bitch for playing men like she did, but the truth was, Katy Sue got bored and resented that men had so many more chances to fuck around.

'Don't stop,' she moaned, her hands rubbing over his strong, corded back. 'I'm almost there.'

'Let go of me, Katy, you want Jake to see this?'

She wrapped her dancer's legs round his muscular cop ass. 'Why not?'

The thought made Katy Sue weak and hot all over. Two strapping men going at it tooth and nail, her little body as the prize. Hot and naked, she would wait in bed for the fight to end, knowing the winner would have her to do with as he willed.

'Jake's not half the man you are.' She nibbled at the sinews of his neck and ran her nails over his broad shoulders. 'You know he doesn't deserve me.'

Mike increased his thrusting. He couldn't resist her. No man could.

'Katy, you're a little witch,' he told her.

'Is that all? I was hoping for the B-word.'

'Let's just get this over with,' he said, gritting his teeth.

Katy Sue's face darkened. 'I don't like being used all in a hurry like some kind of a fuck doll, Cos. It makes me mad.'

She decided to punish him. And Jake, too. Lifting her head she called out good and loud. 'Hey, Jake, I'm up here fu–'

Cosgrove's hand slapped down over her mouth before she could get the rest out. 'You need to wait outside, Jake,' he called out, trying to sound as natural as possible. 'You can't come up . . . it's a crime scene.'

Katy Sue chomped down on his finger, forcing him to release her. He made a face, suppressing the pain.

'That was good thinking,' she whispered, lapping her tongue over his nipple to ease his suffering. 'Now, how are you gonna explain it when we're both shouting and moaning in another thirty seconds?'

'Katy, when you coming home?' Jake wanted to know.

'Just as soon as the officer's done using me, sweetheart.'

Katy Sue bucked her hips, forcing her pelvis against Mike's. His eyes went wide with the mix of desire and pain. Rivulets of hot lust snaked down Katy Sue's belly to her crotch. She wanted more.

'Finish me off.' She slapped his cheek hard. 'Make me come.'

'Till he's done *what*?' Jake asked.

'Done using me,' she repeated, getting off on the sexy dialogue. 'I'm doing my civic duty.' She winked. 'Serving the law.'

Mike began pumping her in earnest, his hands seizing her breasts, mauling them most satisfyingly. The strain in his face as he gave into his animal side was more than a little evident. If he wasn't careful, he'd screw her right into the floor. Or scream out like a wild banshee. Time to push him over the edge, she decided.

'Mike, why don't you tell Jake what a good helper I am,' she called out, loud enough for her husband to hear. 'You do think I'm good, don't you, Mike?'

He looked as if he was ready to kill her, but he didn't have much choice other than to keep playing her game. His dick needed the satisfaction and she was it. 'Uh, yeah, Jake,' he grunted. 'Katy Sue's real . . . good.'

'And tight, too,' she whispered into the cop's ear.

Mike let loose a groan. The bedsprings were starting to squeak under the pressure.

'That's it, baby,' she encouraged. 'Do me. Do me hard, with my husband right downstairs.'

This last little bit was enough to push him over the top. For a second load, it was pretty full. Katy Sue came with him, crying out 'Yes' over and over. It was more than a little blatant, but she knew Jake well enough to know that, if there was anything the man wanted, it was peace. If that meant lying to himself about his wife's fidelity in the face of overwhelming evidence – which it often did – then that's exactly what he'd do.

'That was excellent, lover.' She kissed him on his red, swollen lips, then pushed him back with her palms. 'Now you better get going, before I tell Jake to come on up.'

She suppressed a giggle as the man almost leapt from the bed to find his clothes. 'Be right there,' he assured Jake, hopping into his shorts and running for the door. She put on her own clothes, lazily, and followed him out to the front door. Sure enough, Jake was standing there waiting, just as Cosgrove had told him to do.

'Hi, baby.' Katy Sue sidled up to her husband in her cutoffs and halter. She was barefoot and hadn't bothered to put her panties back on. Wrapping her arm round Jake's thin waist and burying her face in his thick beard she delivered a hot, wet kiss, one that promised plenty of action in the bedroom tonight. If they made it that far.

'I want you to tie me up,' she whispered into his ear, standing on tiptoe and moulding her tight curves to his male hardness, chest to knee. 'I want you to make me helpless, then I want you to invite all your friends over to have me.'

Jake's dick sprang to attention. This was a favourite mutual fantasy, though neither of them had had the gumption to live it out yet. The closest Katy Sue had come was to sleep around behind his back, hardly a fitting substitute.

'Calm down, woman. We ain't alone.' Jake tried to push her aside out of respect for the policeman.

Katy Sue continued to drape herself, in an effort to make Mike jealous. As far as she was concerned, it was a nonstop job controlling and manipulating the men in her life, but the results were more than worth it. Any day she chose, she could run off with any number of them. Doctors, lawyers and businessmen made her offers all the time. And when she got tired of playing around here, why, that's exactly what she'd do. She could picture it now, living the life of ease in a ranch house outside Tallahassee or a high-rise apartment in Jacksonville.

'Who do y'all think did this?' Jake asked Mike, doing his best to ignore Katy Sue's hot hand on his ass.

Katy Sue smiled to herself. The forty-five-year-old twice-divorced mechanic knew better than to fight his twenty-two-year-old wife. He was darned lucky she'd married him at all. It was his laidback attitude and steady income that won her over, along with his steadfast determination to look the other way. Theirs was definitely a marriage of convenience. He got a young trophy wife and she got an occasional shoulder to cry on and a built-in protector when she needed one. Of course, she held her own at Diamond Pete's, too, in more ways than one. By now she was making way more than Jake. Katy Sue let him think she was bringing all her earnings home. If only he knew the half of it. She had two secret bank accounts, both doing mighty nicely.

'I'm thinking it was an interrupted crime of passion.' Mike rested his hands on his gun belt. 'It would only have taken one guy,' he explained, developing her theory. 'Ex-boyfriend, jealous lover, something like that. Nothing was stolen, you see, and –'

Cosgrove cut himself off, probably because he'd just realised he shouldn't be talking about the case to anyone.

'Mike showed me all about fingerprints, honey,' said Katy Sue to her husband.

'Yeah?' Jake narrowed his gaze slightly. Was he starting to figure it out? If nothing else, Jake should be able to smell her all over the man and vice versa. 'How is it you ended up so short-handed today, Cos? Where's the chief?'

'He left me in charge,' Cosgrove said proudly. 'Between you and me, I think maybe he's looking to retire.'

Griff retire? Now that was news. She'd have to make a point of running it through the rumour mill later on at the beauty parlour.

'Hey, here comes the woman now,' Cos said. 'The one who was in the house when it was robbed. She went to get her sister. That must be her.'

Katy Sue watched the rental car pull up into the driveway with the two women in it. Both were pretty – a little too pretty for her liking.

'Officer Cosgrove,' said the casually dressed redhead. 'This is my sister, Diane.'

Cosgrove took off his hat. 'Ma'am.'

'Charmed,' said the dark-haired woman, beaming and looking like something out of a magazine as she held out her hand. 'I've heard all about you.'

The redhead gave her sister a look that translated as 'shut up' in any language. Katy Sue decided she liked this one, but not the snobby one in the black dress.

'This is Jake and Katy Sue Tregan,' said Mike, introducing the happy couple.

'Charmed,' said Katy, mimicking the bitchy sister, whose interest in Mike was more than a little obvious.

'Indeed.' Diane smiled back, a thin and cunning glare that indicated she'd get even later.

Northern women. Katy could spit on the ground for all she cared about their fancy ways and double talk.

'Pleased to meet you.' Jake spoke up, taking off his oil-soaked baseball cap and putting out his hand.

The redhead took it at once, unafraid of the engine grease. 'I'm Maggie. I've heard you can fix anything. I'll be sure to look you up if I run into trouble.'

'Any time, ma'am.'

Katy Sue barely hid her smirk as he took Diane's hand next. The bitchy one didn't like to get herself dirty, that was obvious. Ooh, what she wouldn't give to see her in a cheap bikini, two sizes too small, or better still buck naked, wrestling in the Tuesday-night mud pit at Diamond Pete's, competing like a she-demon with the rest of the no-talent amateurs for the weekly fifty-dollar prize. Katy could picture the look on her face, too, if she actually won and discovered the 'stipulation' imposed by Pete for receiving the money.

Would she ever be desperate enough to take it? Kneeling before the man while he leaned against the bar, his beefy palm slapped down on the lovely green bill, as he expectantly waits for her to unzip his pants, take out his hard dick and put it between her stuck-up Yankee lips?

'I'm real sorry about what happened last night,' said Jake to the redhead. 'It's a terrible thing. We don't usually see that kind of thing around these parts.'

Katy Sue watched the woman closely for tell-tale signs of her trying to hide something criminal.

'I'd rather put it behind me,' she said, passing Katy Sue's visual lie-detector test with flying colours.

'And you will,' said Mike, putting his wide-brimmed hat back over his handsome head. 'As soon as we get the case solved. Jake, ladies, if you don't mind, I'll be on my way.'

'Later,' Katy Sue said, adding just enough sugar to her voice to make them all wonder.

'And I got to get back to the shop,' said Jake.

'Actually, you got something to do at home first,' Katy Sue told him, more than a little suggestively.

The dark-haired one turned up her nose, just slightly, but the redhead was still smiling.

'It was nice to meet you,' Maggie said.

'Will we be seeing you again?' Diane wanted to know.

Katy Sue steered her man towards their two trucks. 'Count on it,' she said pointedly.

6

Ketch had resisted pulling down his shorts and touching himself for as long as he could. He was supposed to be on surveillance, and he was hardly a pervert, but the redhead was just too beautiful to resist. Her nearly naked body was oiled all over, and the tiny string bikini barely covered her maddening curves as she reclined in the lounge chair on the balcony.

He felt guilty, of course. Finding this empty house next door to Heeter's with a third-storey window to spy out of had been a stroke of good fortune and he ought to be thanking Apollo or Athena, not drooling through his binoculars and rubbing his hard, throbbing dick, pretending he was inside the redhead's pussy right now.

By Hades, he could even make out her nipples through the tiny fabric scraps covering her full breasts. And that stomach, so completely concave, undulating with her every breath, her every little motion, the air just above it shimmering like a desert mirage. He wanted to kiss her on that little belly button as it screamed out, here I am, a sexy goddess, come and get me.

Ketch moved forwards to the window frame on his knees, pumping his buttocks as if he was right there on that lounger with her, right between her suggestively parted legs. For a split second he tried to justify it all, telling himself she ought to expect this kind of thing, looking like that, leaving her legs open just enough for the imagination to run wild with possibilities of probing and touching and exploring. And those strings on the sides of her top and bottom – what did they say but come and pluck me, tug me open and have your way? I'm a present, curvy and small, just right for a man to enjoy.

But that was merely a rationalisation for violating her privacy, as well as his own integrity. Playing with his hot, hard dick was the last thing he needed to be doing right now, no matter how edible his little copper-haired nymph might appear to be, with her tiny pink toenails and that little space in the hollow of her neck where a man could just breathe her in, his hands nestled in the full mane of her hair.

No, he needed to stop, needed to pull the elastic shorts Stella had given him back up over his thighs and save his strength. There were cops out there looking for him. Sooner or later they'd get him, too, which meant he had only so long to find his chance to get back over there and find the amulet. The sacred talisman, source of his purity, precious jewel of life so cruelly taken from him, not once but twice.

He pictured the many-coloured stones of the rounded amulet on the gold necklace, and the lovely jade ele-phant that was its centrepiece. Twice it had saved his life, guiding his footsteps on the true path to his des-tiny. When he'd purchased the thing for less than ten US dollars in Bangkok, he had no idea of its value. Not till the fortune-teller had held it in her hand and told him things no one could ever know about him.

'This is the source of your power,' she told him. 'Never let it from your sight.' And he hadn't till Stella had gotten hold of it, along with everything else, in one of her blind rages.

It was no wonder he was floundering right now.

Without the talisman, he wasn't ever going to think straight. He had to get it back. No one would stand in the way, either, not Stella and certainly not that Dark and Callous Buffoon Calvin Heeter Junior.

Revenge. Justice. These were his watchwords. Not thoughts of flame-haired females, fresh from baths, their sex lips full and pouty, wet from the water, and even wetter from their own juices.

Had she been masturbating in the tub last night, thinking of someone? Impulsively, Ketch wanted it to be him, his image burning in her red-gold head and in her complex, mysterious heart.

Blast it, why hadn't he asked her name?

All thoughts of nymphs, elephant necklaces and orgasms vanished as the second woman came out onto the balcony. By the three heads of Cerberus – he froze mid-stroke – who was this new dryad? They couldn't have been more different. Unlike the redhead, the newcomer's hair was dark and tied back with some sort of fancy catch or clasp. She was a little taller, and maybe a tiny bit less curvy, but not by much. There were miles to her legs and the belly was flat as an iron, nicely highlighting her medium-sized breasts. She was wearing a black bikini, very small, very revealing. Ketch gauged her to be maybe five years older, no more.

He felt a little stab of unease as she sat on the edge of the chair occupied by the redhead, who promptly turned over onto her back. The taller one was squirting the oil directly, letting the glistening liquid sluice down the redhead's body, from her neck all the way to her barely covered, quivering ass cheeks. They were laughing, talking. Could they be lovers? Sure enough, the dark-haired one was undoing the ties on the redhead's bikini top for better access. He watched the woman's hands on the redhead's back with envy. The redhead was shivering at the caresses, her buttock cheeks undulating slightly.

After several minutes of rubbing, Red Hair turned back over, allowing Black Hair to help her take her top completely off. Here goes, he thought, bracing himself. But there wasn't any sexual contact. Just some more talking, light and easy, as if they were old, old friends.

Strange.

He didn't know why he was so relieved to find they weren't lesbian partners, but he was. Really, he shouldn't be caring at all who they were. The bottom line was he now had two women between him and the object of his quest instead of one. That wasn't very good odds, given that the clock was ticking towards his inevitable capture, not to mention the eventual return of the home's owner, the great Disrespecter of Property and Amoral Affronter to Civilisation Himself.

Ketch sighed deeply as he confronted the harsh reality. Up to a certain point he could sit back and watch for an opportunity to go back over there, waiting for them to leave for good or even for the evening. But, in the end, it might come down to something more drastic. Something that might involve buying some extra rope.

Chief John Grifford, known to all but his ex-wife and the tax collector as Griff, nearly choked on the half-chewed mouthful of sunflower seeds. The two-seater must have been doing nearly ninety, judging by the ruffled feathers of the blue jay he'd been sharing his afternoon snack with. The crazy bastard would be lucky not to end up rolling into the Gulf, pulling down that kind of speed.

Tossing the remains of the plastic baggie on the ground for the little bird and his friends, Griff hopped up into the modified Jeep the town had bought him for Christmas. For a four-wheel drive, it packed a punch, one he loved to unload on smart-ass tourists any chance he got.

Griff didn't bother with the lights and siren. This wasn't Tallahassee or Tampa; this was Osprey Island, where he'd grown up and his father before him. Before all this bullshit development. Before the million-dollar beach homes and the sham robberies. Like last night at the Heeter place. There was no way in hell that was a bona fide break-in. He'd bet half his sorry excuse for a pension it was a boyfriend who'd tied her up, the whole thing having been orchestrated weeks ago, complete with a fence already lined up to sell off whatever they'd stolen and not reported.

Frankly, he'd expected the young woman to make a run for it already. Instead she'd gone and come back with the sister in tow. The dark-haired woman gave him an instant hard-on. If she'd sounded sexy on the phone, she'd been twice as enticing in person. The fact that she looked so totally out of place, as if she was above it all, amused and intrigued him. City girls weren't his type, but, if they ever were, she'd be the one.

Griff wasn't sure what the two of them were up to, though it was a scam to be sure. Maybe some insurance thing. Or some kind of lover's tiff involving Heeter himself. The man had proven conveniently unavailable for questioning, that was for sure: off at sea without a cell phone. As if assholes of that calibre ever ditched their telecommunications equipment to enjoy the unsullied beauties of nature.

And here was another thing: the so-called robbery had been reported by an anonymous female caller who claimed to be driving past the house when she saw a 'scuffle' through the window. She'd ignored instructions to remain in the area. According to neighbours there'd been a suspicious woman staking out the Heeter place all afternoon in a VW van with South Carolina plates.

No, there was something rotten in Denmark and it wasn't the stale Danish he'd eaten at the diner earlier. It was almost laughable how those two Yankee sisters thought he didn't notice them chattering and conspiring back there. Did they think he wouldn't recognise Diane's voice? Probably thought he was such a complete imbecile that they could sneak out right under his nose undetected, too. Well, they'd be in for a surprise. John Grifford III might be a genuine redneck, but he was nobody's fool.

'Dispatch. This is Unit One,' he called into the radio as he closed the gap almost enough to read the licence. 'Get ready to run me a plate.'

Just a few inches closer and he'd have it. Hopefully it would be a legitimate address. Nope, it was a rental. That figured.

'Scratch that, dispatch. Just get me a cell ready. I'm figuring to bring this joker in on something just for ruining my afternoon nature time.'

'Okey dokey,' chimed Nadine Hawkins, who was married to Griff's third cousin and therefore had the dispatch job for life, despite the fact that she wouldn't know proper police jargon if it whomped her over the head. 'Say, are you still coming for dinner Sunday night, Chief?'

'Can the personal chatter, Dispatch.' He pulled right up behind the speeder's bumper now so there'd be no mistaking his intent. 'Unit one, over and out.'

He pointed to the shoulder for the benefit of the runaway driver, who Griff now saw clearly was not a 'he' but a 'she'. Oh, well, it was a new age, wasn't it?

Whoever this woman was, she wasn't up for a chase. One signal from Griff was enough to pull her onto the side of the two-lane asphalt highway, the only way on or off the island.

Avoiding his Stetson chief's hat, which he hated worse than Nadine's meatloaf and sugar beets, Griff dismounted the white and blue monster, taking stock of the situation.

Damn. This one was a looker even from behind. Long dark hair, done up high on her head, graceful neck, nude shoulders, their smooth ivory colour broken only by the tiniest red straps. A trifle overdressed for these parts, but he wasn't about to complain.

Griff pulled the citation book from his belt before eyeballing the front of her, 'Ma'am, I don't know where you're from, but around here we have a little thing called speed limits.'

'A little thing called speed limits,' she repeated in a light titter. 'That's funny. I never heard that one before.'

Grifford's teeth set on edge. It was her. The sister from Chicago. She must have changed clothes, dolling herself up even more. Griff blinked, trying to figure where to look first. Compared to her front end, the rear view, good as it was, was like the floor of Muldoon's Tavern and Tackle after closing on Saturday karaoke night. For starters, there were the lips. Red as a cardinal, and doing things he didn't even know lips could do. She had to be some kind of model or actress. Hell, she could even be in the magazines he jerked off to when Star Shine, his sometime lover and gal pal, was in one of her meditational downturns.

And that body, the way that tiny red dress made his eyes sweep down past her collarbone to the valley between her generous breasts and below that to her flat belly. But that was only the beginning. The speeder had smooth naked thighs below the hem of her short dress, which if it rode much higher would qualify as a T-shirt. Griff's mouth went dry. He could get himself lost down there in a hurry if he wasn't real careful.

'Am I in trouble?' she crooned, parting her thighs the tiniest bit as if by accident.

'Just show me your licence and registration.' He tried to remember his lines.

Griff watched as she reached for the glove box. Talk about legs. Miles of them, smooth, slender and round in all the right places; like a roller coaster from her hip, moulded to fit a man's hand, all the way down to her flexed calves and gently turned ankles, subtly constrained by the wispy straps of her high heels. He wanted to be down there, sucking those red, red toes. Redder than his roof lights. What a piece of woman flesh! If he could just recline that seat and climb in there, pushing her all the way back and splitting open those chorus-girl legs, his dick jackknifing her like a tractor trailer on Route 10.

And why shouldn't he be so lucky? On the mainland there was action like this to be had all the time, pretty women with cop fetishes looking for a little police brutality, nice and consensual. Yeah, this one would take it hard and deep and she'd shimmy out of that dress plenty fast to avoid getting herself a citation if the officer was anything but buck ugly.

That had happened to him just once, back in those crazy hippy days in the seventies when he and his father, the then police chief, were feuding and he'd gone over to the enemy, temporarily piloting a black-and-tan cruiser for the Highway Patrol on the mainland. The perpetrator in question was a college junior, up from Gainesville, scared shitless of raising Daddy's insurance rates.

'Isn't there any way I can get out of this ticket?' she'd purred, squirming in those cut-off shorts, her tie-dyed shirt peaked by naked nipples.

Griff had accepted the blowjob at a nearby rest area, the curly-haired blonde hot and eager to suck off a genuine star-wearing establishment pig. Her mouth was slick and tight and as he pumped her hard it occurred to him that he liked this a little too much, this having total power over a woman. It didn't seem to hurt her any, though, and, by the time he was ready to shoot off, so was she. They came together, her hand stuffed down the front of her shorts, his hand at the back of her neck holding her in place.

The hippy chick had given him a sweet smile when they were done and had the courtesy to wait till he'd zipped up and turned back to his cruiser before spitting out his semen. The next day Griff quit the state force and moved back to Osprey.

'Officer? You wanted these?'

Grifford jolted back to reality from behind his mirrored shades. Damn, he'd nearly blanked out, fantasising. Had he been out in the sun too long? More likely it was the lack of sleep from having to get up and deal with that phony robbery half the night. Face, it, Griff, you're not as young as you used to be. Sure, you were clever enough to find Diane Quinton's phone number scribbled on a sticky note on the Heeter fridge so you could call and verify Maggie's identity, but still, one of these days, before too many more years, you're gonna have to turn the whole ball of wax over to some pup. Like Cosgrove, perish the thought. Unless he could have himself a grown-up son in a hurry to carry on the family tradition. Now this one right here, she could bear some real healthy ones.

'Turn your engine off and give me the keys,' he said

curtly, accepting her picture ID. He was taking no chances on her running, especially if he found half of what he expected to on her.

The dark-haired beauty smiled coyly as she extended her wrists, palm up. 'Am I under arrest, sir?'

The waft of sweet, womanly perfume nearly knocked him on his behind. 'Just stay put, ma'am.'

It was more than a little difficult to walk back to the Jeep. Hopefully she hadn't seen the erection, the little wench. 'Unit One to dispatch,' he barked into the radio, in no mood for guff. 'Requesting Illinois licence check, number –'

'Chief, is that you?'

Grifford ground his teeth, praying for patience. Ten years of this and she hadn't caught on yet. 'Of course it's me,' he thundered. 'Who the hell else would be running around out here? Elliot Ness?'

'You don't have to yell,' Nadine intoned. 'Say, Chief, would you rather have pot roast or meatloaf on Sunday?'

It was like pulling teeth the rest of the way, but he finally got what he needed out of her. The criminal database turned up nothing extraordinary. More than her share of parking tickets and a few tell-tale 'non-moving violations', which were red flags for speeding infractions pleaded down with the help of expensive lawyers. The really interesting part was her name. Turned out this Diane Quinton Rostov had a few more of them in her past. Apparently marrying was one of her hobbies, along with fast cars. Was one of her ex-husbands part of this robbery scam?

Time would tell. It always did. Until then, Grifford planned on keeping his cards as close to his chest as she did hers. Not that he had a chest to compare.

'We don't take kindly to moving violations in the

state of Florida,' he informed her, handing back the licence and rental-car registration along with the paperwork for the fine. 'Sign here.'

'I've been a bad girl.' She brushed his hand with hers. 'A very bad girl.'

Griff frowned, eyes wary behind his proverbial cop shades. Did she really think he was stupid enough to lay a hand on her and set himself up for a lawsuit for harassment? 'Just pay attention to the signs next time,' he said as he took back the pen.

'I will,' she promised, 'if you'll pay attention to this.'

Griff swallowed. 'This' was her bare pussy, outlined by neatly trimmed black hair, the puffy pink lips pulled apart by her long red fingernails. Damn, the crazy bitch had pulled up her dress and she wasn't wearing any underwear.

Images flashed through his mind of this curvaceous speed freak bent over the back of her own car, dress pulled up to her waist, getting what she deserved from the palm of his red-hot hand. A man would die to see an ass like hers, let alone have the chance to punish it properly. And that would be only the beginning. After that she'd have a nice injection of cop dick. A dick engorged by blue blood, the kind you can only find in uniformed trousers. What he ought to do was spank her and then put her on her knees like the little blonde. Then he could teach her something useful to do with that mouth of hers.

'I'm going to pretend this didn't happen, Mrs Rostov.' He'd used her most recent married name to get a reaction from the woman, but she remained implacable.

'It's Quinton now. I'm divorced. But you can call me Diane. Free As A Bird Diane.'

'Well, then, you should have a wonderful time down

here. The spring breakers will be here any day now. Good day, ma'am.'

'Officer, one more thing,' she called out over her shoulder.

Griff steeled himself. 'Ma'am?'

'You mentioned a good time. Where would a lady go for that around here?'

'You're a little dressed up for Muldoon's. I'd recommend the bar at the Continental Hotel, just across the bridge.'

'Thank you, officer. I'll be there at seven. If you care to join me.'

Griff made no reply. After getting back in the Jeep, he backed it up and headed down the road, taking the well-worn path to Star Shine's place. Looking down at the state of his hopelessly tented shorts, he really hoped her life force was in harmony today because, if it wasn't, the picture would not be very pretty for his manhood, better known as Little Griff.

Maggie knew he was out there, watching her sunbathe. She'd felt his presence all along and now she was sure of it. Just as Diane was getting up to leave, off on her silly mission to bag the chief in her red dress and fast car, she'd seen the glint of light out of the window next door, presumably off the end of a pair of binoculars.

The owners were away and no one was supposed to be over there. How she was sure it was the burglar – her burglar – and not some other random peeping tom who'd broken in to spy on her, she couldn't say. Maybe it was intuition. Or maybe they were connected now on account of what they'd been through together; what he'd put her through, to be precise. Well, now it was going to be payback time. She could have told Diane about her suspicions or, more practically, called the police. Instead, she was going to handle things all by her lonesome.

Her and Heeter's pistol, that is, the one she'd discovered in the closet while looking for beach towels. It was a thirty-eight-calibre police special, and it had bullets to boot. She wouldn't actually shoot him, but she did intend to teach him a lesson whenever he came back.

Yes, indeed, Mister Burglar was going to have himself quite a little surprise. For now, though, she had a different game in mind. Since the boy liked to look so much, why not give him a show? A little taste of the flesh he would never possess. She opted to start with her stomach. Holding the suntan lotion nice and high, the gooey, white kind, she gave the bottle a good hard squeeze, letting a thick stream of it splash onto her belly. It was cool and moist on her hot skin. Deliberately, she circled the bottle, making little squiggles. The stuff looked like come and she hoped it was driving him out of his mind.

Very slowly now, she began to rub it in, arching her back and sucking in her breath. Was he imagining himself touching her, putting his hands all over her warm and willing flesh? She moved up her ribcage now, fanning out her fingers all the way to the bottom of her breasts. He'd be seeing a lot more of them in a minute. She sat up, shaking out her hair. It was time to work on her thighs. A little more lotion, over each one, so very close to her delta, concealing the sex she knew he wished he was inside right now.

Kneading her skin, she let him know just how athletic she was. Maggie had legs to wrap round a man's midsection. The right man. Damn, but it had been way too long since she'd gotten laid. How long was it since her last rendezvous with Bruce, the commodities broker? Two, maybe three months? Now there was a man who knew how to fuck a woman. Bruce approached sex as he did his job, as a feeding frenzy, a bell-to-bell extravaganza, kill or be killed. You didn't mince words with the man, or minutes. Keep up with him and you'd be rocked to the orgasm of your life; fall behind and you were yesterday's quotes. Most women would hate that sort of thing, but not Maggie. He was intense; he cut to the chase and, above all, he had absolutely no interest in a real relationship.

You'd never find his ass lazing in your bed the next morning, no ma'am, and he didn't expect to find your ass in his, either. It was the perfect arrangement for a busy professional with a streak of bad girl in her. And if that didn't do the trick, she could masturbate thinking of Hank, the construction worker she'd met on one of her last jobsites up north last year. He was a brazen one, with a perpetual five o'clock shadow, scruffy auburn hair and a 'hellcat' tattoo on his rock-hard bicep.

Maggie was used to being watched by the men, but with the rest it was something skulking and secret. Hank had looked at her from the start as if he had the right. As if her skirt-clad ass already belonged to him. There was something else about him, too. A kind of intelligence, a quick wit in his brown eyes that made her think he didn't fit with the others somehow.

'Can I help you with something?' she had said, whipping round one day as he was taking his usual gander.

He just stood there, leaning on his shovel, not even caring that he'd been caught. 'That depends,' he replied with a devastating smirk that showed his dimples to full effect. 'Are you asking me as the boss or as a woman?'

Maggie was taken aback. 'Both,' she replied without thinking.

'In that case—' he pushed back the brim of his hard-hat '—I'd say you could help me plenty, 'cause right now I'm wondering more than anything what you'd feel like squirming naked underneath me as I blow your mind with orgasm after orgasm.'

Maggie's knees nearly gave way. 'You're fired,' she told the man.

'Can't do that,' he informed her. 'I'm union.'

Five minutes later he had her on top of the desk in the site office, her frilly pink panties dangling over one ankle as his ten-inch cock jack-hammered fast and furious in and out of her wet hole. He smelled of sweat and dirt and musk and it was the best aphrodisiac she'd ever had in her life. She had to bite down on his shoulder to stifle the moans as he played her, his strong, callused hands squeezing her soft, bare tits mercilessly. It was the most exciting fuck of her life. Any minute someone could walk in and find her like this, her naked buttocks plastered to the metal desk, her legs splayed wide, her jacket on the floor, her blouse unbuttoned and useless, along with her front-clasping bra.

When he bent to bite her nipple she had to stifle the screams of pleasure. She could have taken a hundred men at that point, servicing the whole construction crew.

'This won't be the last time,' he said, breathing the words into her ear like a brand, hot and cruel. 'Say it.'

The bastard had her over a barrel.

'No,' Maggie gasped, putting her palms up to his powerful, bare chest in a vain attempt to keep him at bay 'You can't ask me to be your . . . your girlfriend.'

'Who says I want a girlfriend?' he challenged, pulling her tight once again.

The words made her spasm. It was a sexual claim he

was making on her, pure and simple. What he wanted was the right to do her again, the right to have access to her body for his pleasure. 'I'm not a whore,' she retorted, even as the orgasm began to well, deep within her, unstoppable.

'No,' he agreed. 'You're a woman. The goddamnest, sexiest woman I ever shoved my dick into.'

That did it. Maggie was gone, beyond caring who heard what. By the time the shock-waves finally subsided, she was dripping in sweat, shivering against him. He let her collect herself for a few moments, then backed up.

Here it was, the potentially awkward after-fuck dialogue. It was Hank who handled things, settling the matter in that inimitable style of his, which somehow never failed to rouse her to a sexual frenzy all over again even as it drove her to distraction.

'Same time tomorrow,' he told her, fastening his thick, brown leather belt.

'Give me one good reason,' she challenged, determined to take him down a peg.

'Because,' he said, as he put the hardhat back on his head, 'I'll bet a week's pay that's the best you ever got in your life.'

Maggie was up all night thinking about him. The next morning she changed clothes four times, then decided not to go to the site at all. Finally she threw on some slacks, the most sex-proof clothes she could think of, and ran down. When she saw he wasn't there, she wanted to cry. Then she got mad, feeling as if she'd been used. Eventually, she was flat-out relieved. At least until a familiar hand with a familiar fragrance cupped her eyes from behind.

'Guess who,' he said in his raspy, one-of-a-kind voice.

She turned on him to cuss him out, but when she saw those lips and that smug smile all she could think of was kissing. And a lot of other things, too.

'After work,' he told her, 'we'll get a hotel room.'

'Fuck you,' she said.

Hank laughed, taking her cheeks between his fingers for a lip lock. She could feel her little face literally getting sucked in. Fifteen seconds under the pressure of those hot, dry lips and all her resistance was shot to hell.

'That's exactly my intention.' He released her, panting.

There was no need to check her panties or inspect her nipples for a reaction. Maggie was wet and hot and ready, just as she would be any time this man called for her.

'Five thirty,' he said, dismissing her, 'and don't be late.'

That night they made love five times, soaking the sheets again and again in their fluids. Maggie thought she would die of the sensations, not to mention the lack of sleep. But somehow she never felt the deprivation. For the next two months they kept at it night after night and, when they couldn't wait that long, during the days as well. The newly finished Conover Building would always hold a special place in Maggie's heart on account of the many interesting places in which she'd screwed there.

Was it love? She thought so, at least until the last day. They had a date, right after the ribbon cutting. She wore her best dress and she'd brought him flowers. Hank never showed, nor did he return any of her phone calls. According to his landlord he'd moved on, no forwarding address. The only thing she had left, aside from her memories and the feel of him still lingering between her legs, was the note he'd left with the construction boss.

'Dear Maggie,' it said. 'Thanks just won't cut it and I'm not very sentimental, so I guess this is it. All good things come to an end, don't they? Fondly, Hank. P.S. – You never could get enough of me, could you?'

More than once she'd crumpled up the damn thing and retrieved it before finally filing it away in one of her old scrapbooks – under the heading 'One More Reason Why Magdalene Quinton Should Never Get Serious With a Man.'

But, right now, she had another man on her mind. It was time to take her top off and let her little felon feast his eyes on something really burglar-proof. Reaching behind her, giving a little lick to her drying lips, Maggie tugged at the string behind her neck. The bow gave way with delicious ease, allowing her breasts to spill forwards out of the restraining cups. With teasing deliberateness, she pulled them down over her surprisingly thick nipples, baring the whole of each orb. Now it remained only to undo the bottom tie, pull away the bikini top and, of course, add more lotion.

Maggie poured the cream over her mounds. Tiny rivulets ran down to her ribs. It was ever so much more fun having him as an audience than Diane. Sighing happily, she let her fingers trail along the slick, curvy surfaces. Closing her eyes, she imagined men masturbating over her and ejaculating. The spring break boys, the young hard bodies riding up and down the shore in their jet skis and leaning out of their hotel rooms, screaming for girls to take their tops off or, better still, to come on up and give them blowjobs.

God, Maggie was so horny. Shimmying wickedly, she untied her bikini bottom and pulled down the panel, baring her crotch, the most complex part of her anatomy and yet in some ways the simplest. It knew what it wanted and how to get it. Unlike her heart, which never knew what it wanted.

Ooh, that lotion was going to feel so good in her crack. Digging in her heels, she lifted her ass off the lounger to receive it. The whole of the rest of the bottle was going to go down there and she didn't care who saw it. In fact, it turned her on to think she was being watched.

'Yes,' she moaned to her invisible lover as the cream poured over her pussy. With the fingers of one hand, she spread the lips for better access. She wanted to be filled with the stuff, as if it was the come of all the men who'd ever wanted her and never done anything about it. What a waste. Didn't they realise, nine times out of ten she'd have let them have what they wanted just on account of their boldness?

Diane had always thought Maggie was crazy, the way she carried on with men. Maybe so, but she had her ways of protecting herself. Like work. That was a great way to keep from becoming a nympho. Unfortunately it was also a good way to end up a nun. At least she'd never had to go to divorce court, though, which was more than could be said for her high-rolling sister.

Greedily, blatantly, she shoved a finger up inside herself. She wanted it rough and fast, the way the burglar would do it. She wanted to hump and be humped. She wanted to be totally covered, head to toe, in spunk and then to be taken. Was he up for that challenge? He hadn't been before. He'd run at the first sign of trouble. But that wasn't fair of her to charge. He was only trying to escape the police.

I'm masturbating for a wanted man, she thought, flicking her thumb over her clit. What's next? Conjugal visits at the local prison? Maggie grabbed for her breast, dropping the empty lotion container. She'd be needing more hands in a hurry. Any second now ... any second ...

Ketch Walker groaned as the pressure reached the explosion point. The woman was out of her mind. Did she have any idea he was out here, watching the whole thing? It was wrong to masturbate along with her, but a man would have to be dead in order to stop himself. She was like Aphrodite, goddess of sex, a pure spirit of lust. Stella, intense as she was, couldn't touch this kind of passion. That's why she was so jealous all the time, and why she'd stolen his talisman, the necklace with the tiny, tusked elephant. It hadn't liked Stella from the beginning, which is probably why she'd gotten rid of it.

Without the amulet he was half a man. Could it be, though, that this redhead was channelling the energy back to him? It stood to reason. The necklace was over there somewhere, he was sure of it. That Sphincter of Sphincters Heeter had it hidden there, out of spite. He just needed to get his hands on it, and on her, and all would be right.

Screaming wasn't a good idea right now, but he was past the point of reason. Leaning forwards against the windowsill, the veins in his cock threatening to break, he pressed his cock on all sides, building the necessary friction with his clammy fingers. A few more pumps and it would all come shooting out in the form of sweet, sweet release. Thick and white and creamy, just like the liquid all over the nymph's body.

'Your name,' he shouted as his come blasted free, spattering the wall below the window. 'I don't even know your name.'

7

'Damn it, Star,' Griff shouted into the tangled mass of trees, a conglomeration of venerable pines and weathered palms. 'I'm not in the mood to play!'

If the woman heard him, she wasn't answering. Playing possum, most likely. She'd taken off like a bat out of hell the minute he drove up to her place, one of those big shit-eating grins on her face. The only thing he'd had to go on was a trail of her clothing, and that had just run dry. Feeling like a goddamn fool, his dick harder than Chinese arithmetic, he stood there, holding her panties.

Correction: breathing them in.

Star Shine was one magnificent mare of a woman. At forty-five, she hadn't an ounce of fat on her – nor had she lost much of anything by way of bounce in her 34D cups. The streaks of white in her otherwise hay-coloured hair only endeared her to him that much more. She still had that cheerleader's body and he'd love her till the day he kicked the bucket, just as he had since junior high school.

'Mew?' questioned the scruffy tabby at his heel. It was one of about twenty feral cats that had found refuge out here by Star's tiny, weather-beaten house, an island all its own amid the underbrush and forest of Osprey's interior.

'I found a reefer in your shorts,' Griff said, teasing her, knowing she was somewhere close. 'I'll bring you in if you don't come out this minute.'

He heard a branch snap. She was making a run for it, loud and sloppy, just begging to be caught. That bit about the pot must have got her juices flowing. Star liked the cops-and-robbers game plenty fine. Especially when she ended up in his chains. Crouching low, Griff listened for her breathing.

Out of the corner of his eye he saw her, taking off like a shot. That beautiful naked, pot-smoking ass, white as alabaster. Prettiest sight on the whole damned island. And it would look twice as good when he reddened it up a bit.

'Fuck,' he cried, tripping over a fallen log. The ground smacked him in the face hard. Jeezus, he was getting too old for this. Feeling like an idiot, after pulling himself up by his bootstraps, skinned knees and all, he resumed the chase. Seemed like he'd been doing this his whole life, running after Star. Back when she was Lisa May Evans, the homecoming queen, he'd have run ten miles flat just to taste those saucy lips of hers.

Trouble was, he never thought he was good enough till too late. By the time Griff the gawky boy turned into Griff the rough-and-tumble man, Lisa May had been scarred too deeply for any permanent relationship, let alone one with a badge-toting cop.

He picked up the pace now, detecting her bare foot-prints in the sandy dirt. Tiny and female, shaped just right to set his blood racing. Just let me get my hands on her, he vowed, and I'll show her what for. Right here on the ground, down on all fours, like animals.

Shit. The prints were gone. Vanished, like some kind of alien ship swooped down and gobbled her up. Unless . . .

Griff looked up too late. The naked blonde was already leaping down onto his back, clasping his neck with her hands and digging her heels as if he was a horse.

'Sonovabitch, Star, what the hell do you think you're doing?'

She bore down on his ribs with her feet, spinning him round. This aerial assault had been the last thing he'd expected. Still, she couldn't really expect to subdue him. He let her play with him a little, but when she chomped down on his ear he decided the game had gone far enough.

Falling down to one already bloodied knee, he rolled partially onto his back in an effort to dislodge her. When she continued to hold on for dear life he took stronger measures, grabbing her by her long, wild hair. She yelped like a banshee as he pulled back on her neck. From long experience he knew her limits and there was no danger of him hurting her. Griff, on the other hand, was fair game.

Twice she snapped at his fingers with her pearly teeth before he finally managed to pin her underneath him. He outweighed her by a hundred pounds, but he couldn't take anything for granted. She could and would kick him in the crotch if she had the chance. Securing her wrists over her head in one of his hands, he used the other to help separate her legs. Star Shine was all muscle where it counted and it took some effort to get his knee safely between her legs.

'And that,' he declared, attempting to hide just how winded he was, 'is that.'

The former Lisa May glared at him with deep silver-blue eyes, complicated as hell and some would say flat-out insane. But Griff knew better. It was what she'd been through that made her this way. Her behaviour now was all just a defence mechanism, pure and simple. It was a miracle she trusted him like this to play with her. To exploit the deep, deep sensuality still latent in that gorgeous body.

Griff had to have a kiss. It was a breach of protocol, a careless pre-emptive move for which he'd pay dearly. Her teeth drew blood, as well they should. Fat-lipped and feeling dumber than shit, he returned to the game-plan.

Tame her first. Take the fruits of her love second.

'You have the right to remain silent.' He flipped her onto her stomach. As if Star Shine had uttered a word in ten years. 'And the right to serve my pleasure.'

The cuffs clicked with comforting familiarity round the blonde's wrists. Other than occasional prisoner transfers here and there, these Smith and Wesson hand-cuffs had little if any use except in spicing up the chief's love life.

If you could call these crazy games with Star a form of love.

'You're gonna be the death of me one of these days, woman,' he said as he lifted her to her feet.

She responded with a playful growl, his signal to lift her into his arms and take her back to the house for a little instant discipline. It was a hollow victory. She could run him into the ground these days if she wanted. It had been years since he'd caught her for real. When it came right down to it, she could probably get his gun away from him, too. Sometimes it boggled his mind to think of the trust they had to put in each other to do what they did between them. If he'd had a tenth of that trust with his ex-wife, he'd still be a happily married man.

'Spread 'em,' he ordered quite unnecessarily as they reached the familiar sawhorse in the patch of weeds and wildflowers that passed for her front yard. Griff had customised the thing, nailing cushions over the wood and attaching straps to all four legs. This way he could secure her comfortably for punishment and pleasure alike.

Star opened her legs reluctantly, allowing him to secure her ankles to the horse. The next step was to undo the handcuffs, bend her over the contraption and secure her wrists to the other two legs. This accomplished, she was utterly helpless. Testing her readiness, he ran a finger along the edge of her glistening hole. The yellow fleece was thick with her juice. Star was wet, all right, and hot, too. More than anything he wanted to sink his cock down that pink canal, but first there was the matter of her punishment.

'Running from an officer of the law is a serious offence.' He rubbed her quivering bottom. 'You could draw prison time for that.'

Star clenched her cheeks in anticipation of the inevitable. Griff raised and lowered his hand, the palm landing with a satisfying smack.

She made little protesting noises, cute and sexy. Griff's cock strained in response. Twice more he struck her, pinkening her rounded cheeks before giving in to his fevered desire.

'Sorry, kiddo, I can't hold out long today.'

His cock was already way over-stimulated as he slipped it between the woman's sex lips. Star clenched at him immediately, welcoming him home. Indeed, this was home, or as much of it as he knew any more. Since Jo Anne had left five years ago there'd been nobody steady in his life, and certainly no one to share his house with. With both his parents gone now and his brother moved up to Atlanta, he fully expected to be alone there until his death.

It was just as well. John Grifford was not marrying material.

Grunting heavily, he clenched at her hips. Coming would not be a problem; just a few quick thrusts and it would all be over. For him at least. But that would leave

Star hanging, so close and yet so far. Shit, why couldn't he just be a heartless bastard about these things?

'Ah, fuck it,' he muttered, withdrawing Little Griff.

Star didn't seem sure what he was up to at first. She'd catch on soon enough. After undoing the straps, he slung her over his shoulder, a hundred and ten pounds of naked wildcat.

'Easy, babe,' he protested, wincing as she reached under his shirt to scratch at his back. 'This is for your own good.'

The screen door had been mounted backwards, which meant he could push it open with his foot.

Star didn't use a bed herself, but she kept one, on Griff's insistence. An old brass one with a thick mattress and nice headboards and footboards for ropes and so on.

'I'll be damned if I'll fuck you on the floor every time,' he told her the day he drove up with the thing. It was one of the first smiles he'd gotten out of her since the accident. For some reason not entirely clear to him, Griff catalogued each and every one of these moments between them, storing them in a deep place in his brain, right next to his social security number and his grandmother's recipe for cornbread.

There'd been an unusual sign of appreciation in it for him, too, in the form of an unprecedented peck on the cheek after he'd gotten the bed set up. To his knowledge, she'd never even touched it, except on those occasions when he threw her down on it. Like now. The springs groaned in response to the sudden addition of her weight. She landed on her back, though she went immediately up on her elbows, on guard.

'We can do this the easy way, Lisa May, or the hard way.'

Star kicked up at him. She hated when he called her

by her given name and he only did it to get her riled up. The one thing he'd never do was use her last name. That one was dead and buried, along with her children and her husband.

'That's what I thought.' He grabbed her ankles in mid-air, scissoring them. 'The hard way it is.'

Taking advantage of the open space, Griff climbed between her legs. It was her wrists he wanted. Cuffing her to the headboard was something he could do in his sleep. Though he'd never tire of that look in her eye as the locks clicked shut or the sound of the steel links tinkling across the brass bar as she tested his handiwork afterwards.

Letting her buck and writhe to her heart's content, still kneeling above her, he unbuttoned the khaki shirt and slipped it off his shoulders. Next he pulled the T-shirt over his head, revealing his finely haired barrel chest. Griff prided himself on staying in shape and he could hold his own against any pup, Cosgrove included. He could even beat the lad at arm wrestling, although he had a sneaking suspicion the junior officer was letting him win.

'You look mighty good that way, Lisa May,' he said, admiring her naked predicament. 'Maybe I'll take you home and make you a permanent decoration on my own bed.'

The woman hissed like a snake, adding fuel to the fire as he unhooked his gun belt and went to work on his shorts and underwear. His cock and balls were more than happy to be free of their constraints. Damn, it was a long time since his balls had been this tight. It was a full load he'd be depositing, that was for sure.

But first he needed to take care of Star. Call it a reward for her perseverance, or maybe just more punishment, he dived between her legs head first, winning from the woman a surprised gasp as he pushed his tongue into the hole so recently occupied by his cock. Unlike most men, John Grifford enjoying going down on a woman. The taste genuinely pleased him as did the response he invariably got from his partners. Having the woman a prisoner underneath him didn't hurt either. It wasn't something he did very often with Star, though, on account of her need for faster, more combat-related sex. For some reason, however, Griff was feeling sentimental today.

Star gave in to whimpers and then to genuine moans as he ran his tongue over her clit, back and forth in the way he knew drove her wild. She slid her handcuff chains back and forth over the brass, the sound a sexy timbre in sharp contrast to the soft animality of their conjoining flesh.

'Come on, babe,' he crooned. 'Let it go.'

Lisa May was a fighter, always had been. Not many women could have survived what she had and lived to tell. There were times, like this, though, when he'd rather she fought a little less and yielded a little more.

She was a squirter, too. Which meant his palate would soon be bathed in the sweetest stream of nectar known to man, and the rarest.

Star was tensing up; it was nearly time. The calm before the storm. Taking a deep breath, he knocked on the gates of paradise, ready to be blown down on his motherfucking ass.

The scream was blood-curdling. Juices surged around his tongue, a gurgling honey wash, purifying and electrifying. It was perfect. If only she'd call his name. That was the one regret, the only thing that seemed to be missing from their lovemaking.

'You're the best,' he grumbled softly, climbing on top of her to finish himself off. Star looked at him with those complicated eyes, lost in her afterglow, awash in her own private world. Could she speak any more, if she chose? The doctors said no, that the psychic damage was likely to be permanent even if there was nothing wrong with her vocal cords, but Griff wasn't sure. He had a feeling she could talk any time she wanted, only she didn't have anything to say.

Long steady strokes of his throbbing dick: one, two, three, four. It wouldn't take long. Clamping his eyes shut he set the orgasm free. His hands braced on either side of her ribs, his head thrown back, calling out to the ceiling, the sky, the universe. Nothing articulate from him, either. Just another day on the island. Another day in the uniform. In it and out of it and back in again.

Ten minutes later he was piloting the JEEP once more, smoking a menthol and running details of various cases in his mind. It was the Heeter robbery that kept coming back at him. That gnawing feeling there was something he was missing right under his nose.

Getting on the radio, he raised Cosgrove. 'Unit One to Unit Two, Over.'

Griff counted out the seconds. Mike didn't always answer right away and a lot of that had to do with Katy Sue. For some reason the woman refused to fuck him in his off time, only on duty. If the chief didn't live in a glass house himself, he might toss a stone or two. As it was, he let it go. Truth was, he had the hots for the little blonde himself. And who didn't? The time he found a pair of her panties in the back seat of Mike's cruiser he took them straight to his office. They were fresh and fragrant and he came all over them, rubbing the flowered pink silk all up and down his rough and ready shaft.

'Roger, Unit One.' He heard Cos clear his throat. 'This is Unit Two.'

Griff recognised the sound of granola being shoved down his throat. Oh, well, at least the boy could use proper police jargon. And he seemed to be alone at the moment, which was a plus.

'Unit Two, did you run those fingerprints over to the county crime lab yet?'

'I just got back, Chief.'

'Good. Here's hoping those dickheads in Marston don't fuck this up the way they do everything else. Listen, I want you to get right on over to the Heeter place. Keep an eye out there the rest of the day. The redhead has a sister in town now, dark hair, about five foot five. I want you to watch them both.'

'Yes, sir,' he replied solemnly, eager beaver that he was. 'You can count on me. Over and out, sir.'

Grifford felt a slight pang of guilt as he clicked off the radio. He probably ought to do the job himself. But he wanted to go home and put his feet up, maybe drink a couple of cold beers and catch a game on TV.

Then again . . .

His eyes had just now fallen to the citation book he'd left on the seat. All over again he was remembering Diane Quinton Rostov. The black-haired siren with the racy red dress and the bare pussy and the fast car. Seven, she'd said. That's when she'd be at the Continental. There was no way he'd go. For one thing she was related to Magdalene Quinton, victim in a case he was working on. For another she was a perpetrator herself, someone he'd given a ticket to and theoretically might have to testify against in court.

On the other hand, there were the legs to consider, and what lay between them. Griff looked down. Damn if he wasn't getting hard all over again. Back-to-back erections. How long had it been since that happened? Maybe he would just check things out at the Continental after all. Not for social purposes, but as part of the investigation. Undercover, so to speak.

It was a bullshit excuse for trying to get his rocks off with the gorgeous Diane, but it sure sounded good.

8

'Are you sure you'll be all right here by yourself tonight?' asked Diane for the fifth time.

Maggie popped one eye open, just long enough to see her sister dressed for sex in a low-cut, backless blue dress that left nothing to the imagination. Where did her sister get so many clothes from, anyway?

'Yes,' she grumbled, throwing the pillow over her head. 'The question is, will you be OK out there?'

'Me?' Diane laughed. 'It's the natives who ought to be shaking in their alligator-skin boots, not me.'

Maggie sat up in a tangle of bedsheets feeling a hundred years old. Was it the sun that had wiped her out today, or the wild masturbation session, or was it all just fallout from last night?

'You're not really going to meet that cop again, are you, Di?'

'If he shows up.' She sauntered over to give her baby sister a goodbye kiss on the cheek. 'Hell, yes. Good grief, Mags. I feel like I'm tucking you in again like when you were little.'

Maggie rolled her eyes. 'I'm quite capable of tucking myself in, thank you very much.'

'Yes, well, I can still worry, can't I? You promise me you'll call 911 at the first sign of trouble, right? And me. Call me, too.'

'Yes, mother.'

Di narrowed her gaze, noting the oversized pyjama

top, Maggie's only form of bodily covering at the moment. 'That's his, isn't it?'

Maggie hugged herself defensively. 'So what if it is?'

'I thought we were over him?'

'*We* are. This is just for sleeping in, OK?'

Hank, they were talking about Hank. As for the pyjama top, it was the only thing of his she'd managed to keep. She'd bought it for him and he'd worn it all of one time, just to humour her, but it was still his in Maggie's mind.

Maggie was ready for a fight, but Diane just wrinkled her nose, her attention having been thankfully diverted back to herself. She sniffed the air. 'I used too much perfume, didn't I?'

Glad to be out of the spotlight, Maggie giggled. 'No, you smell perfect. Now would you get out of here?'

Di was still talking as she left, going on about her shoes and whether she should have gone with the slingbacks instead of the pumps. Smiling to herself, Maggie collapsed back down into Heeter's oversized bed and gave in to the sleep that had been calling her name all afternoon. The fact that she was being watched again, this time from up close, escaped her purview. At least for the moment.

It was now or never. The redhead was sound asleep in her bed and the other one was gone, presumably for the evening. Ketch hadn't intended to vacate his safe little perch next door till both women were gone, but 7he hadn't much choice, not once that cop had shown up. At first Ketch thought the man knew he was there, but it turned out he was at the house next to Heeter's for the same purpose he was: surveillance. After slipping out the back window, Ketch had found his way over here. He'd been hiding under the boardwalk, waiting for his opportunity.

Slipping off his flip-flops, Ketch slid open the unlocked window and stepped through, barefoot on the plush carpet. Thank the Sirens for the low crime rate that made locks and alarms unheard-of on the island.

Ketch felt a lump in both throat and groin at the sight of the sleeping Maggie in the bedroom. Should he tie her up again just for safekeeping? No, that was a very bad idea. Tying this woman made him want to have her. Then again, so did looking at her. She would probably think herself a wreck right now, lips puffy from sleep, her hair all tousled, her body half burrowed in the sheets, barely covered, except for her thighs, by a man's pyjama top, the sleeves too long. In reality, though, this was when a woman looked her sexiest. The most natural, the most ready for love. It was all he could do to keep from crawling into bed with her and brushing the hair back from her tiny ear to give her a little kiss on the earlobe. He'd start there and work his way down. Down and across to the hollow of her neck and the valley between her perfect breasts.

Concentrate, man. You have to concentrate. Where could the amulet be? More to the point, where would the Conniving Scoundrel Heeter hide such a thing, worth nothing to himself but everything to Ketch? Spite jewellery, that's all it was for the man. Kept out of pettiness, as a sign of the man's ability to cheat people out of whatever he wanted from them.

Perhaps it was in the den. In a desk drawer, where he could take it out any time he liked and run his unworthy, money-grubbing fingers over it.

Ignoring the obnoxious Neanderthal décor, complete with bearskin rug and hunting trophies, Ketch went right for his objective. He was already deep into the second drawer, bent forwards on his knees, when he heard a familiar, disconcerting sound from across the mahogany desk.

Looking up he saw the realisation of his worst fears. The redhead was no longer sleeping but standing there in front of him, pointing a gun, the trigger of which she had just now cocked.

'One false move, asshole, and I'll blow your head off.'

Ketch straightened himself, very, very slowly. Three years in the Marines had taught him to respect and fear firearms. Especially in the wrong hands. 'Miss, I would advise putting that down before someone gets hurt.'

'If you mean you, ask me if I give a flying fuck.'

Admittedly, she did not seem overly concerned at the danger to his person.

'I really think it would be best,' he repeated more emphatically, 'if you put that down so we can talk like grown adults.'

The redhead shook her head. 'I'm giving the orders, Ace. For starters, I want you out from behind that desk where I can see you. Hands over your head.'

Ketch complied, feeling as if he'd been stuck in some horrible spaghetti Western.

'I see you're dressed tonight,' said his spunky captor, looking him up and down in his shorts and T-shirt. 'To what do I owe the honour?'

He could say the same of her, but thought it prudent to restrict his remarks to an apology. 'I meant no offence.'

'None taken,' she said. 'Now strip.'

Ketch hadn't expected this turn of events. 'Did I hear you properly?'

'If you heard me saying get naked, yes, you did.'

He attempted a wry laugh, rather on the subtle side. 'You can't be serious.'

'As a heart attack,' she assured him. 'I figure turnabout is fair play. Last night you got to see me, tonight I get to see you.'

Ketch's cock was threatening to burst through both his underwear and his shorts. What was it about a sexy, dominant filly with a firearm?

'I want you to know –' he pulled his shirt over his head '– that I never meant you any harm. My dispute is with Heeter, not you.'

'I feel so much better about being violated now that I know that,' she assured him.

'I can tell you're angry.' He unzipped his shorts. 'And I don't blame you.'

'Oh, so now I'm angry.' She laughed. 'Last night you said I was just a horny little slut looking to get raped.'

'I recall saying no such thing.'

'Less talk, Junior Gangster, and more action.'

One wave of the pistol was enough for him to peel, letting free his rock-hard dick and tight balls.

'Ooh ... got a little arousal problem,' she teased. 'Or is that just another adrenalin rush?'

Ketch did not appreciate having his words thrown back in his face, nor did he like it when she made him put his hands at his side to keep him from covering himself.

'So what happens now?' he wanted to know.

For the first time he saw hesitation in her eyes. She was enjoying the sight of him, but following through on one's desires with a stranger was entirely different from merely having them as fantasy.

'We tie you up,' she decided. 'As you recall, there's plenty of rope in the house.'

'You don't need to do that, you know.'

'Oh, no? And what the fuck makes you the expert on what I need to do?'

He'd hit another nerve.

'I just know.' He shrugged. 'Like I know that you don't really intend to call the cops.'

'Never said I would in the first place, did I?' she challenged.

By Hera, but she looked fetching in that pyjama top. What was it about a man's top that made a woman look so good? Was it the fact that it functioned as a short dress on her small, lithe form, baring her thighs and legs, or was it the way it pointed out so markedly the clear physical differences between men and women?

'I made a logical assumption,' he said defensively.

'You assume a lot, don't you? When you're not spying on women, that is.'

Ketch felt the colour creep into his face. So she had known he was out there today after all. 'That was, um, . . . inadvertent.'

'Did you get off on it?' she demanded. 'Were my sister and I good jerk-off material? I'm sorry we didn't screw each other for you. I'll bet you would have liked that.'

'Seeing you was enough. Tantalising yourself with the lotion, squirting it on you and in you till you were forced to bring yourself to orgasm with your fingers.'

She aimed the gun at him again. 'What's to stop me from making you a eunuch right now?'

'I would assume your innate aversion to shooting innocent men?'

'Innocent my ass,' she snorted.

'You do realise,' he offered by way of diversion, 'that

we don't even know each other's names? Mine's Ketch. As in To Catch a Thief. Kind of ironic, don't you think?'

She didn't seem to think it was ironic at all. In fact, she looked more prepared than ever to follow through on that eunuch threat. 'If you must know, I'm Maggie,' she supplied with a cold shake of her curls. 'Not that I'd socialise with you if you were the last man in the galaxy.'

'There was a spark, though, you have to admit.'

'Excuse me?'

'We kissed, Maggie. You can't deny that.'

'I've been trying to forget it, actually. Unfortunately I can't find a big enough bottle of mouthwash.'

'Personally, I found the taste pleasant. Pinot Noir, was it not? The wine you were drinking?'

Now it was her turn to blush. 'Aren't you the clever one. Unfortunately, I don't have time for idiot savant surf bums who don't have enough common sense to keep from robbing the same house two nights in a row.'

'I'm not a robber. I'm here to recover stolen property. If *you* must know, your Calvin Heeter Junior has a necklace of mine, a sacred amulet. Something of value only to myself, but which he refuses to part company with.'

'A sacred amulet? What on earth are you talking about?'

Ketch proceeded to explain to her the history of the jade elephant on the jewelled chain and how it had spared him an untimely death in a Cobra helicopter accident in the Marines as well as a near-drowning off the coast of Tortuga. Never once had he slept apart from it till the fateful night Stella Sawgrass had gotten him drunk and stolen it from him along with all the rest of his possessions. He'd awoken nude somewhere on a beach in South Carolina. By a minor miracle he'd managed to track Stella down, following her all the way to a flea market outside of Orlando. She confessed to having sold the necklace there along with the rest of his largely worthless belongings.

He got to the vendor too late, although he did find out that the jade necklace had been sold to a wealthy-looking northerner out for his jollies. The man was none other than Calvin Heeter Junior. Ketch proceeded to track him down, having to go all the way to his office in Chicago, only to be told after pouring his heart out that Heeter had become 'attached' to the 'trinket' as he put it and intended to keep it on Osprey Island with some other items he'd picked up. After refusing Ketch's offer to pay him fair market value, he had him thrown out of the building.

It was out of this sequence of events that his current course of action had evolved. Heeter had left him no option but to take the law into his own hands. Having concluded his tale of heroic woe, he now waited for Maggie's response, which he expected to be one of great sympathy, if not outright awe at his stalwart resolve. What he got instead was a blank stare.

'I can honestly say,' she replied flatly, 'that that is the strangest, most mixed-up story I have ever heard. And you're honestly telling me you think that is going to keep you out of jail?'

Ketch stiffened, justifiably affronted. 'I cannot say. I only know that I will face my fate as would any martyr.'

'Martyr? Lunatic, more like.'

'Is it me that's crazy, Maggie? I'm not the one paving over a beautiful island and turning it into a neon parking lot so some neurotic tourists can come down here and act like they never even left home.'

Maggie wasn't sure which cut worse, hearing the man insult her life's work or say her name, making her feel like no one before him had ever said it the right way. 'All right,' she sighed. 'I've heard enough. It's time to tie you up and call Sheriff Andy and Deputy Barney.'

'As you wish,' he said nodding, though in his mind he was already going over what he'd have to do next. Somehow he was going to have to get that gun away from Maggie and turn the tables on the whole situation. And fast.

Cosgrove hated stakeouts. Sitting in lonely rooms, spying in people's windows, stuck eating stale baloney sandwiches from home. It was, however, good for building his resumé as a genuine crime fighter, the up-and-coming hero of Osprey Island's finest, and one day, hopefully, chief of the whole shooting match.

To really shine, all he needed was to make a bust tonight. The chief had seemed pretty sure that the robber would come back, but Cos didn't figure it. Odds were he'd moved on, either to the other side of the island or, if he was really smart, back to the mainland. Then again, there was that old thing about criminals returning to the scene of the crime. Unscrewing a bottled water, Cos leaned back. Yeah, this was his big chance. The only thing that could go wrong now would be if . . .

He looked down at his flashing cell phone, which was set to vibrate so as not to blow his cover. Damn it all to hell! It was Katy Sue, the very interruption he'd been afraid of. What was she doing calling him after five, anyway, when she was supposed to be at work?

'Katy Sue, I can't see you right now. I'm on top secret police business at an undisclosed location,' he said before she'd even managed to get out a hello. 'And that's final.'

'Everybody knows you're staking out the Heeter place, Cos. Besides, I'm right downstairs, standing next to your patrol car.'

Fuck me hard, thought Officer Michael Cosgrove.

'No, Katy Sue, and I mean it.' Cos was on his feet, trying to keep his voice as low as possible while still conveying his deepest displeasure. 'Now I want you to turn around and head back where you came from. For crying out loud, girl, ain't you supposed to be at work, anyhow?'

'I got the night off,' she offered cheerfully. 'On account of the stakeout. Figured you could use some company. I got Rayleen with me, too.'

'You got who? Jumping jackrabbits on a spit, Katy Sue, are you plumb crazy? What do you think I'm holding here, a party for strippers? Why don't you just have the whole club down while you're at it? We'll get Diamond Pete to cook up some ribs and have us a good old time.'

'But wouldn't the smoke let the robber see you were there?'

Cos slapped his palm on his head three times in succession, lamenting his wasted sarcasm. 'Gee, Katy Sue,' he deadpanned. 'I hadn't thought of that.'

'That's what you got me for, baby. Now hang tight, we'll be right up.'

Cos wasn't sure whether to laugh or cry. The only thing he knew for sure was that it was stuff like this that was going to wind him up Chief Trash Collector instead of Chief of Police.

'Hey,' greeted the girls in unison, bearing brown sacks filled with six-packs of beer and barbecue chips.

If pretty little Katy Sue was a distraction, Rayleen Carter was a distraction and a half. Standing five foot six with wild red hair, Rayleen was a stripper's stripper.

Hers were breasts a man could get smothered in, and there wasn't a hint of sag anywhere on the girl's flesh, although she'd had three kids, which made her unblemished appearance all the more amazing.

'Aren't you a sight for sore eyes,' said Rayleen as she jiggled her way over to him in her cowgirl skirt and vest and a western shirt tied high on her midriff.

'You, too. Dressed for work,' he observed. 'You coming or going?'

'Just got off shift.' She pressed her full bosom against his chest. 'Oh my, Michael. I think somebody's been working out again.'

'I got me one of those new workout machines,' he ventured, hoping the explanation would fare better with her than it had with Katy Sue. 'Like that fella on TV has. Chuck Norris. He plays a cop, but he isn't really one.'

'Of course he ain't, silly. He's an actor. And a martial arts fighter, too.'

Cos was duly impressed. Why hadn't he noticed before how smart she was? 'That's right, Rayleen.'

'I watch TV, too,' said Katy Sue, in a vain attempt to keep up. 'I've seen every *Simpsons* episode at least twice.'

'That's nice, Katy Sue,' Rayleen purred, letting her fingers trail over Cos's, washboard stomach. 'Isn't it, Michael?'

Mike's cock was throbbing against Rayleen's pelvis. If he didn't act soon, he was going to be blowing this stakeout bigtime. 'Sorry, ladies.' He pulled her off him gently but firmly. 'But this is not going to happen tonight.'

'Why not?' asked Katy Sue, attaching herself to his right hip, well within ear-nibbling range.

Cos frowned. The little blonde was dressed as a

schoolgirl, her act at the club. With that tiny little plaid skirt and white shirt tied up right under her breasts, she looked anything but virginal.

'We could play together,' Katy Sue murmured in his ear, ever the voice of temptation. 'You can have both of us if you like. That'd be something new.'

'Nothing new about that, honey, that's what you call a *men-age*. It's French,' he said expertly, drawing on the knowledge he'd acquired on a trip to Mardi Gras two seasons past. For most people on Osprey, saying you'd been to New Orleans was pretty much like saying you'd been to Paris or the moon.

'Ooh, I love it when you talk foreign.' She kissed his neck, her long fingers sliding across under his shirt. 'Will you say some more foreign things while you're fucking me and Rayleen?'

Rayleen was busy unbuttoning him, trying to get at his chest.

'Watch the badge,' he complained.

Her nibbling fingers had already worked their way down to his belt line. With Katy Sue's help, they pulled the shirt over his shoulders.

'Katy Sue, you were right about these muscles,' Rayleen commented, exploring his biceps as though he were some kind of department-store mannequin.

'You ain't seen nothing yet,' said Katy Sue, ripping open the front of his white cotton T-shirt.

'Katy Sue, for crying out loud, you know how much these things go for down at the Super Mart nowadays?'

'I'll buy you a fresh pack for Christmas. Rayleen, turn that chair around. I believe it's time we gave the officer here his own private show.'

Rayleen elbowed the plush recliner into position and Katy Sue shoved him down into it. Cosgrove was in for it now.

'What you want to see first?' asked Katy Sue.

'Your ass on the way out of that door.'

'You don't mean that.' Katy Sue began to gyrate in front of him.

'Yes, I do. You two are interfering in a police investigation. That's obstruction of justice.'

'Seems like you got a nice obstruction right here.' Rayleen bent forwards to rub his crotch. She had a nice gentle touch. Why hadn't he ever really noticed her before, the way he did Katy Sue? Sure, he helped her out some with a domestic violence problem and he wasn't blind to her looks, even back in high school, but he'd never thought of her as a bed partner. Maybe it was on account of her always seeming to hang with the wrong crowd.

'Baby, you watching me?' Katy Sue had her eyes closed in tune to the music in her head. She could do this routine in her sleep by now. Placing her hands over her bare belly, just below where the white blouse was tied, she began to rub at her smooth skin. Meanwhile Rayleen was letting her long, silky red hair wash over his face, obviously not yet ready to let Katy Sue have his undivided attention.

'You like that, Michael?' Rayleen wanted to know.

'Uh huh.' The smell of her perfume, strong and cheap, was flaring his nostrils.

'Don't go shooting off early on us,' teased Katy Sue, unbuttoning her mockery of a schoolgirl skirt. 'The show ain't hardly begun.'

Rayleen knelt between his legs, her smouldering brown eyes locked on his as she unbuckled his utility belt.

'Watch the equipment,' he complained, immediately realising he'd set himself up for another joke.

'Oh, we'll treat it just fine,' Rayleen purred.

Katy Sue's skirt slipped to the floor. She was wearing a G-string – the minimal garment allowed in a strip club in this jurisdiction. Hers was a pussy he knew inside and out, tight, shaved naked and doubly ringed in gold. Still, the mystery was there every time, the anticipation of getting past whatever sheer layer of silk – in this case sky-blue – was blocking his view, and his access.

Cos licked his lips, imagining himself doing things to her. Sometimes he went to the club just to see her flirt with the other guys, knowing he didn't have to stick money in her waistband for a little peek because he was going to get the real thing.

Rayleen finished unzipping him then straightened. It was time for her to lose some clothes, too. Joining in the silent dance, she ran her hands up her thighs, underneath the hem of the short imitation-rawhide skirt. Unable to help himself, Cos finished the job she'd started, fumbling for his throbbing cock under his boxers. Unabashedly he began to stroke the long, uncircumcised pole. Mike wasn't a small man and he made no apology for those few times in his life when he'd bragged a little. Supposedly size didn't matter to the modern woman but, down here in 'gator country, females still liked things king-sized, and he didn't mean the French fries at Burger World.

'Take the rest of that shirt off,' said Katy Sue as she undid her own. 'Let's see them pecs.'

Mike obliged, no longer concerned with how much the replacement would set him back.

'Mm, that's it, baby,' encouraged Katy Sue as he tore the shreds from his chest. 'Show us what you got.'

Katy Sue had plenty going for her, too, that was for sure. The blouse was fluttering to the floor and now she was reaching for the strap of the bra. Rayleen, meanwhile, had shed the cowgirl vest and top and was holding up her breasts, which were barely contained in a thin, plum-coloured bra.

It was hard to know where to look next. Of course he ought to have been looking out of the window over to the Heeter place, but an empty house took a distant third at this point to the two strippers.

But could he really be sure it was empty? It occurred to him now that he'd assumed both women had left, but he'd only seen one of them come out by the side door. Oh, well. Time to worry about that later.

Rayleen was down to a purple G-string and white cowgirl boots and Katy Sue was in white-and-black saddle shoes, white socks and a sultry smile.

'Does the chief pay you enough to afford a lap dance?' Katy Sue teased.

'I don't know, do you take checks?' Mike quipped.

'We take dicks,' Rayleen grinned, slipping to her knees in front of him. Grasping the end of his cock, she blew gently over the tip.

'Easy.' He gripped the arms of the chair, fearing a loss of control. 'I'm only human.'

'You're not just human.' She kissed the tip, running her finger along the vein underneath. 'You're a cop.'

For her part, Katy Sue had hardly let up on her efforts to drive him out of his mind. Hands in her long blonde hair, eyes closed, she was slowly turning, her body responding to the invisible touch of a dozen lovers, soft and gentle. Her nipples were peaked and as she arched her back and thrust out her pelvis he could see the glistening of her pink pussy lips, more than ready for entry. The woman was worked up already, and he hadn't laid a hand on her.

'I ain't never tasted a cop before,' mused Rayleen, licking him like a lollipop. 'I did a mailman in St Augustine once, though.'

'We're pretty much the same,' Mike said. 'Except mailmen taste stringier on account of their cocks being bit by dogs so much.'

'Really?' She was looking up at him, big brown eyes aglow.

'It's a joke, Rayleen. How the hell should I know what a mail carrier's pecker tastes like? Do I look gay to you?'

She shook her head.

'Then get back to what you were doing and cut the small talk.'

Rayleen popped his dick in her mouth. He didn't mean to be impatient, but there was a time and place for conversation and this wasn't it. Clenching his fists, he noted the layer of sweat on them. He was itching to get at Katy Sue over yonder. That fine little body, the woman all lost in her own little world. She wasn't half bad as a dancer. Stripping was hardly her first choice in life. She'd danced jazz and tap as a kid and even went to New York for a while after graduation, till her old man found out and went up to drag her home. A few months after that she got herself married off to Jake and that was pretty much the end of her ambitions. Mike's own theory was that everything she was doing now, as far as screwing around left and right, was to get back at her father and all the other men in her life she thought were keeping her from living out her dreams.

Cosgrove understood this. There was a time in his life when he wanted to join the FBI. Although he wouldn't have gotten the fringe benefits that he did here.

Mike cocked his head for a second. Had he just heard someone screaming? He ought to get up and look, but this felt so good. Maybe he'd just imagined it. It might have been birds, too. Maybe a crane or a screech owl, up early. That was it. Katy Sue and Rayleen didn't seem to have heard anything, so why worry? Mike settled back in his seat. He'd check it out, in just a few minutes. As soon as he finished up here.

'Damn,' he muttered as Rayleen took him deep. 'You're good at this.'

Almost as good as he was at being a cop. If he did say so himself.

9

If there was one thing Magdalene Quinton hated doing, it was screaming like a girl. Unfortunately the man had caught her off guard, which meant she needed a moment to recover her usual aplomb.

'Get the fuck off me!' she shouted as he spun her about, his hand around her waist.

The burglar – Ketch – lifted her off the ground like a rag doll. He was stronger than he looked, and he'd looked pretty darn strong to start with.

'I'm not going to hurt you,' he said, attempting to pry the gun out of her fingers.

'I swear, I'll shoot your balls off!'

'I don't think so,' he said, lifting her arm over her head and taking the pistol away. 'Not tonight.'

'Let go of me,' she repeated, not liking at all the feeling of being pinned back to front with a naked man whose body resembled that of Michelangelo's David.

OK, well, maybe she did like it. Just a little. But the point was, she couldn't afford to be liking it right now. This man was the enemy. A crazy person who'd broken into her temporary home not once but twice. She could kick herself now for not immobilising him when she had the chance.

'I don't want to have to tie you again, but I will if you can't get control of yourself.' The condescension in his voice was definitely the last straw.

'Fuck you,' she managed, sinking her teeth into his shoulder.

Ketch yelped and all of a sudden she was free. Taking her opportunity she ran like hell. He was right behind her, grabbing at the back of her – of Hank's – pyjama top. The material ripped in his hand. Bastard. That was one more thing he'd pay for later. The phone, she had to get to the phone. Her cell was in her purse in the bedroom. She'd lock herself in and call 911.

Ketch managed to get a foot in the doorway as she was trying to slam it. Was there no end to his plaguing of her life? She pushed on the door for all she was worth, but he didn't yield. One final burst and he was through. Her last refuge was the closet, but he had her by the waist again. This time he swung her up and over, face down onto her own bed.

'Rape!' she screamed, the word cut off mid-syllable as he clamped his hand over her mouth from behind.

'Woman, you are impossible,' he growled, sounding riled up for the first time since she'd met him.

Good, maybe she was getting to him after all. A little more surreptitious searching with her hand for a certain sensitive part of his anatomy and she'd really give him something to be pissed off about.

He cried out again as she squeezed, this time from a pain and shock that ran a little deeper than having his shoulder bitten.

'Now will you get off me?' she asked with surprising sweetness, her hand still tightly wrapped round his naked balls.

'OK, OK,' he groaned. 'Just let go and I'll get up.'

She let him back away on all fours, though she switched over to his cock, grasping it for all she was worth. At this point, it was her only leverage, so to speak, and she couldn't afford to lose it.

Maggie felt a little fluttering in her stomach. She hadn't counted on his organ feeling so good in her hand. Iron wrapped in velvet. Pulsing and very, very manly. She had to feel him inside her, at the same time putting him in his place once and for all. 'You think you're such a hero?' she challenged, turning herself over and sliding her hips directly underneath his crotch. 'Bullying a small defenceless woman? Well, let's see if you can handle it when I fight back a while, shall we?'

Ketch was breathing fast, his sculpted chest rising and falling quickly. She hadn't noticed before just how tanned he was, how bronzed and rugged in comparison to her own soft, white skin. She loved the look of his muscles, too. Entirely natural, as if he'd earned them the hard way, through honest work, not by spending hour upon hour in some gym like Bruce did.

Hank had muscles like this, though his smacked of the harsh world of steel and bar-room brawls. Ketch looked and smelled of the sea, like some kind of merman washed onto her own personal seashore. Above all she was transfixed by those eyes, so complicated, sometimes like a little boy's, all innocent and waiting for Santa, sometimes imbued with real pain, the nature and depth of which she couldn't begin to imagine. She had the impression it wasn't so much what he'd been through as how it had affected him. For all his rugged good looks, this Ketch bruised more easily than the rest of the world. He could be hurt and disappointed where others could just shrug it all off.

A lump formed in her throat as she realised the awesome responsibility she was taking on, making love to a man like this. For her it would be casual sex, an impulsive release, not very well thought out and probably downright stupid. For him, though, it might represent something entirely different.

'Maggie, what are you doing?'

She guided his penis between her legs. God, was she ready.

'Shh,' she whispered, stilling his objections. 'Don't think right now. Just ... take.'

It was the first word that popped into her mind, and it reflected exactly what she wanted. To be taken, by her strong, mysterious burglar. Her hands trembled as she positioned him, just at the entrance to her glistening lips. What a cock he had, thick and long, as if it had been carved out of living stone. Carved as the great Italian masters used to carve, finding living flesh in seemingly inanimate pieces of marble. This cock was very much alive, though, with veins and tiny ridges, and an owner who was making the tiniest little gasping noises as she encouraged him to finish the job she'd started.

'Fuck me,' said Maggie, spelling out the obvious.

He fell upon her, a mix of wonder and confusion on his face. It wasn't as if he was any kind of virgin, but somehow it was like entering a fairy-tale world in his own mind. Once, twice, he lifted and lowered himself, tentatively.

Maggie pulled at his upper arms, his smooth biceps. 'Come on, I won't break.'

She wanted it, needed it, faster. They were enemies, after all; they'd wrestled, fought over a gun, nearly killed one another. Surely that deserved a good and proper ploughing on his part.

'Or don't you have it in you?' she taunted. 'Are you all talk and nothing to back it with?'

'You don't know me at all,' he countered, slamming down his pelvis.

Maggie's eyes lit. Now he was talking. 'Introduce me, then.'

He swallowed her left breast whole, devouring the

flesh as if he'd been waiting his whole life for it. At the same time he began to establish his rhythm. Fast, but still not fast enough.

'When you're done,' she said, 'I'm still going to turn you in.'

He released her tit, a string of saliva running from the corner of his mouth. 'The hell you will.'

'Change my mind, then.' She clutched at him with the muscles of her well-stretched pussy. 'Fuck me into submission.'

'Is that all you understand?'

She thrust her crotch up to meet him. 'I'm a female. Isn't that all any of us understands?'

'I'd hoped better from you.'

'Screw you.' She tried to wriggle out from underneath him.

Ketch easily put her back down, pinning her hands over her head. 'I wanted you from the first moment I saw you.'

Maggie felt a fresh rush of female heat as she saw the set of his jaw, the light behind the eyes. She might just make a man of him yet.

'It wasn't mutual,' she lied.

'No? And why's that?'

'You're not my type.'

This might or might not be true. She'd yet to figure that part out. To be really sure she'd have to wait for him to spurn her and run out on her once he'd gotten what he'd wanted sexually. Then she'd know for sure.

'Women like you don't have a type. You fall in love once, hard, and that's that.'

She laughed. 'You don't know me very well then, either, do you?'

He arched a brow. 'Better than you think.'

Maggie didn't have an answer to that. Who knew

what a merman like Ketch might know or not know. She'd seen strange enough things on this island already not to doubt anything. 'Oh, God,' she moaned. 'Don't make me wait any longer.'

'What's the matter? Tired of sparring?' he rejoined.

Bastard.

'Just ... just do it.' Not very articulate, but that was where she was at.

Ketch seized her nipples, first one, then the other, in his teeth. Her body rose to meet him, well past listening to her brain. She had her own primal rhythm going, curves to meet his angles, liquid softness to meet his hardness, flesh yielding to his teeth and lips and cock. Moans came from deeper and deeper as he shifted, managing to find her clit with the top of his penis. The man knew what he was doing, she'd give him that.

'Yes, yes, that's it,' she cried, grasping his upper arms. 'That's what I need.'

Maggie locked her feet behind him, wanting his ass tight against her, wanting him all to herself, the feel of him, the taste. He gritted his teeth as she put her mouth over the open wound on his shoulder. The pungent taste of blood permeated her lips from where she'd bit him earlier. Adversaries always did make the best lovers, didn't they?

'Turn over,' Ketch growled, her action seeming to awaken something even more primal in him.

He pulled himself out, giving her room to flip onto all fours. He recaptured her open pussy with minimal delay, ramming himself home like the outdoor creature she'd imagined him to be. Was this how he lived? Taking what he needed on the run, including his loving?

'Maggie,' he rasped, sweet as sin. 'You're incredible.'

She felt incredible, deep guttural groans emanating

from her throat as he reached round to grasp her breasts in his hands.

'Come on,' she encouraged. 'Finish me off.'

In and out he slammed himself, her tailbone pushing backwards to meet his every thrust.

'Oh, God,' she moaned. 'I'm going to –'

The words were lost in sensation as they exploded together, the combined tension of the last twenty-four hours, of life and death, released in this single explosion of human lust. Of its own accord, Maggie's pussy fluttered and squeezed and spasmed, communicating in its own language to his erupting cock. Spurt after spurt jetted from him till she felt as full as she'd ever been.

And as exhausted.

'Oh, Ketch,' she collapsed onto her stomach. 'That was . . .'

'I know.' He fell beside her, reading her mind. 'For me, too.'

They lay together several long minutes, just listening to one another's heartbeat. It was the kind of plateau you didn't want to come down from, especially in this case, because there were going to be too many questions. Not the least of which was: which one of them would take command now and who would end up being a prisoner for the rest of the night? Or maybe forever.

Katy Sue was beginning to feel very sorry she'd invited Rayleen along to the stakeout. This two-women-on-one-guy thing was proving to be a lot less fun than she'd thought. Especially with Rayleen getting all the attention from the one guy.

'Rayleen, ain't them titties tired yet?' Katy Sue complained.

'They're. fine,' The other woman smiled as she switched nipples, taking the left out of Mike's greedily sucking mouth and putting in the right. 'But you're sweet for asking.'

Katy Sue frowned. At the moment Mike was sprawled on his back on the king-size bed with Rayleen crouching above his head, bending over to let him feed on her swinging teats.

'I just figured they'd get worn out,' she said spitefully. 'With those kids sucking on 'em day and night.'

The insult seemed to pass her by. Mike just gurgled, taking no responsibility. If he wasn't careful, he'd end up all alone with nothing but his own hand for relief. Honestly, she'd picked Rayleen to come along with her because she was so needy. Katy Sue had expected the woman to be grateful just to be there and to take all her orders from her, and here she was making moves on her lover, trying to shut *her* out.

'Mikey, if you're still worried about that noise you heard,' said Katy Sue, as she tossed her hair back and forth possessively over his huge dick, which at the moment he seemed to care less about than his slurping lips, 'why don't you have Rayleen go and check it out for you?'

Mike was shaking his head, though he wasn't making a whole lot of sense, what with Rayleen feeding him like a little man-stealing bitch. 'Damn it, Katy Sue,' he garbled at last. 'I ain't sending no woman out there. I need to do it myself.'

Rayleen guided one of her milk-white tits deeper between his full lips. 'Hush, baby,' she crooned, with all the expertise of a three-time mother. 'You need to stop all your fussing. Nobody has to go anywhere. That woman you heard next door wasn't crying in pain, she was having sex. And leave Katy Sue alone, too, she meant well.'

Like hell I did, she thought, as she dragged her teeth

over the main underside vein in the man's cock. And why did Rayleen have to be all sweet and nice about everything?

The big cop let out a moan in response to her nibbling that made Katy Sue feel wicked and naughty and horny as hell. What female wouldn't want to be in this situation? Having a big strapping lug at your mercy, buck naked, with a humungous cock ready to be ridden till the cows came home. She loved the man's body. The way his nipples stood out so keenly on his pecs, the way his six-packed abs tapered so beautifully to a tight and narrow waist. The way his neck tasted when she kissed all over him. The way his balls did that cute little retracting thing when she weighed them in her hand.

'Bet you'd like to have a nice warm, wet place to put this big old thing, wouldn't you?' she teased, kneeling beside him to run her fingers along the underside of his cock.

'Get on up here,' said Mike, lifting his head and reaching for Katy Sue.

Rayleen tried to distract him with her bosom again, but he was all about Katy Sue now. Good. Let the washed-up milk cow do what she was supposed to be doing, watching and fetching and generally playing second fiddle.

'Rayleen, get the gun belt. There are handcuffs and a taser, too.'

For the moment the cop was pliant, right where she wanted him, but she was going to have to do something a little more permanent if she intended to keep him in line.

She showed Rayleen exactly what to do to help her and they worked on connecting his wrists through one of the wrought-iron bars on the headboard. He didn't realise what they were up to until too late.

'Hey, what the –'

Rayleen gave him a full-mouthed kiss, designed to knock any man down in his tracks. 'We're just playing a game, baby,' she said huskily.

Mike yanked on the cuffs. 'You call that playing? I'm stuck here for real.'

'Oh, what's the matter?' teased Katy Sue in a baby-girl voice. 'Is the big bad cop afraid?'

'So help me, girls, when I get free, I'm gonna –'

Rayleen silenced him with a nipple.

This gave Katy Sue the opportunity to grab one of his legs. For her little plan to work, she needed to have him completely immobilised. The thing was, even without his hands he was more than a match for her.

'Let go,' he snapped, kicking her away as she tried to grab his ankle.

'Mike Cosgrove, don't you be a bad boy,' chastised Rayleen.

'That's right,' said Katy Sue, standing over him. ''Cause I'd hate to use this.'

Mike's eyes got real huge at the sight of the taser. 'Katy Sue, that's not a toy. You put that down right this instant, you hear?'

'I think this end points forward,' she remarked to Rayleen. 'Don't you?'

'Only one way to find out,' said Rayleen with a shrug.

'Keep that away from me!' he yelped. 'Just tell me what you want me to do and I'll do it!'

Katy Sue treated him to a big smile and a peck on the cheek. 'Thank you, baby, I knew you'd come around. OK, here's what I need. You gotta spread your legs real wide while we tie you down.'

'While you what?'

'You heard me,' she said crossly. 'Don't make me repeat myself.'

Cos scowled in protest, but the big beefy thighs parted, leaving his cock and balls deliciously exposed.

'Rayleen, go find some rope. I'll keep him occupied.'

'Yes, ma'am,' Rayleen said with a grin, running from the room.

'You gonna be a good boy for me?' Katy Sue asked.

Mike looked less than thrilled.

Katy Sue gave him the old carrot-and-stick approach, massaging his dick with one hand and aiming the taser with the other.

'Damn it,' he said between gritted teeth, 'you ain't fighting fair.'

'Who's fighting, Mikey? We already won.'

Rayleen came back with some nice cloth rope from the utility room. It was just right for securing his ankles to the feet of the bed.

'Go on,' said Katy Sue when they were done, 'try and get free.'

Mike gave it his best effort, his every muscle deliciously tensing and squirming. After a few useless minutes she stopped him cold with a dig to his balls with her fingernails.

'That's enough, boy. Time to get down to business.'

Mike was out of breath, but his eyes weren't leaving Katy Sue or her hands for a second.

'Pretty worked up, huh?' She played lightly with his penis. 'Bet you'd like a little relief.'

Mike moaned, raising his ass off the bed, unabashedly humping the air.

'Down!' Katy Sue ordered, as if he was a dog. The big cop collapsed, shocked.

'You want any relief, boy, you have to earn it, is that clear?'

Mike stared at her till she flayed his nipples with a loose piece of rope. She managed to do it just hard enough to make him howl.

'I asked you a question.'

'Yes, it's clear, Katy Sue. Jeezus, have you lost your mind?'

She whipped him another time with the cord. 'You speak when spoken to and that's it. Got it?'

Mike nodded, his face contorted with new fear and respect for the little stripper. Wow, she thought, I could get to like this.

'You earn your pleasure by licking pussy. You do me and Rayleen good, and I mean real good, and maybe we'll let you have an orgasm.'

Mike licked his lips, eyes passing back and forth between the two beautiful girls. 'Yes, ma'am.'

'Don't get cocky with me,' she warned. 'We ain't gonna be faking it the way females usually do. This is gonna be for real. Rayleen, you're up first. And by the way, Mikey, if you come before we say you can, you can plan on staying here all night this way. That way the chief can find you in the morning all tied up. Just like the little redhead next door.'

Cos tensed but said nothing. She wouldn't really do that to him, but for the purposes of the game she had to sound like a totally heartless bitch.

As part of her plan, she intended to keep on teasing Mike while he serviced the milk cow, Rayleen. The woman was anything but shy in climbing up on the man's face. Katy Sue felt her own pussy tighten in anticipation. She hadn't gotten much oral pleasuring in her life. Once she and Mike had tried it, but it was too rushed and too cramped to really enjoy. There were just some things that weren't meant to be done in a squad car and that was one of them.

She could forget about ever getting anything that exotic from Jake. His idea of foreplay was stumbling into the bedroom after a six-pack trying to find her pussy to shove his dick into before he passed out. Could you blame her for looking around for a little action? Never mind something on the side, she was just trying to get her main dish each day.

That's what pissed her off so much about these tourist women, like dark-haired Diane, coming down here and trying to horn in on what few good men there actually were on this island. Didn't she get her fill in the big city? Katy Sue had watched enough TV to know there were hunks on every street corner up there, growing out of the darn trees, for gosh sakes. The little time she'd been in New York she'd seen enough herself to confirm that. She'd still be there, too, if it wasn't for her deadbeat old man. Never lifted a finger to raise her, barely darkened her and her mom's doorstep for the better part of ten years, and then he has the nerve to go and get all paternal, fetching her back home as if she was still a little kid and not all grown up and eighteen. Legally, she could have told him to go to hell and a lot of times she asked herself why she hadn't.

None of the answers she came up with were good. At some level, she was afraid she'd gone along with him because she had the same demon inside her as everyone else in the family. The one that said she wasn't good enough, that she wouldn't amount to anything, so she might as well just go ahead and fuck up now and save everybody the trouble. An unhappy marriage to Jake was a real good start. Secretly taking birth-control pills so she couldn't have any kids by him was even better. Then there was her habit of screwing around with Mike on duty.

'That's it, honey, lick it good,' Rayleen encouraged.

Mike was breathing the woman's pussy at this point. If the man needed lessons, he was getting a crash course.

'Is he getting your clit?' Katy Sue asked, licking the bottom vein of his neglected sex tool.

Mike arched his back. She could only imagine what torture this was for him. And it was only the beginning. She intended to have the man crying and begging before it was all over.

'Take your time, Mikey,' Katy Sue coached putting her head down to swallow one of his balls whole. 'We got all night.'

Mike moaned his response. Katy Sue could almost feel all that testosterone pumping through his veins. This was a mountain of manhood and at the moment she had total control over it. What a great idea, tying him down like this. She should have thought of it ages ago. Definitely a good way to level the playing field. Men had such an unfair advantage otherwise. Not only were they physically stronger, but they also could make women want them, getting them all weak-kneed and silly. She'd had that problem in high school, and again in New York when that Broadway show producer had wanted to give her an audition in exchange for a little physical affection.

He'd started by making her feel like a queen, taking her out to a fancy restaurant. There were things on the menu she'd never even heard of and when she asked why there were no prices on hers he just laughed, saying that wasn't for the lady to worry about. The food was good and the wine was even better. Not quite the same as the homemade she was used to, but pretty fine all the same. It seemed to go straight to her head, too.

The producer, whose name was Lyle, took her back home and offered to help her back upstairs to her cheap one-bedroom apartment. He was just like some hero out of a movie, carrying her over the threshold and laying her down on her bed. When he started undressing her, rolling her over to unzip her black dress, the one good one she had, Katy Sue didn't think much of it. She didn't think much of it when he kissed her, either, or when he sat her up to take the dress off, leaving her in nothing but a slip and bra and panties.

'I don't feel so good,' she said, but he told her she'd be feeling real fine in a minute. Lyle kissed her deep and hard and made a strong play with his hands, using one to form-fit her throbbing breast while he slid the other unabashedly up her thigh to the top of her panties.

'Lyle, don't,' she remembered saying without a whole lot of conviction. The thing was it had gone too far already and she was hot and willing even if she was a little scared because he was old enough to be her father and because he was so much more sophisticated than any man she'd ever met.

'Shh,' he'd said, stroking her forehead, his cock poking at her through his silk trousers. 'Just let it happen, it'll be all right.'

'But why me?' she'd asked foolishly, as if it weren't obvious that a man would want to put his hard dick into the hole of any pretty, naïve young thing he could get his hands on.

'Because you're beautiful,' he told her with his sparkling blue eyes and sparkling white teeth. 'And because I see in you all the potential in the world.'

Later on she learned that Lyle murmured things like that to young women on a regular basis and that his promises were about as shallow as his smile. At the time, though, it was all too real, body-to-body, and his wasn't half bad for a man pushing sixty. There was something especially naughty about being with a fifty-eight-year-old, something scandalous in a way. And with all his experience to guide them, she knew she could let go and let him carry her where he wanted.

Taking his sweet time, laying her back down on the bed, he played over her curves, teasing with his fingers, up and down her thighs, over her pussy, then up to her breasts. He made her beg him to take off each article of clothing as, step by step, he freed her skin for loving. She was on fire and his hands were ice. By the time he pulled down her panties she was beside herself, thrashing her head back and forth on the bed, her pussy gaping, craving to be stuffed with dick. Any dick. For as long and hard as the man wanted her.

But Lyle had only just begun. Now he was tickling her nipples with his tongue, lapping her full young breasts as he gradually worked his fingers down to her sex. He didn't insert them at first, but just laid them over the top. She was arching, try to make contact, but he made her lie still, enforcing his decree with gentle bites of her swollen, sensitive nipples. Put in her place, she collapsed, moaning, a nervous wreck. Over and over he made her tell him what she wanted, in coarser and coarser terms, till she was screaming to be fucked.

Then he silenced her with a kiss, fusing their lips and plunging his tongue like a cock in its own right. The first touch of his finger to her clit made her explode, a mini orgasm in preparation for the three more that he would shamelessly tease from her overheated, broken body.

When at last he took his place above her, she was looking up to him like a subject to a king. His face puffed with self-satisfaction, Lyle settled himself to the hilt, enjoying his conquest. Katy Sue set in to spasming all over again from the pressure and now she turned the tables a tiny bit, forcing him to rush to his own climax. Unable to rear back for a final thrust, he simply clutched at her, shivering as they came together, sexual equals.

Lyle said not a word to her afterwards. Either she'd pissed him off or else he'd already gotten all he wanted and was done with her. Either way, the slamming door sounded the same, as did the tears she cried into the cheap, tattered pillow provided by her landlord. It was no wonder she hadn't put up too much of a fight when her father came three days later to take her home.

Rayleen was bucking like a bronco rider now, giving out some pretty good hoots and hollers as she steered Mike's face into all the right nooks and crannies. Katy Sue was curious how it would end. There was no telling how a woman was gonna come till you heard it for yourself. Personally, Katy Sue was a screamer.

'You tell him,' she giggled, encouraging the wildly undulating face-sitter.

Rayleen's juices were pouring down Mike's chin. Katy Sue sure hoped the man liked the taste, 'cause right about now he was drowning in the stuff.'

'Best save your appetite, honey,' she told Mike. 'Cause I aim to give you a nice little drink myself in a minute here.'

Enjoying her own joke, she gave the tip of Mike's cock a nice big kiss. He was a good sport and somewhere down the line, real soon, she intended to reward him for that in a big way.

10

Diane was beginning to wonder if Chief Grifford would ever show. Did the man really expect her to sit around in this awful bar all night waiting? She'd already had to shoot down propositions from half a dozen margarita-soused insurance salesmen who'd made their predatory approaches to her little corner table like rabid sharks. It wasn't as if the atmosphere here was anything to make her want to hang around by herself, either: black leather stools, black leather-trimmed bar and walnut-panelled walls, complete with signed photos of various players from the Florida Marlins baseball team.

They didn't even have any decent gin in stock. Checking her overly expensive watch, a gift from Manuel the bullfighter she'd sort of married and then divorced in San Castillo, she noted the time: seven forty-five. If this had been a college lecture she was waiting for, she'd have been excused twenty minutes ago. Not that she intended to let this cop do any lecturing to her. She had something else in mind, something that didn't involve talking.

Honestly, she would probably have left by now if not for her own vanity. Diane Quinton had never been stood up for a date in her life and she did not intend this backwater lawman to be the first. Didn't he have any idea what she could give him in bed? Dumb as he might be, he certainly had eyes and from what she'd seen she was like caviare in a dish of chopped liver around here. Or was it chopped alligator?

Maybe she should call and check on Maggie. Honestly, you just had to wonder about that girl sometimes. She really needed to get laid, that was her problem – moping around in Hank's old pyjama top mooning for a robber. She didn't know what she wanted. Heaven forbid some sensible, stable, halfway respectable man ever did show an interest in her. She wouldn't know what to do with herself. Playing the field was one thing, but you had to be practical, too. Money or love, you needed to get something long-term from a man or else there was no point in giving a second thought to him once the sex was over. Take this police chief . . . he'd be great between the sheets, a fine holiday hump, but as soon as she had her narrow behind back in Chicago she'd be looking for someone with a little clout, not to mention a couple of hundred thousand tucked away in stocks and mutual funds.

It was women like Maggie who made her gender look bad, earning all their own money and acting as if they didn't need men to support them. How was she supposed to keep on exploiting the male half of the species with those kinds of bad examples floating around?

'So, you showed up after all.'

Diane felt a shiver down her spine and promptly tried to hide it. It was him, standing over her shoulder, talking to her with that deep, rich-as-cocoa voice of his. Hell's bells, did she ever love that accent, too. Slow and meandering, deceptively languid – like a panther casually touring his territory.

'I think I should be asking that question of you,' she corrected, greeting him with a smooth urban smile.

Chief John Grifford ran his hand through his short, sandy-brown hair, looking more like a schoolboy dressed for church than a high-ranking civil official. 'I was detained on business.'

She looked him up and down. He was wearing shiny black cowboy boots, brand new jeans and a white, western-style shirt with pearl buttons. The effort he'd obviously made on her behalf went a long way towards appeasing her anger. So did the clean, fresh scent of the man: soap mixed with musk.

'Buy you a drink?' He waved his cowboy hat towards the vacant bar.

Diane watched a toupeed man abruptly pay his tab and walk out. He'd been about to hit on her until the tall cop had shown up. 'That would be lovely, thank you,' she said.

'What you got there?' he wanted to know.

'Gin and tonic.'

Griff went up and relayed her order, adding a whisky for himself.

She ogled him on his way to the bar. The man's ass looked even better in denim than it did in khaki, she decided. And his front end didn't look so bad on the return trip, either.

'I want to thank you for today, Chief,' she said as he put the drinks on the small table and sat down across from her.

'Thank me for what – giving you a ticket?'

'But that's what opened my eyes. You see, I hadn't really stopped to think how selfish my behaviour was, or how I might be endangering the lives of others.'

Griff raised an eyebrow. 'Is that right? I must be one helluva cop to get through to you after – how many tickets is it you've gotten again, Mrs Rostov?'

'It's Diane,' she reminded him. OK, so he was no fool and easy flattery wasn't going to get her anywhere. Her low-cut Gurelli dress, however, ought to get her any-where she wanted.

'You're a sly one, Chief Grifford,' she said, leaning forwards slightly. 'May I call you John?'

His eyes strayed for the briefest second to her cleav-age and then back to her eyes. He was a disciplined son of a bitch, that was for sure.

'You could but, being as you're not my dear departed mother or a bill collector, I'm not apt to answer you back. Around here folks call me Griff.'

'Where I'm from they call me Di.'

'And where's that?' He picked up the shot glass, making a ritual of it. 'Chicago?'

'Originally. Though I've had quite a few other addresses since, thanks to my various ex-husbands.'

Griff downed the whisky and replaced the glass on the table. 'Yeah. I noticed from the records you've had a few of them. Surnames, that is.'

'A sad story, really. When all I've ever wanted to do is to make men happy.'

He smiled thinly. 'And what do you think it is makes men happy, Mrs Rostov . . . Di?'

Good boy, he was finally getting with the pro-gramme, using her nickname and flirting all in one sentence.

'It's quite simple, really. They want someone who's a lady in public and a whore in the bedroom.'

'Really? Around here, I'd say it's pretty much the opposite.'

Diane laughed. 'You're quite the card, Griff. Here's to your quick wit. May it never defy any speed limits,' she toasted.

'That calls for a refill,' he said, signalling to the bartender.

'I am puzzled by one thing,' she said after he'd

downed the second shot. 'Today, when we were out there on the road, you could have had me. Why didn't you take advantage? And don't tell me you're gay – I wouldn't believe it for a minute.'

'Wouldn't,' he said with a smirk, 'or couldn't bear to?'

My my, so the old tiger had claws after all. 'The question is purely academic,' she shot back playfully, 'I assure you.'

He shook his head. 'I've seen plenty of women like you. They need to be adored. Need to have men fawning all over them. The thought that a man could possibly find them unattractive is far too devastating for their egos.'

'Oh, lord,' she said, rolling her eyes. 'Don't tell me you're going to turn out to be one of those intolerable drunks who insists on telling the truth about everything, because, if you are, I can assure you things won't turn out well at all.'

She saw the mirth in his eyes, though he was trying hard not to have a good time. 'And how exactly would you like things to turn out?'

'You and me in bed,' she said bluntly.

'Hmm, so I see you're an honest drunk, too.'

'Oh, no.' She slipped off her shoe to run her stocking-clad foot up his leg. 'I'm an incurable liar when I drink. I'm also a pathetically easy lay.'

He made no move to dislodge her as she pressed her toes into his crotch. 'As opposed to when you're sober and you play hard to get?'

'Admit it,' she purred, wiggling her big toe over his rock-hard dick. 'You were beside yourself today. I saw you waddle back to your truck. I bet you had to run right off and jerk it, too, didn't you?'

'Is that how you get your kicks up in the big city? Getting law officers to masturbate for you?' He was remarkably stone-faced for a man who was getting an expert foot-job.

'Just tell me the truth. Tell me how after you saw my pussy all out in the open like that you had to go off and shoot your wad. Tell me, or I'll make you lose it again, right here.'

Griff pulled a pack of cigarettes from his shirt pocket. 'Please. Do I look like a seventeen-year-old punk? I've had women twice as hot as you come onto me and never batted an eyelash.'

'I thought this was a no-smoking state.'

'Only in establishments where ten per cent or more of the receipts are from food. Now, are you going to remove that weapon of yours or do I have to arrest you for assaulting an officer?'

'Why not? I'd love to see how you wrote this all up on a police report.'

'Who the hell cares? No one reads a damn thing I write. The city clerk is a blind scrap-dealer who hasn't been outside his yard in ten years and the mayor is so senile he walks around with his air-raid helmet on half the time because he thinks it's still 1945. Smoke?'

'I'm trying to quit.'

'Suit yourself,' he said with a shrug. 'If you're really interested, I went to see a friend this afternoon. A lady friend.'

'A lady friend? Well, those are two words you don't hear in the same sentence very much any more.' Di licked her full red lips. 'So she took good care of you, then?'

'She knows how to handle Little Griff.'

'Little Griff? Don't tell me you're one of those guys who actually names his dick?'

'Why not? I'm a hell of a lot closer to it than I'll ever be to a living human being.'

Diane took back her foot. 'I believe I'll have that cigarette after all.'

Griff handed one over and gave her a light.

'Here's the deal, cowboy.' She steeled herself with a good long puff. 'I want it. Long and hard. And you do, too, or you wouldn't have come here tonight. So why don't we cut through the bullshit?'

Griff took a deep puff on his own cigarette, looking sexy as hell. 'They told me you northern gals were direct. I guess they weren't kidding.'

'That's me. A Yankee gal all the way. Now, you want in my panties or not?'

'You're actually wearing some? That's a switch.'

'I got them special, just for you to take off.'

This last quip actually made him laugh. It was a small one, but it was low and raspy and it curled her toes. She'd get more out of him, she decided, if it killed them both.

'Sorry, I'll have to take a raincheck.'

'Why's that?'

'Because you're part of an ongoing investigation.'

'Like hell I am. I wasn't even in the same goddamned state.'

'You were in on it, sure as anything.'

'In on what? I haven't a clue what you're talking about.'

'You think I'm really that stupid, don't you? You think because I talk slow and wear short pants to work means I can't add two plus two?'

Di felt her warm belly full of lust turn to bile. 'I don't care what you're adding, you're still getting the wrong answers. My sister was robbed last night, and that's all there is to it. And if you were any kind of cop, or any kind of a man, you'd be out looking for the man right now.'

'Maybe I will.'

'You found your way in here,' she said dismissively. 'I'm sure you can find your way out.'

They fell silent, back in neutral corners. For a while they puffed on their cigarettes. Griff ordered another round of drinks.

'What's so special about me, anyway?' he asked after a fresh whisky. 'You got your pick of men, I'm sure.'

'Is that a compliment, Chief?'

'Not on your life.'

'In that case, there's nothing special about you at all. I'm just slumming.'

'A lot of men would call you a smart-ass bitch, you know that?'

'Now that,' she noted sarcastically, 'just has to be a compliment.'

He shrugged. 'I didn't say I was one of 'em.'

'No? And what would you call me?'

'A lonely, mixed-up woman who needs a strong man in her life.'

Diane swallowed. She wasn't sure which blew her away more, the audacity of the remark or its startling proximity to a truth she herself had been trying to avoid for years.

'Oh, please, spare me the chauvinist propaganda,' she said with a laugh, desperate to shore up the vulnerability she was suddenly feeling. 'You don't really believe this stuff that comes out of your mouth, do you?'

He pulled a couple of twenties from a hand-stitched wallet. 'Actually, I think I'm gonna call it a night if you don't mind.'

Diane's heart was pounding. She wasn't used to chasing, still less to begging. 'Wait, I really do want to hear the rest. Tell me what you'd do if you were the man in my life. Tell me how you'd make things all better.'

She tried to coat the request with a sprinkling of irony for self-respect's sake, but she was half-afraid she was sounding pathetic. Damn it, what did they put in the drinks down here to make them so strong?

Griff regarded her coolly. 'For starters, I wouldn't let you run around half-naked, teasing every cock from here to Tallahassee.'

Diane pressed her thighs together. No man had talked to her like this. Ever. 'So you'd be jealous, then? And controlling?'

'If you're implying I'd be some goddamn lunatic trying to shadow your every move, no, but I'd sure as hell want a woman of mine conducting herself like a lady.'

A lady in public, she thought, and a whore in the bedroom. So her words had sparked something in him after all.

'And if I didn't?' she asked huskily. 'You'd have to correct my behaviour, wouldn't you? I bet you wouldn't hesitate to put me over your knee, even, would you?'

Griff snorted. 'Lady, you're a real piece of work, you know that? I'd tell you it's been fun,' he said as he rose to his feet, 'but I'd be lying.'

Diane sat there stunned, watching him walk out. She was on the verge of tears. She ought to be furious, or else just laughing at what a fool she'd made of him, but instead she just felt hollow and empty inside.

'Griff,' she cried. 'Wait. Please?'

She caught up with him in the parking lot. He had his hand on the door handle of the oversized police vehicle which apparently doubled as his personal transportation.

'Griff, I'm sorry.' She tugged at his arm. 'I was being

a bitch and I don't blame you one bit for walking out on me. If you'll please just give me another chance to –'

She was swept up into his arms before she could finish the sentence. Griff's kiss was like a hot, silencing brand. His arms around her waist drew her up and into his orbit, leaving her instantly breathless and dizzy. It was as if she was being punished, forgiven and redeemed all at once. Her body grew so weak there was no way she'd be able to hold herself up any more. If he let her go now, she would slide straight down onto the asphalt. To say she was burning, wet and ready would be the understatement of the year.

'We'll go back inside and get a room,' he told her when he finally released her lips.

Diane managed a dreamy little 'uh huh'. If this one-night stand had started out as her own idea, it had been taken over by the tall, dark and handsome Florida lawman. She had to hang onto his arm, literally, in order to walk back across the parking lot and inside to the front desk.

Everything was a blur. Standing there at the imitation-marble counter with the young African-American clerk behind it, Griff could have been signing them up for a week's stay in the deepest bowels of hell and she'd have happily followed him.

The only thing she could do – and this was possible only when they were safely alone inside the elevator – was to throw herself at the man in the hope of receiving another of his unique and devastating kisses.

'Hold your horses, woman,' he chided, though he made no serious effort to keep her from rubbing her body against him.

'No. I can't wait,' she breathed hotly into his neck. 'I need you to take me now. Please, Griff, fuck me.'

'In the elevator? Are you crazy, Diane?'

Yes, she was, and yes, she was going to manage, hell or high water, to get herself screwed somewhere between the first floor and the eleventh.

'Do it to me,' she gasped, slapping the emergency stop button with her palm. 'Show me what a bad girl I am. Put me back in my place.'

This time she took the offensive, offering up her small hot mouth to be plundered. A pair of torpedo breasts with rock-hard nipples against his chest couldn't hurt either, nor could her fingers flying over his belt and pants.

'You need a good spanking,' he breathed, the words passing directly between her close-pressed lips.

'I want it, Griff,' she panted, urging him on. 'I want it all.'

His hands moulded her ass cheeks, hard and firm. She could tell by the look in his eyes that the foreplay would have to wait till they got upstairs, and that was just fine by her.

'Take off your panties,' he growled.

Diane wriggled obediently out of her sopping wet silk underwear. Feeling like the sultriest hooker in the world, she handed them over to the hard-eyed lawman.

'Turn around,' he commanded, tossing them to the floor. 'Face the wall and bend over.'

Diane had visions of being arrested, of being patted down prior to being cuffed. The chief wasn't interested in searching her, though, except for that magic spot between her legs.

'Grip the railing,' he said, flipping up the hem of her hot little blue dress – the one that was about to more than pay for itself.

Di clenched the thin brass rod, her knuckles white. She was bare-assed now, naked and exposed. There'd be no more talking, no more taunting of the chief and playing with him. She'd poked at the sleeping tiger long enough and now he was awake. She was going to get fucked, good and hard and on his terms. Which, amazingly enough, were her terms, too.

'Jeezus,' he rasped, slipping his dick inside her more-than-ready opening. 'You're as tight as a fucking teenager.'

'And you're as hard as one,' she praised him back. It was good when you could feel young again, as if you were starting over, experiencing all this for the first time.

'Oh, God,' he moaned, sliding himself in and out. 'You're so fucking good.'

For some reason the words seemed to mean more to her than just sex. 'I am good for you,' she agreed with a sigh. 'And I want to be even better.'

Her soft, feminine plea seemed to trigger something in him, strong and masculine. Seizing her hips, he took responsibility, controlling the event completely. Diane hadn't come this way in ages, with no warm-up, but she was going to now. It was something deep inside, something emotional. The man made her feel safe and wild and horny all at once.

'That's it, John.' She dared to use his Christian name. 'Take me, oh, God, please ... yes ... I'm going to ...'

He groaned over her, drowning her high-pitched cries with low ones of his own. They were climaxing in unison, inside the small metal box, suspended dead centre of the elevator shaft, the alarm bell dinging in the background covering all but the most animalistic of their screams. She could only imagine what someone outside listening might think.

The orgasm went on and on until finally Diane felt herself drifting back to earth. Little details of the surroundings came flooding to her senses, things she'd missed before, like the colour of the Persian-style carpeting, the mirrors on the walls that reflected Griff standing behind her and in her. And the look on his face, that sweet, angelic look of peace. She'd never thought the man capable of it, but she was more glad of it than just about anything else she could remember in her life.

'Mmm, baby,' she murmured, straightening her spine and reaching behind her to stroke his cheek, 'that was to die for.'

A wicked idea crossed her mind. The man was a cop. Why not take advantage – in a kinky sort of way? 'Darling, do you have any handcuffs?'

Griff chuckled. A moment later she felt it, the click of cold steel on her wrist, the very hand she was using to caress him.

'That's it,' she encouraged. 'Show me what a naughty girl I am.'

Griff easily manoeuvred her other wrist into the companion cuff, securing them both behind her back. 'You realise I can exploit you to my heart's content now?'

Diane tugged ineffectually at her wrists, marvelling at the feeling. 'Oh, I'm counting on it. Make love to me again, right now, please?'

'No, we're going back to the room first.' He zipped up his pants and smoothed down her dress.

'B–but what if someone sees us in the hall?'

Griff pulled out his wallet and flipped it open to reveal an official-looking ID with a star. 'I'm the police, remember? I'm allowed to do this.'

'Not with innocent people you're not.'

'You just said what a naughty girl you were,' he reminded.

'That's in private, not in some hotel corridor.'

He laughed. 'Relax. It's not like you know anyone around here. I'm the one who'll have to do all the explaining.'

'Good,' she said, pouting, 'and I hope it lands you in hot water.'

'Be careful,' he teased, steering her out of the elevator and down the deserted corridor. 'You don't want to make me unhappy, do you?'

'As a matter of fact, it has just moved to the top of my list of things to do on this god-forsaken island.'

'Yes, well, before too long, you'll be busy working on something else, something designed to make me pretty damned ecstatic, as a matter of fact.'

'Arrogant prick,' she said accusingly, knowing exactly what he had in mind.

'Why, thank you, ma'am,' he drawled, hand on the room door. 'I believe that's the nicest thing anyone's called me all day.'

'Must be a slow one.'

'Was till you came along.'

'It's too late to impress me,' she said haughtily. 'You've lost that privilege.'

'We'll see.' He grinned with that damned sexy smile of his that was forever turning her knees to jelly. 'We'll see.'

Katy Sue had told Rayleen not to touch Michael while she was off taking a piss, but the woman couldn't help herself, the way his hard cock was just begging for release. Crawling on top of his spreadeagled body, no muss no fuss, had just seemed the most natural thing in the world, and so Rayleen did exactly that, sliding her slick, sweet-as-honey pussy down over the officer's shaft.

He was pulsing inside her and she wanted him to

come fast, before Katy Sue got back and started teasing him again. At first it had been fun, but after a while she started feeling sorry for the man. She supposed he liked it, though, since he could have fought them off before they'd tied him down if he'd really wanted to. A man this strong could fight off a dozen other males, let alone a couple of frail women. It wasn't the first time Rayleen had noticed this. In fact, she had to admit, she'd had a crush on Michael for a long time now. Not that he ever seemed to notice her. Even in school, she'd been invisible to him. He was always into his sports, and she, well, she was into trouble.

Getting knocked up at the age of sixteen was her first mistake. Marrying Acre Foley was her second. Michael – she always called him this because she wanted to think of him differently from how everyone else did – probably didn't even remember the time he came out to her place and set Acre straight, drunken son-of-a-bitch that he was. The only good thing that man ever did was to leave the state for good to be a shrimp fisherman in Louisiana. Unfortunately he cleaned out her savings and stole her car to do it.

Michael was like a rock that night, never once raising his voice. He took one look at Rayleen's eye, all swollen, saw the crying babies and gave Acre two choices. One of them involved leaving town in one piece, for good, and the other, well, that was something that Michael would have done to Acre man to man, without his badge on. Coward that he was, Acre chose exile.

Most everyone else looked down on her for how she took care of the kids after he left, working for Diamond Pete and all, but it wasn't as if she had much choice. Not if she wanted to stay here on the island where she'd spent her whole life. What else could she do? Where else could she go?

'Untie me, Rayleen,' said the police officer, 'and get these cuffs off me.'

She felt a stab of disappointment. 'Ain't I good for you, Michael?'

'It's not about that. I got work to do is all.'

Rayleen's hands trembled as she undid the ropes on his ankles and unlocked his handcuffs. Katy Sue was not going to like this one bit. In a last-ditch effort to hold him, she planted her lips on his, firm and passionate, trying to tell him with a kiss everything that was on her heart, how she was sorry for what they'd done to him tonight, how she was so grateful for his help with Acre and how he'd always made her feel fluttery inside whenever he'd looked at her.

Mike gripped her upper arms, holding her at bay.

Rayleen whimpered at his touch, strong but not hurting. Her pussy was aching and empty, but not as much as her soul. 'Let me love you, Michael, please?'

'Why do you always call me that?' he wanted to know.

'I ain't never tried to explain it to nobody,' she confessed. 'I guess it's so I can think of you in my own special way.'

'And what way is that?'

'Like a hero.'

The answer seemed to stun him. He was looking at her with new eyes, like he'd never really seen her before. And that, in turn, made her eyes weepy.

'You OK, Rayleen?'

'I will be,' she replied, 'if you make love to me like there's no tomorrow.'

The cop lowered her gently so their lips could reconnect. Rayleen sighed, welcoming his mouth on hers as if it had belonged there always.

'I never knew this,' he told her. 'How you felt and all.'

Rayleen felt a tear trickle from her eye onto his cheek. 'I love you, Michael Cosgrove.'

He gave no answer, except to roll her onto her back so he could mount her, treating her as gently as if she were a piece of china. He felt ever so much bigger this way and, when he began to move in and out of her sex, she was tempted to cry his name out to the world. But she knew it was still a stakeout and that she better be quiet.

'I love you,' she repeated, her voice soft as a raindrop. 'Michael Cosgrove.'

'Rayleen,' he grunted, his body quaking in release. 'I – I never knew.'

She lay beneath him, deeply satisfied as he orgasmed on top of her. She'd had more than her share already, and anyway this moment was not about sex. For the first time in her life she'd had something to feel that wasn't dirty or painful and, even if the man never felt anything back, she'd be able to hold her head high for the rest of her days.

11

Maggie was biting her lip to stay awake. Ketch was spooning her and he was snoring. She could only hope he wasn't faking sleep like she'd been. Playing possum on her part had been a brilliant manoeuvre, lulling him into a false sense of security where her person was concerned. Even if it had been a bitter-sweet feeling, letting the half-conscious man reach round from behind to take hold of her breast so possessively, as if somehow one fuck made her his.

The thought sickened her. No, wait ... that was too strong an emotion. Strong negative feelings could all too easily turn to positive ones. She was grossly indifferent to the man, that's what she was. She could care less that he'd given her the best sex in ages or that her pussy was already crying out for more of his dick, hard again and agonisingly pointing between her ass cheeks.

The man was a brute: breathing in her ear, breaking into Heeter's house and into her life. Spying on her. Screwing her. Tying her. Who cared about his stupid old necklace? She was working on a hundred-million-dollar project and he was quibbling over some flea-market-grade jade elephant charm that supposedly gave him mumbo-jumbo powers. What a lot of nonsense. How sentimental and soppy could a man get? Not to mention demented. She almost wished he were just some run-of-the-mill break-in artist whom she could have fucked and forgotten. A fool like this would probably end up falling in love with her or some other ridiculous thing.

Well, he'd be doing it from behind bars as far as she was concerned. Just as soon as she slipped out from under his arm, she'd be on the cell phone calling for help. It was a bit of a squeeze working her way out and she did not like at all how she had to rub her already sensitive nipples on the sheet. Damn, she was still wet down there, too. And not just from his come, so insolently deposited, but from her own fresh juices as well.

Get a grip, girl, she chided herself. Just think like Houdini.

A few moments later, she was standing over him, a free woman once again. He was cute in his sleep, though, the way his mouth was moving and the way his hair was all tucked in behind his ear.

Uh-oh. He was stirring. Maggie took a quick step backwards, as if he was somehow going to leap off the bed and grab her out of a sound sleep. Shit, he was rolling onto his back. She ought to run, but something was keeping her feet locked right where they were. It was as if his body had this mesmerising effect on her, overriding her normal instinct for self-preservation.

A lot of it had to do with his cock. She'd never seen one quite like it. It was so natural looking, like the rest of him, and yet so perfect, like some primeval piece of clay that everyone should be worshipping. She licked her lips. There was only one way she knew to worship a cock and that was to put her money where her mouth was.

Maggie stopped herself before it was too late. What was she doing, thinking of fellatio, when she should be finding the gun and taking the man prisoner again? She had to get the upper hand, or else he'd tie her again or, worse, make love to her however he wanted, for however long. She'd never be able to endure it, having to do whatever he told her to, no matter how perverted.

He could even call over his friends – assuming a weirdo like this had any friends – and then she'd have to service them, too. And she'd have to satisfy them, too, or else she'd be in trouble. Then he might get even more men. One by one, she'd have to lick and suck their big dicks, right down the line, shuffling on her knees from man to man.

Maggie looked down. She had her hand in her pussy, stroking her juicy wet opening. The fluids were trickling down her inner thigh, fresh and warm over the already solidified layers from her earlier session with Ketch. Was she turning into a nymphomaniac or what?

The gun. She needed to get the gun. That would help her think more clearly. Without some kind of mental protection, she did not trust her own body to resist for a second. Her pussy and even her breasts were traitors to the cause, like every other inch of her skin, still tingling from Ketch's touch. More than anything, she craved to jump back in that bed and kiss the man awake so he would take her again, consequences be damned.

Putting temptation behind her, she returned to the den and found the pistol where it had been dropped in the scuffle. What was that, about a hundred years ago? Next she went out to the balcony. The moon was up. How had it gotten so late? She headed back to the bedroom, properly armed if not clothed, and flipped on the light switch to wake him up.

'Come on, Robin Hood. Rise and –'

Fuck. He was gone.

'Ketch, this isn't funny.' She held the gun in both hands, elbows locked, the way she'd seen them do on TV. 'You better come out here right now, before I do something we'll both regret.'

Regret was right. If she hadn't wanted to shoot him

before, she sure as hell didn't want to now that they'd shared bodily fluids.

'I wouldn't worry about it. I took out the bullets.'

Ketch was right behind her in the doorway. 'But ... but how ... when?' she stammered.

He took the pistol from her suddenly limp hands. 'While you were sleeping.'

'I didn't fall asleep,' she protested.

Ketch, who was still naked, tossed the gun onto the bed. 'Sure you did. Right after we made love. You snored like a little baby. I was tempted to make love to you again, but I thought you needed your rest.'

'How fucking considerate of you.'

'I also took the liberty of finding more rope,' he continued, showing her the coils in his left hand. 'I'm afraid you're going to have to spend a little more time in bondage while I make my getaway.'

Maggie felt herself moisten all over again at the word 'bondage'. Whether he intended it or not, the concept carried heavy sexual connotations.

'No, wait,' she said, backing up at his approach. 'Let's talk about this.'

'I think we've already covered this from every angle, don't you?'

'We haven't tried anal,' she replied, stalling for time.

'Maggie, you're a very desirable woman.' He brushed the hair back from her face. 'Hell, you're the most beautiful I've ever seen, let alone touched. But I can't risk your safety by being here any longer.'

Maggie's knees went weak. OK, so he talked a pretty good game, and he could back it up with some pretty nice touching, but this was hardly a reason to diverge from *her* game plan. If she could just remember what it was.

Her hand went to his chest, smooth, solid and so very male. 'Please,' she said huskily, no longer sure if she was acting or not. 'Can't you stay a little while?'

His moment of hesitation cost him dearly. Catching her breath, she moved in to steal a kiss, just one, to prove he wasn't the only burglar of the pair.

Ketch stiffened but didn't recoil. He smoothed his lips to hers and their mouths met with a deep intensity, a kind of communicated need Maggie had never before known with another human being.

He let her go, not a moment too soon.

'Maggie, if we do this again –' he held her by her upper arms '– I don't know if I'll ever be able to let you go.'

'I – I don't want you to,' she heard herself say.

How crazy was that? The man was a sneaky, mixed-up, incompetent thief whom she hardly even knew, and here she was pledging herself to him in exchange for – what? One more fuck, a little extra bit of nookie before he high-tailed it for Mexico or wherever the hell else he was going to hide out from the police?

There was a thought: she could run with him and play Bonnie to his Clyde.

Oh, God, he was lifting her into his arms, carrying her to the bed like some romance-book heroine. Put to a stop to this, her brain screamed. Right now, before it's too late.

'Tell me you really want this,' he whispered, laying her down soft as a cloud upon the mattress.

Maggie opened her mouth, her brain trying to form the words. No. No. No.

'Yes,' she rasped back, lost in those jade-green eyes of his. 'Oh, God, yes.'

* * *

Officer Cosgrove straightened his Stetson hat, adjusted his gun belt and knocked on the front door of the Heeter place. It was past midnight now, a good two hours since he'd first heard the noises. It might have just been an owl, or someone having sex, like Rayleen said, but he had a duty to check these things out. There had never been any kind of foul play in living memory on the Island of Osprey and he sure as hell didn't want it on his watch.

More importantly, he didn't want anything to have happened to one of those two sisters – whichever one might be in there. He knocked again more loudly. Frankly, this was one of the more confusing nights of his career. Katy Sue had really done it this time. Cuffing him on duty, practically gangbanging him along with Rayleen Carter.

And wasn't that a surprise. Who knew the lovely Rayleen had feelings for someone like him? Mike hadn't even figured she knew he was alive, what with all the fancy types and high-rollers that came into Diamond Pete's. He sure felt sorry for her, though. She'd gotten a raw deal with that scumbag husband of hers, first getting beat up on for five years and now having to raise all three of his kids by herself. He'd have run the man out long before if he'd known what was going on. That was the problem with folks in these parts. Sometimes they kept things a little too private, things that ought properly to be dealt with by law enforcement.

Which meant Griff and him. If you could count a junior officer who lapped pussy for hours when he was supposed to be taking care of business. Damn that Katy Sue, anyway. And on top of everything else she had the nerve to give him the cold shoulder when all was said and done, like he'd somehow offended her. What more did the woman want? He'd lost count of how many orgasms he'd given her. She sure was a good cock-tease, though. He had to love that about her. Sometimes a man just craved that sort of thing.

Come to think of it, Katy Sue was kind of bitchy towards Rayleen there at the end. Was it on account of the private session they'd had together while Katy Sue was in the bathroom? Nah. Katy Sue couldn't possibly be jealous. She was a married woman. Jeezus, he sure hoped they hadn't left any evidence behind. The chief had gotten permission to use the Shiffler place to run surveillance, but he very much doubted whether Mort and Ida Shiffler would enjoy strippers fucking on their king-size bed.

Damn it, why was no one answering this door? He was almost certain somebody was in there. Things were looking more suspicious by the minute. One hand on his holstered revolver, just in case, he tapped the windowpane with the back of the flashlight.

'Open up,' he said, good and loud this time. 'It's the police.'

Cos's heart was pounding. Maybe he ought to call for backup. No, he'd gotten himself in this mess and he'd have to get himself out of it.

'You hear me?' he repeated, pulling the pistol out halfway. 'I said it's the police and you better open up right now.'

Aw, hell, had he put bullets in the gun this morning? Talk about a bad time to remember something.

'Lord, just get me and everybody else out of this alive,' he whispered, saying a quick prayer, 'and I swear I'll never take out my dick on duty again.'

* * *

'Ketch, do you hear that?'

'Hmm?' Ketch mumbled, his mouth half full of Maggie's breast.

'Get off me, Ketch. I heard something. Someone's at the door.'

The banging was repeated, this time with a voice, announcing itself as the police.

'Ketch, get up!'

The man was lost, having just taken the promised nether plunge, his flesh completely conjoined with hers, cock to pussy. It was the storybook union, the start of their life together – happily ever after, on the lam, knocking off convenience stores into the sunset.

'Snap out of it,' she said, pounding his unmoving back. 'You have to make a run for it.'

Ketch rolled to his side, blinking his eyes clear. 'I'd never make it.' He shook his head. 'Who knows how many of them are out there?'

'Hide in the closet, then, while I stall them.'

'Sorry, honey.' He stroked her cheek. 'But I can't do that, either. How do I know you won't give me away?'

Oh. So they were back to that game again.

'Scout's honour?' she suggested, raising her hand in her best rendering of an official pledge.

'You weren't a Scout, Maggie. Which leaves us only one option.'

She didn't like the look on his face one bit. 'What's that?'

'We'll have to fool them into thinking I'm someone else.'

'Like who? It's a little late at night for the postal carrier and I don't think they deliver milk any more, even around here.'

'We'll have to convince them I'm your boyfriend. Shouldn't be too hard, right?'

She slapped his hand off her breast, her brain firmly back in control. 'Forget it, buddy. Maggie's all awake now and playtime is over.'

'Tell me you don't quiver at my touch,' he challenged, giving the barest brush to her nipple. It was like fire, shooting down to her toes.

'All right,' she conceded. 'We'll do it your way but, I swear, if you say anything to embarrass me, I'll kick you in the balls, and I don't care if every cop in Florida is watching.'

'You can count on me,' he said with a grin, hopping off the bed like a small child. 'Do you think we should hold hands?'

'To answer the door? Yeah, like that wouldn't look suspicious. Where did you grow up, anyway, in a turnip patch? Never mind –' she held out her hand, forestalling his answer '– I really don't want to know. Let's just get this over with.'

To Maggie's amazement there was only one cop, the younger one from before.

'I'm sorry we took so long,' she said with a smile, wrapping the hastily donned silk robe more tightly about her flushed and oversexed body. 'We were, um, sleeping.'

'We were making love, actually.' Ketch put his arm around her waist from behind. 'I'm afraid my girl's a bit of a screamer. You know how that goes.'

The cop looked quickly at Maggie, sharing her embarrassment. 'I'm, uh, sorry to have disturbed you.' He cleared his throat. 'I just wanted to make sure everything was quiet after last night.'

'It's fine now,' said Ketch, clenching her tighter. 'Now that we're back together. You can bet I was worried sick about my Maggie after the robbery. I came down here as quick as I could.'

'I'm sure you did.' The cop was looking straight at the towel around his waist. Was he wondering if Ketch had a hard-on?

'Would it be all right if I looked around a little? Assuming you folks don't mind.'

Maggie's heart thundered in her chest. She wanted so badly to shout out this fool's identity to the policeman. 'Sure,' she said instead. 'That would be fine.'

The officer tipped his hat and brushed past. Maggie waited till he was in the next room to chew Ketch out.

'What the hell was that all about?' she whispered fiercely. 'Who said you could tell anyone we were making love?'

'Well, it's true, isn't it?'

'A lot of things are true, you asshole, but it doesn't mean you blurt them out to every Tom, Dick and –'

Ketch yanked her in for a kiss to silence her just as the officer came back down the hall. She squirmed to get away, which only induced Ketch to grab her ass, locking her in place. She wanted desperately to kick him, but things were bad enough already without a struggle to complicate things, what with her poor, barely concealed breasts pinned against his chest. Not to mention what was happening between her legs as his cock rose to take its all-too-familiar place against her pelvis.

The cop cleared his throat, more loudly than before. 'Everything seems to be in order,' he said to announce his presence.

'Sorry, officer, she just can't seem to keep her hands off me.' Ketch pulled her alongside him, hip-to-hip, close enough to make sure she had no option but to confirm what he was saying about her. The worst part was that she really did want to sex him up now, on account of how worked up he had gotten her. And the fact that she was being made to show off her sexuality in front of the policeman, shameful as it was, only seemed to inflame her more.

'Are you down from Chicago as well?' the cop asked, facing the two.

'Actually, I'm from South Carolina by birth.' His hand slid up under the back of Maggie's robe, this time to cup her bare ass. 'But I've been around quite a bit since.'

'Where'd you two meet?' he asked Maggie, who was trying her hardest not to squirm.

'On the beach. We were both vaca–' She broke off mid-syllable as Ketch's finger wormed its way up into her pussy from the rear. Surely the cop had to be seeing what was going on? 'Vacationing.' She completed the word, fighting to keep her voice steady.

'It was lust at first sight,' added Ketch, wiggling his index finger back and forth. 'I took one look at her and I had to have her. Who could blame me?'

'I gather you felt the same,' said the cop dryly.

Maggie was moving her ass against the penetrating finger, bittersweet invader that it was. 'He was hard to resist,' she confessed huskily.

Oh, God, she thought. Please don't make me come like this, totally exposed, in front of a strange man.

'You'll have to forgive all the questions,' the cop said, maintaining his demeanour remarkably well under the circumstances. 'It's just we don't get many robberies here. Especially involving off-islanders.'

'Perfectly understandable,' said Ketch, motherfucking, pussy-tormenting bastard that he was. 'I'd want to know the same things in your position.'

'And I can promise you,' the cop said gravely, 'we are

doing everything in our power to find the low-life coward that broke in here last night.'

'It's a funny thing, though, isn't it, officer?'

The cop had been about to take his leave. 'What's that, sir?'

Shit, why couldn't Ketch let well enough alone? Did he want them both to end up in jail?

'The effect that ropes can have on a woman. The right kind of woman, that is. I mean, there are some who enjoy that kind of thing. Isn't that right, Maggie?'

'I – I couldn't say.' She smiled tightly, trying to keep the waves of pussy pleasure at bay.

'Well, just speaking for yourself, honey, what does it feel like, being constrained by rope?'

I'm going to kill this man, she thought. I am going to find his infernal necklace myself and I am going to use it to slowly choke the life out of him.

'That's private,' she retorted. 'Don't you think, *sweetheart*?'

The cop was licking his lips. He looked as if he wasn't sure whether to run off or get involved himself. 'I think I should be going. Thanks for your time, folks.'

'But you haven't answered the question.' Ketch shifted his finger to her clit. Maggie tried to suppress a gasp. He had her now and she knew it. His finger was on the trigger and, if she didn't cooperate, he was going to pull it.

'Yes,' she said, opting for the lesser shame of verbal confession. 'The feeling excites me. I – I like to be tied.'

'There you have it, officer,' Ketch said as Maggie leaned back helplessly, her head turned, her eyes closing. She was his now, to play with as he chose, to be danced with upon the fine string as he plucked the deepest pleasures of her soul.

'I think all that rope talk got her a little too worked up,' said Ketch, laughing lightly at her reaction. 'What do you think, officer?'

The officer was silent. What was the man thinking? She didn't dare look. He was seeing it all, her obscenely covered body, helplessly responding to the commanding touch of her lover.

'I think I'll go check the perimeter ... sir.'

'No problem, and thanks again for your service.'

'I'll see myself out.'

'Yes, I'd appreciate that,' he gloated. 'I'm afraid the little woman won't part with me at the moment.'

As soon as the cop closed the door behind him, Ketch pushed Maggie forwards, pinning her against it. Immediately, he sank his finger to the hilt in her silky hole.

'You complete and total bastard,' she hissed, launching into a string of every curse word she could think of, as well as a few made up just for the occasion.

'Tell me what you need, Maggie.' Ketch was nibbling at her ear, holding her damp hair in his fingers. He had his body tight against her, fitting her and filling her, but denying her the motion she needed to get off.

Impotently, she clenched her fists. 'You know what I need, damn you.'

'Say it, Maggie. I want to hear the words.'

'Please,' she panted. 'Please ... Ketch ... let me come.'

Ketch gave her the pay-off she was looking for, his talented finger finishing the job. Maggie's lips sealed against the windowpane and her nipples pressed to the wooden door. She was shuddering, pushing herself back against him. Their orgasm was like a pair of snakes twisted in mortal combat.

'Oh, Ketch,' she moaned. 'Oh, baby.'

He stayed very close behind her afterwards, seeming to know how vulnerable she'd be. Kissing and nibbling at her neck, spoiling her with kisses, he treated her as if he were a real lover and not just a manipulative, sex-stealing intruder. A girl could get used to this, she thought.

Mike was going to blow a load in his pants. What in the blazes was wrong with that guy, groping his woman right in front of him? He ought to run the two of them in for lewd and lascivious conduct. Not to mention making an officer of the law way too horny for his own good.

He had half a mind to call Katy Sue back for another quickie. Or maybe Rayleen. Sex with her had been damned good, better than anything he'd ever had before, actually. Why exactly was that? The woman was sexy, sure, and she had the moves of a pro, but he'd had a lot of good-looking women before. Katy Sue was just as pretty in her own way, and even more kinky. What was the difference? Could it be he felt something for Rayleen Carter, the way she did for him? He'd never been aware of loving anyone before and he didn't even know what it felt like. He supposed he could go and fuck her again, just to do some more comparison.

But he had his duty and this time he wasn't going to shirk it. Not this time. Shining the flashlight around the corner, he continued his perimeter search. It didn't seem likely the burglar had come back, but he needed to be sure. The chief would want a full report in the morning, first thing. It was the fine points of a case that made it or broke it, the chief was always saying.

'Criminals always overlook something small,' Griff had told him. 'It's the nature of the beast. Call it guilty conscience or just God's way of keeping evil in check, but there's always a clue to be had if you know where to look. The devil's in the details, every time.'

The other thing Griff was always telling him was to be suspicious of everyone right off the bat and then make them earn your trust. Trust is easy to give away, but hard as hell to get back once it's stolen.

Was there anything suspicious in what he'd seen tonight, other than the fact that this dude was feeling up his girlfriend right in front of him? Not really. In fact, a man would have to feel pretty sure of his innocence to draw attention to himself that way in front of a cop.

That Maggie Quinton sure was a sex kitten, though. It had taken all the restraint in the world not to reach right out and grab those barely contained tits. And those nipples, like little rocks, pink and sweet under the silk robe, waiting to be popped in a man's mouth. Was it his imagination, or was she coming on to him, too, telling him how she liked to be tied and how it made her all hot and bothered to be constrained by a strong man? Maybe he'd come back one night when lover boy was gone and do a little solo investigating, beginning with what lay underneath that tiny little robe she was wearing.

Mike stopped in his tracks. It just occurred to him he hadn't seen a suitcase in the master bedroom, just the ones in the guest room, but they had to belong to the sister. Shouldn't the boyfriend have some luggage, too? Or, at the very least, a pair of shoes or a wallet on the dresser? Something to show he belonged there? Then again, maybe he was just a neat freak and had everything packed all away?

Sure, that was probably it. No big deal at all. There was such a thing as being too suspicious, he chuckled to himself.

Mike was about to call it a night when he saw the footprints. A single set of them, man-sized, flat soles. Tracing the flashlight along the ground he followed them straight to Maggie's bedroom window. Those sure as hell hadn't been there last night. And, given the absence of another set pointing in the opposite direction, that meant there was a good chance whoever owned those prints was still in the house. Somewhere.

Officer Cosgrove pulled his revolver, fumbling to check the chamber for the bullets. His hands shook. It was loaded all right. Time for another little visit to the Heeter place, he thought, and this time he wasn't going to be knocking.

12

'This is police brutality,' Diane informed the chief, doing her best to appear angry and not aroused as he locked the hotel room door behind him.

'Is that right?' He dug his hand in his pocket for the key and removed the cuffs. 'In that case, I might as well make the most of it. Take off your clothes and get on the bed. It's time for a little cavity search.'

Diane decided to make him work for it this time. 'Go to hell, Grifford. I'm not your prisoner ... or your whore.'

'Obviously not. Or I'd have to pay you. Now are you going to do as you're told or do I have to put you over my knee – just like you've been practically begging me to all night?'

Her pulse was racing. He couldn't possibly be seeing into those old fantasies of hers, could he? Fantasies of being put under the control of a loving but domineering man who would compel her to feel wicked pleasures she was too scared to feel on her own?

'I'm not a child,' she said defiantly, though the heat was already pooling between her legs at the prospect of having the man's strong, punishing hand on her helpless flesh.

'No,' he agreed, a twinkle in his eye, 'you're a spoiled brat.'

Diane's felt butterflies flip in her tummy. No man had ever treated her this way, even in jest. None had dared to take control, to try and beat her at her own game of brazenness. It was thrilling, arousing and just a little bit scary all rolled into one.

'You have a lot of nerve.' She decided to test his limits. 'Treating me this way.'

'Nerve enough to give you to the count of five to get over here and give me a kiss.'

'And if I don't?'

He hid his smirk, but just barely. 'Then I'll know you're afraid of me.'

'Maybe it's you,' she cooed, 'who should be afraid of me.'

Diane waltzed up to him, intending to bring him to his knees with a couple of well-placed caresses. Instead she found herself exactly where he'd threatened, her crotch down on his lap as he sat on the corner of the bed. The manoeuvre had been smooth, painless and totally unexpected.

'Stop it!' she squealed like a banshee, squirming. 'You have no right!'

Grif delivered the first smack right through her dress. It was light enough, though it certainly stung her pride.

'Ow!' she cried, exaggerating the pain. 'That really hurts, you big brute!'

He rubbed the sore spot, delivering delicious and maddening heat. 'I'll stop if you like. Unless I miss my guess, though, you've fantasised about this before, haven't you?'

'Yes,' she whispered, unable to lie fast enough.

'Lots of women do. Why don't we try going to ten and see how it feels, shall we?'

'I'm sure it will feel great for you,' she grumbled, flushed from head to toe, feeling humiliated and horny as hell.

Grif chuckled and proceeded to spank her just as he

193

liked, striking at will, obviously enjoying the sight of her and the tiny whimpers he was eliciting between each stroke.

By five she was so wet, she feared she'd soak through her dress and his pants. By nine, she was pressing herself against him, on the brink of orgasm. When it came to ten she was relieved he hadn't made her come in such a degrading way, but also a little disappointed.

'You may get up, Diane, and strip.'

The command jolted her from her tiny dream world of pleasure and pain at the man's hand. It was a sudden reminder of what was really going on. A battle of wills. A contest for sexual supremacy.

Grifford punished her delay with a mild pinch to her hot behind, just hard enough to make her yelp but not enough to make her want to call it quits.

'I'm waiting, Diane.'

He let her go. Really the only thing being bruised was her ego, though even that was more a turn-on than anything else. What was it about this man that made her trust him to have this kind of power over her? Seizing a ragged breath, she readied herself for the next stage in this session of most unusual foreplay.

'You asked for it. I'm gonna blow your fucking mind.' She stood in front of him, posing like the whore she'd just gotten through saying she wasn't. 'I'm gonna make you come harder than you ever have in your life.'

He made no comment as she arched her back salaciously, running her hands through her hair. She felt like a hot little alley cat, her hide freshly tanned by her tom. Diane was pure oozing sex now and she still had every intention of seducing him.

'Nobody's ever done that to me,' she said as she unzipped the back of her dress, pushing out her braless breasts, the nipples tight and hard against the bodice. 'That means you get an extra special reward.'

Slowly, tantalisingly, she pulled at the hem of her dress, almost all the way up to her naked crotch, but not quite. 'I know you want some,' she said huskily. 'And you'll have it – all of it.'

Griff said nothing, nor did he stand up, though he did begin to undo the pearl buttons of his shirt, revealing a bronzed chest covered in fine dark hair. The sight of it made her feel faint.

'Oh, yeah, baby,' she cooed, shimmying the dress over her hips. 'Show me that body, show me what I'm going to be crawling all over tonight.'

Griff slipped the shirt over his shoulders. His stomach was flat and muscled, his biceps firm and strong. She wanted to kiss at him and lick every inch of his weathered skin.

'Meet you on the bed?' she murmured, tossing the dress over her shoulder.

'No.' He shook his head, his face still expressionless. 'We're not done with your punishment yet.'

She took a step backwards, feeling suddenly nude. 'What?' she exclaimed, her hand resting lightly over her pussy.

'Your spanking,' he said, his fingers splayed over denim-clad thighs, right beside the swollen crotch. 'It isn't over.'

Diane looked at his lap, trying to imagine herself across it again, this time with no protection whatsoever.

'But I can't.' She spelled out the obvious. 'I'm naked.'

'You can, Diane, and you will. You are past the point of resisting me. You know that. We are both well aware what you need and we know I'm the one to give it to you.'

His words just turned her to butter. It wasn't about the action, the spanking, so much as it was about him wanting her, caring, desiring. This was about pleasure, not only his but hers.

She shuddered at the touch of the denim, rough on her nipples as she slid down till her pussy was over his hard penis. She tried to hold herself like a bridge, elevating her sex, but he put her rebellion to an end with a single word and gesture.

'Down.' He smacked her lightly, sending her crashing into his crotch. Diane's moan was helpless and feminine, but it was only the beginning.

'Women like you amaze me,' he said, running his hand over her already exploited terrain. 'You want men to see how beautiful you are, to praise you, but you're never sure enough. Never loved enough. It always goes back to the daddy you never had.'

She winced as he smacked her. It started out as mild pain, but grew into a warm, pervasive sexual tingle.

'I'll wager yours was away a lot. On business. A salesman, maybe. Came home once or twice a month to dote on his pretty little girl, saying how beautiful she looked. A lot of pressure for a child, I'd imagine, to always be perfect for him, wouldn't you say?'

Diane was still back on the part where he'd said she was pretty. 'I – I suppose.'

'You suppose?' His finger entered her pussy, adding a whole new twist to his game of cat and mouse. 'I'd have thought it would strike quite a chord.'

'M– my father's a lawyer,' she managed.

He masturbated her to the brink and then stopped. 'That would have been my second guess.'

Diane raised her ass in the air, trying to impale herself again.

'Lie still,' he chided, spanking her hard.

Diane submitted, her swollen breasts squashed against his leg. When he found her clit again, she cried out. The outburst earned her a pinch. After that she went limp as he worked her efficiently: three crisp, though less severe, smacks, followed by full finger penetrations. At no time was she allowed to climax.

'Let me come, Griff,' she begged at last, no longer caring what he did to her. 'I need to so bad.'

'No fun being teased, is it?' he asked pointedly.

She thought of herself out there on the road, in her little red car and dress, flashing her pussy when there wasn't a goddamn thing he could do about it. 'I have it coming, I know. But I'll make it up now. Let me please you. Use my body. I'm yours, anyway you want me.'

'In the ass,' he decided. 'I'm going to have you in the ass.'

'Oh, yes, Griff.' She was breathless, rubbing her pussy. 'Take me in the ass. Shove that big, beautiful cock as deep as you want.'

'Are you any good?'

He was treating her like a sex toy, making her reduce herself to a creature of pure pleasure-giving, and she was loving it, needing it. 'Oh, yes,' she gasped, feeling her pussy spasm. 'I'm good. I want to be a good ass fuck for you.'

'I want you on the bed on all fours,' he said huskily. 'You may crawl there, on your hands and knees.'

'Yes,' she replied, feeling something deep and primal well up within her.

The carpet tickled her palms and knees. It was electric down here, another world of sex, one that was dark and wicked and male-dominated. Here Diane Quinton could be as sexy and lusty and naughty as she liked. The man – John Grifford – would keep her in hand. But really, she had power, too, because, as long as he'd put her here, he had to watch over her, protect her and cherish her. She was as much the centre of his world now as he was of hers. His sexuality was consumed by her flesh, and also his mind. And she'd take advantage, too, making him use all his energy, all his patience, all his resources.

Yes, Diane Quinton planned to be a very naughty little girl, a complicated, exasperating wench, and, when she was done, it would be him and not her begging for mercy. In the meantime there would be sensation, pure and unbridled.

'Face down,' he commanded as she crawled catlike onto the bed. 'Ass in the air.'

Griff had lotion, which he rubbed into her sore ass cheeks. It was cool and soothing. See? The man was catering to her already. But he had some gel, too, which he applied inside her. So it was real. He intended to bugger her.

'Griff, there's something you should know.'

'You've never done this before?'

'No, I have, it's just that I've never done it with anyone I wasn't married to.'

'Doesn't narrow the field very much.' He pressed the tip of his dick to the tight, tingling opening.

'I'm serious. This is something intimate.' She stretched out her arms in front of her, her cheek to the bedspread. 'Don't you think?'

'A lot of things are intimate, Diane.' He pushed himself an inch inside her. 'And they don't lead to marriage.'

'Oh, God,' she moaned. 'Why are you such a prick about everything?'

'The same reason you're such a bitch, my dear.'

'I guess we're a match, then, aren't we?'

Griff grabbed her narrow hips. 'I really wish to God you wouldn't talk so much.'

'Guess you should have spanked me harder ... *sir*.'

'If I didn't know better,' he grunted, making himself completely at home in her ass, 'I'd say you were mocking me.'

'Perish the thought.'

Griff's breath came thick and fast. He was chewing at her neck, straining to make them as close as possible. The man was into her hopelessly deep, and not just between her ass cheeks.

'I'm going to fuck the daylights out of you, Diane Quinton. You won't walk straight for a week,' he vowed.

'If I don't break your dick off first,' she said, as she slammed against him.

She had managed to get the last word. Now it was moans he was coaxing, and feelings, too, strange ones that left her wondering, for the first time ever, if she could fall for the wrong man, like her sister. Could her need for this underpaid civil servant's body somehow override her normal gold-digging sensibilities? Or even cloud her heart?

As she'd said, perish the thought. Perish it, indeed.

Mike found the front door unlocked and no one in sight as he snuck into the house. There was no telling where the robber might be. Clearly he'd hidden himself from the horny young couple, not that they'd have noticed anything that didn't involve sex. He'd have to rely on stealth, alerting no one to his presence. This burglar was sneaky and he had balls to come back two nights running. Maybe he should have called for some backup. But then he wouldn't get all the credit. It would go to the chief or, worse still, a couple of county dicks who just happened to be cruising by sucking down dough-nuts and coffee.

Cos hated coffee and he never touched doughnuts. Anybody who said he did was a dirty liar, a cop-stereotyper of the worst order. Shit, he wished he could turn his flashlight on to cut the darkness. That would be a dead giveaway, though. He'd have to stay in stealth mode.

There was moonlight shining into the living room. Making his way along the wall, he did an indoor perimeter check. He and Griff had taken a class on this over at the academy sponsored by the county sheriff's department. What a bunch of losers they were. The only ones who joined the county force were the ones who couldn't make it on the state force and didn't have connections to get taken on by some town. There was this pretty blonde, though, with really yellow hair and a hell of a shooting hand. Griff said it was her big tits let her hold the gun that steady. She'd accidentally overheard him and challenged the chief one-on-one. She cleaned his clock and he had to buy her drinks all night. With every scotch, though, her little denim skirt seemed to ride higher and her crop-top got lower. By the end of the night she was throwing herself at him, laughing at every one of his stupid jokes and dancing close enough to the man for him to wedge both his hands down the back of her underpants.

Being a conscientious supervisor, Griff shared his good fortunes. The female deputy was insatiable, insist-ing on taking her own nightstick in not just one but all three of her orifices as the two island cops did their best to fill in the gaps. Aside from Rayleen, she was the hottest screw he ever had and by far the best cock-sucker. After that he and Griff looked to sign on for training with the county every chance they got.

The living room was clear. Ditto the kitchen. He ought to check the carport, but he had a sneaking suspicion about the bedroom. If the burglar was in the closet, Mr and Mrs Fuck-Like-Rabbits could be in one hell of a lot of trouble. Besides, he was damned tired of hearing them moaning.

'Police,' he said as he flipped on the bedroom light.

The two got one look at him and froze midstroke, like one of those old porn photos out of old man Johnson's collection up by Seashell Bay.

Cos trained his gun on the closet and yanked the door open, quickly determining it was empty except for a large, meowing cat.

'Officer,' said the young man with surprising aplomb, considering he was in the process of getting a blowjob, 'you're back.'

'No shit, buddy. There's a burglar somewhere in here and we need to get the two of you out of here.'

The woman, who was lying face-down between his splayed legs, popped her mouth free. 'Here's your robber,' she gasped. 'It's him. I wanted to tell you before, but he wouldn't let me.'

Cos levelled the pistol. Sure, it sounded pretty bizarre, but he'd seen worse on the island. 'Is that true?' he asked the suddenly ghost-white character with the saliva-covered dick.

The man looked at the woman like a beaten, betrayed puppy. 'Maggie, why?' he whispered. When she said nothing, he just frowned. 'Yes, officer. I'm the robber.'

Maggie was on her feet. Cos was disappointed. He had had this wicked notion to make her stay down and keep on sucking for his own viewing pleasure.

'All right,' he said to the sorry-ass burglar. 'Get your hands over your head. You and me got a little appointment down at the jail.'

'The jail!' she gasped. 'You're not really taking him to jail, are you?'

He looked at Maggie in disbelief. Could this night possibly get any more ridiculous? 'No, lady, I'm gonna take him out for ice cream and then I thought we'd go to the circus.'

'It's just that he's not a hardened criminal, that's all. Look at him, officer. He wouldn't hurt a fly. He didn't really want to steal anything. He was just after this necklace that Heeter stole from him. He wasn't going to touch anything else. Were you, Ketch?'

'No, sir,' the man said solemnly, raising his right hand. 'On my honour as a gentleman.'

Unbelievable. The woman was actually trying to win his freedom after just turning him in. The two of them needed a rubber room as far as he was concerned. On the other hand, there might be one of those win-win situations to be had in a case like this. After all, they did owe him for getting him so worked up before.

'I'll tell you what, folks. I'll walk on out of here and pretend I didn't see anything. Provided you two give me a little incentive.'

The pair looked at each other. 'What are you talking about?' Maggie asked for both of them.

'Sex,' said Cos with a grin. 'I want to see the two of you get it on. No holds barred. I get to watch it all, start to finish.'

'Are you out of your mind?' Maggie scorned. 'What kind of cop are you?'

'The kind that believes in creative justice.' He put his gun away. 'Now quit fighting me. You both know you haven't got any choice.'

'I'm afraid he's right,' said the burglar whom she had called Ketch. 'He's got us over a barrel. Besides, it's not like it's something we don't enjoy doing anyway.'

Cosgrove's dick pulsed in his pants. He had total power over them. Anything he wanted from them, they'd have to give it. So long as it turned them on, of course.

'Get down on the floor, babe,' he said pointing down. 'I want to see you suck again, nice and slow this time.'

'My name is Maggie,' she protested, but she knelt anyway.

'You're up to bat,' he told the man, directing him into position right over her. 'Good, now get to work, sweetheart. Kiss it first. Then rub it all over your face.'

The woman did as she was told, the rapidity of her breathing indicating she was more turned on than she wanted to admit.

'That's it. Rub that dick good, all over your cheeks, your eyes. Now I want you to slap your face with it. You heard me, slap yourself with that hard cock.'

She gave him a look, a sexy little pout of protest, before swinging the man's penis at her cheek. Mike couldn't help himself. He had to take out his own dick and stroke it in time to the little scene he was creating. This was incredible – it was as if he was one of those big-time directors, the guy who did *Star Wars* or that other film he loved, *Pussy Snatcher from Venus*.

'OK, Mr Breaking and Entering, let's see you get into this a little more. Pinch your nipples for me. Nice and hard.'

The longhaired robber did just what Cos wanted, further reinforcing the cop's sense of invincibility. It was funny, he'd never thought of himself as gay but, being able to hang back like this, he could almost appreciate what a woman saw in a man. Nice tight buttocks, hard tube pumping the woman's mouth, tight abdomen undulating, biceps curled, his fingers tweaking tough little man nipples. It didn't make him gay to jerk off to this, did it? Hell, no, not as long as there was a female involved.

'Time to switch,' he announced. 'Burglar, I want you to muff dive, and you, sweetheart, show me how you play with those titties.'

'They are known as breasts,' she corrected.

'Around here they are titties and I'm giving you ten seconds to start honking them or you'll both be spending the night in the lockup.'

'It doesn't matter,' she said haughtily. 'When people hear what you've done to us, you'll be going to jail, not us.' Her tune quickly changed as the kneeling Ketch put his head between her thighs. 'Oh, baby,' she whimpered. 'Don't make it so real. I can't hold out.'

'Oh, it better be real,' Cos warned. 'I want orgasms all the way around.'

Maggie was making her nipples into tight, rubbery little nubs with her fingers, moaning as she let her pretty head go back, her hair trailing down like a flame. Meanwhile the burglar was gobbling like a pro on that flaming patch of hair between her legs.

'Careful,' Cos snickered. 'You might end up with spontaneous human combustion if you're not careful.'

Watching the man suck gave him a wicked idea. What if he tried the burglar's tongue on himself? It wouldn't be gay exactly, just to try it. Not with the girl watching. It was an important distinction because, in Cos' world, real men liked women and that was that.

'Hey, buddy, why don't come here a second. And, tell you what, little lady, why don't you sprawl yourself out on the bed and you can watch us while you're playing with yourself. Only keep those knees up, so I can see the action.'

Ketch crawled on his hands and knees. The son of a

bitch had a beautiful back, nice and corded. Taking his hand away from his dick, Cos got hold of that long hair, guiding the man's head onto the tip of his spear. It was nice, smooth hair he had, real silky-like.

'Fuck,' he muttered as the man's lips slid sweetly over his shaft. 'You sure you never did this before?'

It was amazing, really. You had to wonder – in a blindfold test, could the average man really tell the sex of the person giving him head? Did that make all men potentially gay?

'I'm going to fuck you in the ass,' he blurted, and then couldn't believe the words had just come from his mouth. 'I want your little fake girlfriend to watch while I do you.'

Ketch sucked him with a little more gusto, as if this was turning him on, too.

'Let's go, sweetheart,' Cos urged his leading lady. 'Let's see some fireworks.'

Maggie's eyes were glued to the two men as if she'd never seen anything so good in all her life. 'That's it, Ketch. Lick him. Suck him,' she sighed.

She was propped up on a pillow, facing them, lifting her ass up to meet her fingers, deeply probing the pussy splayed wide for the cop to see.

'I'm gonna have me some of that muff, too,' he said, serving notice.

'Both of you,' said Maggie, her eyes lit like a wild woman's. 'I want both of you.'

Well, shit on a shingle. Who was directing this picture, anyway?

'Just you mind your manners,' he scolded her. 'Or you'll get left high and dry.'

'Like you could resist me,' she taunted.

Mike closed his eyes, trying to concentrate on what the burglar was doing. Maybe this two-boys-and-a-girl thing was going to be harder than it looked. 'All right,' he said, and took a deep breath. There was a fresh portrait of lust in his mind, ready to be enacted. 'It's time we put our leading lady in her place. On all fours, if you please, missy.'

Maggie didn't offer up much protest. Whatever it was he'd started here, it was turning them all into sex fiends in a hurry.

'Put your dick back in her mouth,' he commanded, pulling Ketch to his feet. 'Let's see if she can handle two at once.'

Maggie was more than happy to take her lover back down her throat. In fact, she seemed hell-bound on making him come as quickly as possible.

'Slow it down, you two,' he chided. 'I don't want any premature endings to my work of art.'

Using just her tongue now, she commenced licking, keeping him right on the razor's edge. Meanwhile, Mike was shedding his clothes at lightning speed to get at the tight little pussy.

Damn, but she was soft and silky. Tight, too.

Maggie slid her body back and forth, trying to fully please both men at once. She was a regular little fucking machine. Mike had her by the hips, holding on for dear life while Ketch was groaning, his hands on top of her head.

'Now we're talking,' Cos growled, hardly believing he was finding the stamina to do the act yet again tonight. 'That's what I want.'

Maggie moaned out her need. What a woman. And that burglar, he was good enough to eat. Wow. Had he just thought that? Was he really thinking about sucking off a man's dick?

Yes, he was, and tonight he was just crazy enough to follow through. Call it the moonlight, this wacky case or maybe just all those mixed-up feelings he had for Rayleen, but he was ready to cross every line.

And maybe he wouldn't come back once he'd crossed them, either.

Diane pretended she was still too drunk to drive her car, so Griff took her back to Maggie's place.

'So will I see you again?' she asked softly, breaking the silence about midway into the trip.

Griff took a good while to answer, which she was learning meant he was trying to sort out difficult emotions. She'd learned a lot about him tonight, and she was more than a little afraid of how much more she wanted to know.

'Not sure there's much point,' he replied, driving the police vehicle back over the bridge to Osprey. 'What with you going back to Chicago and all.'

'Definitely,' she agreed with all the verbal haste of a city dweller. 'I'll be going back any day, I imagine. In the meantime I'll be busy catching up with my sister. We hardly ever see each other as it is.'

The metal grating of the bridge rattled rhythmically under the Jeep. Griff let it work its way into the conversation like some kind of jazz riff before saying, seemingly at random, 'So you really don't have any idea about who's behind the robbery, do you?'

Coming from any other man, fresh after a mind-blowing, soul-baring sexual encounter, his question would have seemed insulting. From Griff, though, it came across as a compliment, as if somehow she was being given a chance to earn his trust – a thing she knew instinctively he did not grant lightly.

'No, the whole thing makes no sense to me, John. And I'll tell you, what really has me worried is how attached Maggie seemed to be to the guy.'

'You think she knew him from before?'

'Definitely not. He was a stranger, but there was something about him that, well, got her hot, to put it bluntly. I'm afraid danger turns her on.'

'Yes,' he noted dryly. 'The tendency seems to run in the family.'

She slapped his forearm. Solid muscle. Steady, manly flesh clutching the steering wheel. 'Be nice. And for heaven's sake, don't you dare let on to her what happened between us.'

Griff looked at her head-on for the first time since they'd left the hotel. 'You mean you won't tell her yourself? You seem like the type of sisters that share everything.'

'What makes you ask? You hoping to get in her pants, too?'

The little smirk was back, the one that made him look half boy, half devil. 'Methinks the lady's jealous bone hath been pricked again.'

'You can't prick a bone. As for your attempt at Elizabethan English, may I say heartily, sir, that it sucketh.'

'You *are* jealous,' he teased, putting his hand on her bare thigh. 'You're afraid I'll go to bed with your little sister and forget all about you.'

She peeled off the hand, only to have him put it right back, this time higher up.

'Do that again,' he said with mock sternness, 'and you'll find yourself bent over the hood of this fine Osprey police vehicle faster than you can say Willie Shakespeare.'

Diane stopped fighting him, but she registered her protest with a snort.

'Be a nice girl,' he chided, tapping her rapidly heating skin. 'Open those legs for me.'

'Griff, no. I'm putting my foot down this time. Sex is done for the night. You want any more, you make a date with me, like a normal man.'

Diane was powerless to stop him snaking his way under the waistband of her panties. For all her squirming, she was a sitting duck and he knew it. The fact that his finger found her sopping wet and ready all over again certainly didn't help her case any.

'If you're trying to get revenge for the shower,' she said, harking back to when she'd gotten him all worked up with the soap then run out of the bathroom, 'this is a pretty childish way to do it.'

'I already had my revenge,' he reminded her. 'Over the desk.'

As if she could forget being captured and taken from behind, soaking wet, his hand twisted in her hair, his cock subduing her to the level of a moaning, panting bitch. It made her flush right now just thinking of the things he'd made her say, the way she'd had to beg for release on his terms, primitive, raw and animalistic. She would never tease the man with soap again.

'All the more reason to lay off me now.'

'Tell me to take my finger away,' he said, calling her bluff, 'and I will.'

Diane bit her lip. The bastard had to know what he was doing to her, the way he was making her move and grind and need him all over again. 'You're impossible,' she cried. 'Why are you doing this to me now when you just said we'd never see each other again?'

'Call it a little something to remember me by.'

Di grabbed the door strap for support. He was working her shamelessly, making her writhe and shimmy against his hand. 'Oh, I'll remember you all right.' She was out of breath, but she had to get the words out. 'As the biggest ... most pompous ...'

'I want you to come on my hand, Diane. Come on, baby, give it to me.'

The combination of his treacherous touch and his murderously soft words were more than any woman could bear. She gave in to it all, the paroxysms, the fresh surrender laid on top of so many others in this long, long night of surprises.

'It's OK, baby,' he said, tilting her seat back, when she was done. 'Just close your eyes and get some rest.'

She looked at him, limp as a dishrag, as open as a woman could possibly be.

'Sleep,' he murmured, stroking her forehead, brushing back the sweat-soaked black hair. 'Just go to sleep.'

Instinctively, she turned towards him, clutching his arm. Slipping away on a deep black raft, she listened to the lulling sounds of the road, feeling like a small child in the protection of a big grown man, the way she had when Daddy used to drive them places and she and Maggie would lie down head to head on the big back seat of the family Cadillac.

This man is a total paradox, she thought. The most aggravating, infuriating, totally delicious man I've ever met. I can't afford him – but then again, can I live without him?

OK, so Cos had fucked up again. But had he really done any harm? One of the things the chief was very fond of pointing out was that sometimes justice had to turn a blind eye. In other words, you had to just let things be, every now and again, for the sake of the larger picture, even if a statute or two was broken along the way. Mike wasn't totally sure how to apply that to his having sex with the burglar and his fake girlfriend instead of arresting them, but he was pretty sure everything would sort itself out in the end, if for no other reason than Rayleen Carter had confidence in him. Hell, he was a bona fide hero in her mind. That had to count for something.

Straightening out his uniform for the zillionth time, he waited for the chief to drive up. Griff had called him over the radio and told him he was on his way back from the mainland and that he had Diane, the sister, with him. He was giving her a ride because she was too drunk to drive. That sure didn't sound like regulations either, did it? Hopefully that meant the big guy wouldn't be asking him too many embarrassing questions. Everybody on the island knew the main perk of being an Osprey cop was the pussy, anyway. It sure as shit wasn't the pay. Or the glory, either. Rescuing baby sea turtles. Jump-starting old ladies whose thirty-year-old mothballed Cadillacs had broken down on the way to bingo. Yeah, there was an exciting career.

Damn, what a night, though. In just a few short hours, Michael Lawrence Cosgrove had gotten himself tied down by two sexy strippers, been told by a beautiful woman that she loved him and performed in a bizarre threesome, the highlight of which involved having a strange man fuck him in the ass while an equally strange woman drowned his face in pussy juices.

In typical bad-luck Cosgrove fashion, he'd never gotten to fuck Ketch himself. The chief had called, spoiling the show. He had gotten the feel of a dick inside him, though, on both ends. It was a weird sensation, but not entirely unpleasant. The hottest thing was having the woman watch, knowing she was getting turned on. Mike liked to turn women on. That's why he worked so hard on his body and why he made sure never to say no when they came calling on him. Women like Katy Sue, and now Rayleen. Maybe he ought to say no a little more often? Nah. Where would be the fun in that?

Mike saw the chief coming down the road and straightened up. At first he thought the boss was alone, but as the Jeep pulled up he saw the woman reclining in the seat next to him, soundly snoozing with that freshly fucked look on her face.

'Evening, Chief,' he said, tipping his hat, making a show of not noticing what was painfully obvious. 'A bit colder tonight than last night, wouldn't you say?'

'Cut the bullshit, Cosgrove. What did you find?'

'Nothing, sir. The place is clean as a whistle. Inside and out.'

Griff looked at him, his arm on the window frame, eyes narrowed to cop width. 'That's good,' he said, taking a long time to answer. 'Because I'm not about to send the lady here into any danger.' His tone indicated that Cos had better be damn sure about the report he'd just given.

'Clean as a whistle,' Cos repeated. 'I'm sure that the, um, *lady* will be fine.'

Griff blinked. Now it was his turn to pick up on the other's tone. 'You got something on your mind, officer?'

Mike cleared his throat. This really would have been a fan-fucking-tastic time to have kept his mouth shut. Unfortunately, he was a Cosgrove and the Cosgroves had been known on the island for being loudmouths since Moby Dick was a minnow. 'It's nothing, Chief,' he said, trying to cover for himself. 'It's just she's real sexy and all, and –'

'That give you any ideas, does it, officer?' he interrupted, getting way too worked up about one of his casual screws. 'Because, if it does, you and me have a problem. A personal problem.'

'No problem at all.' Mike backed off. 'You're just being a Good Samaritan. Any idiot could see that.'

'Just check the perimeter again, Cos, and then go home. I'll be handling the stakeout till morning.'

'Yes, sir,' he saluted crisply. 'I'm on it.'

Holy shit, he thought, climbing the mound of sand to get to the back porch. If I didn't know better, I'd say the old man was in love.

'That's enough, Griff.' Diane was trying desperately to stop him kissing her. 'I need to go inside and you need to do ... whatever it is you're going to do all night.'

He had her pinned against the outside wall of the house like a schoolgirl. 'I'm going to be keeping you safe. Watching you all night from that window over there. If you want, you can give me a little show later.'

'It's four in the morning,' she protested, trying to push his hand off her breast, 'and my sister's in there. In case you forgot.'

Diane was still groggy, having woken up in the chief's arms as he carried her to the front door. For a split second, when she'd opened her eyes, she'd imagined there was something permanent in this, that he was caring for her like this because he loved her. Then she remembered what he'd said about never seeing her again. Did he still mean that?

'It'd make a whole lot more sense to just pick up where we left off tomorrow,' she said, testing the waters. 'Don't you think?'

Griff angled his lips, his eyes unreadable. 'Don't worry about it, Di. What's one more recreational screw in the scheme of things, right?'

The man's rebuff, light-hearted as it might have been intended, cut Diane to the quick. 'Screw you,' she said, slapping him. 'And your recreation, too.'

The chief held his cheek. 'What was that for?'

'For being a man.' She shoved him away, both hands flat on his chest. 'Now get out of my way.'

She slammed the door behind her hard enough to rattle the glass in every window. The noise brought Maggie out from the bedroom, wild-haired in a long robe. 'Um, is everything OK, sis?'

'Everything's just splendid, Magdalene,' she replied, tearing past. 'Just tell me you have cigarettes in your room and that there's no law against smoking in a house in Florida.'

'Di, you can't go back there!'

Diane stared at her baby sister, who had run up like a madwoman to block her way. Of all nights for the kid to weird out on her. 'What are you doing, Mags? Do you have a death wish or something?'

Maggie swallowed hard, looking like a little girl again. 'It's just that ... it's a little complicated, and ...'

'Magdalene, stop beating about the bush. I hate when you do that. Just come out with it.'

Maggie took a deep breath. Now it would be run-on sentence time, which meant yet another problem had arisen. 'Diane, I know I should have asked, but I needed somewhere to put him for the night, and he's not dangerous at all, he's just trying to get back this neck- lace that Cal Heeter took from him, and, anyway, he'll only be here till morning and then he'll be gone, I swear, and don't tell me I don't know what I'm doing, because I do. I'm old enough to make up my own mind about men, no matter what you say.' She paused to gulp air.

'The burglar.' Diane filled in the blanks, amazed at her sudden serenity under the circumstances. 'You've bedded him. Well, isn't that a smart thing to do? Of course, you do realise Chief Grifford has had a man watching the house all night, which means you'll probably get yourself arrested as some kind of accessory?'

Maggie looked down at her bare feet, toes wiggling in the plush carpet. 'Um, actually, Di, a cop was here, too.'

'A cop here? What do you mean, he was *here*? Look at me, Magdalene.'

Maggie had her lower lip between her teeth, a guilty look on her face, just the way she had the day she'd told her about Hank and how he was screwing her daily at the job site.

'Jesus, Mary and Joseph,' said Diane, reverting to one of their Irish grandmother's expressions. 'The cop fucked you, too?'

'I had to let him, Di. He was going to arrest Ketch.'

'Ketch? Who in blazes is Ketch?'

'The burglar. The one who's not really a burglar. He made love to me, sis, it was beautiful.'

'Oh, I'm sure it was.' She folded her arms. 'And how was the policeman? Was he beautiful, too?'

'Don't make me feel like a tramp, Di. It's been a long enough night as it is.'

Diane sighed. What could she really say to her sister, anyway, given her own exploits with the cop's boss?

'So what happens now? Dare I ask?'

'I say we order pizza. There's a twenty-four-hour place on the mainland,' announced a chipper male voice.

Diane's eyes turned to the lean man with the swimmer's physique who'd just come out of the bedroom. He was wearing a pair of shorts and nothing else. A half-hard dick poked out alluringly. The effect was rounded off by an attractive set of balls. She had to hand it to Maggie, the girl sure did know how to pick the pretty boys. But pretty boys always break your heart in the end. Even the older ones.

'You must be Diane,' he said, and shook her hand as if they were meeting at a family barbecue. 'I've heard all about you. I'm Ketch Walker. But most folks just call me Ketch.'

'Ketch. What a charming name. Now, if you don't mind, I'm going to call it a night, seeing as how I just spent eight hours in the company of the most obnoxious, arrogant man I've ever met, who, after turning my world upside down, never wants to see me again. Naturally, I went ahead and fell in love with him first because I'm the biggest idiot on the planet.'

'Di, wait,' her sister called after her, but Diane wasn't in the mood for company, not even with her closest confidante in the world. She had an appointment with her pillow. Face down for a good old-fashioned cry.

13

'Just a goddamn minute!' called out Cos, throwing on a shirt over his running shorts. Who the hell would be knocking on his door at six in the morning? Didn't anybody respect a man's right to a decent night's sleep any more? Especially since he hadn't even gotten into bed till nearly five.

'Whoever the fuck is out there better know how to run fast, that's all I can say!'

He swung open the door, spoiling for a fight. Seeing no one at eye level, he looked down.

'Rayleen.' He felt the anger dissolve in a pool of soft warmth. 'I didn't realise it was you.'

'I made you something,' she said, holding out her hands shyly, offering a covered glass dish with something yellow and delicious looking inside. 'I'm sorry if I woke you. I'll just leave it and go.'

Mike ran his hands over his hair. Suddenly he didn't feel tired at all. 'No, come in, if you got a minute. Place looks like hell, but maybe you could close your eyes.'

She smiled sweetly. Her teeth were dazzling and so were her green eyes. She was wearing a green and white print dress, knee-length and sleeveless. A ribbon was holding back her long cascades of hair. Jeezus, how come he'd never seen how truly beautiful she was – not just sexy, but downright lovely?

'Damn it,' he muttered, just standing there in the kitchen like a fool. 'Ain't nothing this good ever been in here before.'

She set herself to bustling about, messing with the stove. 'It's just a little breakfast casserole, that's all.'

'I didn't mean the casserole.'

The compliment brought colour to her cheeks. It made him furious to think that men looked at her naked every night and thought she was some kind of cheap floozy. Even if she had to make money with her body, she was still a lady in his book.

'How'd you find time to make this?' he wanted to know. 'Here, I'll get the plates.'

'Sit,' she ordered, pointing firmly to one of the two beat-up kitchen chairs. 'I'm doing the serving, you're doing the eating.'

Mike watched her bend over to put the casserole in the oven. He was hungry, all right, but not for food.

'Michael,' she cried. 'What do you think you're doing?'

'You said you were going to serve me, didn't you?' He had his hands on her waist from behind. His hard dick was pushing between her soft ass cheeks and his tongue was having its way with her ear lobes and neck.

'I didn't mean that.' She giggled.

'What'd you expect?' he rasped, wrapping a hand around her flat belly. 'Coming around here looking and smelling so good first thing in the morning?'

'I expected you to act like a gentleman, Michael Cosgrove.'

'I am,' he challenged. 'I'm being a man, and I'm going to do you real gentle ... maybe.'

'Oh, baby,' she crooned, craning her neck to reach his lips. 'Do you have any idea what you do to me?'

'Nope. But you're going to tell me.' Mike turned her so she was facing him. She looked at him with hot, lust-filled eyes. Her quick breathing was making her breasts rise and fall enticingly. A few more seconds of this and he'd be stripping her naked with his bare hands.

'You make me want to give you everything, Michael. My heart, my body, my soul. You make me want to pleasure you, with my breasts and my pussy and my mouth.'

'And you make me have to have you.' The cloth dress tore in his hands, right down the bodice. Rayleen gave a little cry of approval, her body slack with need. She offered no resistance as he ripped apart the clasp of her bra and shredded her feminine panties. Scraps still clung to her as he lifted her into his arms. He was taking her to bed. To his bed, to make her his woman.

Forever.

They didn't have to say a word. It was understood. In the way she opened her legs as he set her down on the quilt, and in the way her hands naturally fell above her head, palms up, and in the way her hip turned, ever so slightly inviting him to her ravishment. Understood, too, in the way the young cop took his place on top of the lovely stripper, wasting no time in piercing her wet and ready pussy, plunging to the hilt with a casual but decisive authority. And in the little moans, soft and female, encouraging him to go faster, to take liberties with her breasts, to taste the nipples offered up just for him, to bury his hands in her long hair, torn free of the ribbon, to clutch at her buttock cheeks, spasming and pulling him in tighter against her.

'Oh, Michael, you don't know how long I've waited.'

Mike melded their flesh, two bodies into one. 'Me too, Rayleen, me too.'

The heat was incredible. A fine sheen of sweat filmed their bodies. There was no more talking now, just the age-old tangle of limbs, the sinking of teeth into flesh, the aching and yearning ... and finishing.

They shouted out their ecstasy together, climaxing in a rage of rushing fluid, pounding blood and primeval screams. Mike clutched at her, half-afraid she'd leave, half-afraid she'd stay. There was no backing down, though, no retreating from the plateau they'd reached. Falling into silence, still on the bed, they lay together, Mike's head on her breast, Rayleen stroking his hair, half mother, half wanton.

'This could get to be a habit,' he muttered.

She slapped him playfully on the ass. 'It darned well better,' she chided. 'Especially once you've proposed to me.'

Maggie leaned on her elbow, watching Ketch sleep. He was like a little boy, puffing air out his mouth, his eyelashes fluttering. Except that Ketch Walker's body was all man, from the rising chest to the lazy cock sprawled limply across his hip. Having this guy in her bed was feeling strangely natural. And so was the sex. Again and again they'd gelled, the last time just half an hour ago.

Diane obviously thought she was crazy and it was clear they'd have a lot of talking to do today, not only about her own situation but also about the matter of Diane falling in love. Clearly she meant the handsome police chief, but that didn't sound like Diane at all, giving her heart so quickly and impractically. Not to put the woman down, but John Grifford could hardly have the portfolio or connections she generally looked for.

Lord, they were a pair of siblings. Between the two of them they'd never once made a right choice. Daddy was too hard to live up to, she supposed. Or was it just that he'd been too emotionally unavailable to teach his girls how to interact in a healthy way with the opposite sex?

At any event, she needed to get this mess cleared up today. She had work to do. There was a geological survey to be completed on the north side of the island and the high-rise construction site was now two days overdue for a supervisory visit.

A note would suffice for the man, she decided, lifting herself gently out of the bed. But what to write? So long and thanks for all the orgasms, don't let the door hit you on the way out? She really did want him gone, though. By the time she got back, if possible. He needed to be in Mexico, not with her. And God help them all if he got caught here, in her bed, by the chief or some state patrolman who wouldn't trade sex for keeping his mouth shut. Diane was right. What had she been thinking, taking this kind of risk? She might go to jail, or lose her job. A man like Heeter didn't take kindly to adverse publicity, nor would he enjoy knowing his house had been used to stage orgies featuring his chief architect.

Grabbing a pencil, she scribbled a note, read it over and then promptly crumpled it up. Words on paper would just make it worse. After giving him a tiny kiss on the forehead she dragged her nude body to the shower. Let him figure it out on his own after she was gone, Maggie decided, ignoring as best she could his erect cock. Lord, but the man was insatiable.

Standing bravely under the faucet head, she turned the water to full cold. It wasn't waking up she needed, but a chance to cool down. Shivering, she parted her legs, letting the water sluice over her tight breasts and into her moist pussy. Her sudden state of arousal was his fault, of course. Even sleeping, the man didn't play fair. How was she supposed to resist someone who looked and felt and fucked as good as him? Not to mention someone who made her feel so thoroughly annoyed, frustrated and . . . alive.

Ketch was awake the whole time Maggie was writing. He saw her struggling with the note, but didn't dare open his eyes. He was too ashamed of himself. The last thing she needed after his disgraceful performance of last night was to have to deal with him all over again. It was no exaggeration to say he'd behaved worse than Stella ever had. Using the woman for his own pleasure, humiliating her in front of the policeman and then in front of her own sister, parading half-naked like a satyr.

How this one redheaded woman had caused him to sink to such lustful depths, he had no clue. But the fault was his and his alone. Watching her with one eye closed, he felt the lust rekindling all over again. The way she'd bent over the desk as she wrote, her breasts depending so sweetly, her little feet crossed as she stood, and that sexy tongue peeking out between her lips as she tried so hard to concentrate. How could a man not want a female like that in his bed every night? How could he not want to wake up next to her, that wild flame of hair, that soft little body? If he had his way, she would wake up every morning with his hard cock inside her sweet, wet hole, so that the first expression on her newly awakened face would be one of lust.

But a man like Ketch could never have a woman like her. She was out of his league. She would marry some doctor or lawyer, somebody big in Chicago or Tallahassee, some pinstriped business type whose children she would bear. A woman like her would look lovely pregnant, her belly swollen, her cheeks flush and full of love.

Not trusting himself, he had turned onto his stomach

as she came back into the room. The pressure of his cock against the mattress nearly made him come. Out of the corner of his eye, he watched her shed the towel, shake out her hair and pick out her clothes for the day. White bra and panties. A white blouse, navy blue skirt and a matching jacket. Ketch drooled as she shimmied into the panties, hooked the bra and stepped into white patent leather heels. The skirt and blouse and jacket made her look totally professional on the outside, but he'd seen underneath: the little firebrand, ready and willing to be loved, needing to be taken hard and passionately.

If he'd hoped for another kiss, he was to be disappointed. Maggie had no sooner finished her makeup than she was out the door, carefully closing it behind her. Childishly, impulsively, Ketch proceeded to hump the bed, building enough friction with his dick to achieve ejaculation. He tried to justify soiling her bed as fair punishment for her unwitting teasing of him, but in his heart he knew this was only one more act of boorishness on his part. Gathering up the sheet, sticky with come, he thrust it deep into her pink, lace-covered hamper.

'I deserve Stella,' he told his reflection miserably, 'and all the abuse she doles out.'

Grabbing his shorts and T-shirt, Ketch put his ear to the door. He could hear her out there, talking to her sister. Avoiding the door, he climbed out the bedroom window, not caring any more if the cops were watching or if they were going to catch him as a result of his rash daylight departure.

He needed fresh air. He needed to clear his head. Before it exploded.

Maggie was surprised to find Diane awake and fully dressed in the kitchen. 'I expected you to sleep in.' She noted the black tank-top, jeans and sunglasses. The last time she'd seen her sister this dressed down was in junior high school. 'But I guess you have plans?'

Diane was occupying herself wiping down the already clean counter. 'I'm going back home, Mags. You know, you really need to keep up with the chores. You're letting the place go to the dogs.'

Maggie put her hand over her sister's flying wrist. 'You're wearing out the Formica, Di. Now how about telling me what's really going on?'

'Nothing,' she said, her voice way too flat to be believed. 'I have things to do back in Chicago, that's all.'

Maggie knew it was about Grifford, but she was afraid to broach the topic. 'I thought you were concerned,' she said instead, 'about the burglar situation.'

'Look, Maggie,' Di snapped, surprising her sister with her sudden sharpness. 'You can't have it both ways. Always goading me into worrying, then wanting me to back off when I do. It isn't fair.'

Maggie felt the flare of her Irish temper, a gift from her mother's side of the family. 'I never asked you to do a damned thing for me, Diane. So you can crawl off your high horse. And, for your information, I'm just fine, so you can take your skinny, over-marrying, self-absorbed ass back to Chicago as soon as you like.'

'Fine.'

'Fine,' echoed Maggie, feeling and sounding more like a five-year-old by the minute. 'I'll be more than happy to drive you to the airport.'

'Don't bother, I have a car. Besides, I'd hate to interfere with your day's leg-spreading. Who is it going to be today? The local mafia boss?'

'Fuck you, Diane.'

'Right back at you, little sister.'

Diane picked up her suitcase, which was by the front

door, already packed. If Maggie thought last night's door slam was loud, that was a mere whisper compared to this.

'And don't come back!' Maggie shouted stupidly after her.

Diane ran smack into John Grifford outside the door. The very last man on earth she wanted to face right now.

'Well, well,' he rasped. 'I guess you made me a liar – about not seeing you again, I mean.'

'I'm not in the mood, John. As for seeing me, get a good look at my ass as it fades away because I'm about to bid farewell to your pathetic little island forever.'

Her legs were shaking as she walked past him, but she hoped it didn't show through the confident sway of her buttocks. The last thing she could afford was to stop. One deep look into John Grifford's baby blues and she had a strong suspicion she would be bawling like a baby.

'If you're going to the airport,' he called out, 'I can get you there faster.'

'And be your little sex toy the whole way? No, thank you,' she said, shaking her head. 'Goodbye, John Grifford.' She gripped the door of her little rented speedster, the car that had gotten her in all this trouble in the first place. 'I hope you find what you're looking for in life.'

She managed to hold back the tears till she reached the bridge. What a silly woman she was. After all the things she'd been through in her life, why was this affecting her so badly? Diane had always been the strong one, using her quick wit and natural grace to keep everyone else in line: Daddy with his affairs, Mother with her drinking, and little Magdalene, always the goddamn innocent one, too young and impressionable to be stained by the cold, ugly truths of life. And yet she had ended up as the whipping girl, the lightning rod for everybody's sins: Diane the slut, Diane the gold-digger, Diane the intellectual lightweight, Diane the flighty social butterfly. As if she didn't have a heart to be broken like all the rest of them. As if she wasn't killing herself keeping them all happy, being the clown, the whore, the party girl, whatever it took. That was the one thing that had seemed different about Griff. He didn't know her from Eve and he didn't seem to want anything, except what she wanted to give. And it had really seemed as if that was OK with him, as if he wasn't going to have impossible expectations of her.

Unfortunately, he had no expectations at all, because evidently she wasn't anything more than a casual fuck to him. Of course, that was exactly what she'd wanted and received. Congratulations, girl, she told herself spitefully. You're a success at last.

Diane's last words were burning a hole in John Grifford's heart and he didn't even know why. How could anything coming from the mouth of a one-night stand make that big a difference? People said all kinds of screwy things to avoid a plain goodbye; wasn't this just one more catchphrase?

Have a nice life. It's been real. Call me, we'll do lunch. All of it was just a code, a cover for the awkwardness of an aborted relationship. Now there was a thought: what if one-night stands were the premature termination of something that was supposed to unfold gradually? Was it cheating nature to grab the sex up front and run? It wasn't that way with Star. They had sex all the time, and a kind of relationship, too, but neither of them had any illusions that it was ever going to be anything other than what it was. Convenience. A male and a female, compatible enough, mutually attracted, making use of each other's body. Warm bodies. Steaming hot ones, even.

Christ – he kicked the tyre of his own truck – what did Diane Quinton Rostov want from him? She came to him for a fuck, plain and simple. She wanted to be used by a redneck cop – the flavour of the month, something to add to her collection of exotic encounters. And then she had to get all uppity about things, angry because he told her he wouldn't see her again, as if he was some kind of dick for insinuating she was going to keep on sleeping around. What did she even care what he thought about her, anyway?

'Chief Grifford?'

Griff looked up from the blacktop, his eyes vacant holes. It was the sister. Maggie. Come on, buddy, get it together.

'Miss Quinton.' He nodded politely, acknowledging his second Quinton sister of the morning.

Her head was cocked, as if she was trying to figure out what he was doing out here.

'I'm still on surveillance,' he explained.

'Oh.' She frowned slightly and then tried to hide it. 'Good,' she said, nodding hastily. 'I'll feel better knowing that while I'm away today.'

Griff's radar was up. The woman was hiding something. Unfortunately, so was he, in the form of a whopper of an erection. For some reason Diane had that effect on him, doubly so when she was angry with him.

'That's what we're here for. Officer Cosgrove will be here any minute to relieve me.'

And he would, too, as soon as Griff called him in, half a day early for his shift, so Griff could make an emergency trip to Star to deal with his penis problem.

'Cosgrove. The young officer, yes.'

Another reaction. Interesting. What, did she have a thing for Cos and the robber both?

'Cos is my best man,' he assured her. 'Of course, he also happens to be my only man.'

The redhead laughed, her eyes twinkling in a way that reminded him of Diane. Dimly, he was aware of how poorly his brain was functioning. Something fishy was going on here and he hardly cared. 'Be careful today,' he said, feeling suddenly protective of the little sister. 'Don't take any unnecessary chances.'

'I wouldn't hear of it.' She smiled cockily. 'Chief.'

He watched her walk off to her car. It wasn't till she'd pulled out and he reached for the cell phone to call Mike that he realised something truly terrifying. As sexy as Maggie was, he wasn't thinking of her as a bedmate. She'd become off-limits, because of Diane. As if there was something serious there, between him, John Grifford III, and the black-haired demoness from Chicago.

Impossible. Absurd. Talk about being overdue for a trip to Star. His whole world was unravelling.

Cosgrove's phone went to voice mail. He had to call back twice to get an answer.

'Cos,' he barked without preamble. 'Pull your dick out of whatever pussy you're parked in and get your ass over to Heeter's. You're pulling stakeout duty again. What's that?' He listened to the man in disbelief. 'I don't give a fuck if you're in love this time. What am I, your fairy fucking godmother?'

Jumping Judas on a tortilla, he thought, clicking off the phone, was this whole island losing its mind?

It was the sea turtles that changed everything for Maggie. She was turning off the main road onto the path leading to the job site, and there they were, the tiniest little things, scurrying across the sand. Ten, eleven, a dozen of them, making a desperate dash for the sea. At first she wanted to run them over, on account of the time being wasted, but then she remembered something Ketch had said to her at one point while they were lying together in the dark.

Stop running, Maggie. Everything you need is right around you.

Just like those turtles finding their way to the sea. Home. And peace.

Suddenly she knew what she had to do. Basically, she wanted two huge do-overs. One with her sister, on account of what a brat she'd been, and the other with Ketch Walker – because, for all his idiosyncrasies, and in spite of all the craziness, Ketch had been totally up-front and honest with her as no man had been before. Plus he'd loved her body with gusto and respect, and he'd managed to protect her person through both of the break-ins, which was more care than any of her so-called boyfriends had ever been able to provide.

And besides that, she loved him.

As for the business of the necklace, what was so strange about it, really? Everybody has their special treasures, valuable only to them, that make them who they are. Most people simply forgot those simple, magic things in life when they got older, pursuing money and cars and houses instead. That's what made Ketch special. He still knew who he was and what life was for. A man like Cal Heeter would never understand that kind of commitment in life, or that kind of vision. And, if she kept on her present path, Maggie wouldn't understand any more either.

Damn, Diane's cell phone was off. She tried the house

and got no answer. There was only one thing to do now. Putting the car in reverse, she determined to go and find him, before it was too late. For both of them.

'Going somewhere?'

Shivers went down Maggie's spine. Icy fingers trailed down her body, all the way to her toes. Sweat collected on her palms. She was paralysed. It wasn't possible, not in a million years of bad dreams. Not here, not now.

'Hank,' she whispered, scarcely daring to say his name aloud.

It was him all right, leaning on the window frame, physically altered but unmistakably the same man.

'I told you, baby, you'd never get enough of me,' crooned the clean-shaven, bald-headed man with the gold earring and muscle shirt.

'What are you ... doing here?' she gulped.

'I'm a construction worker,' he replied with a grin. 'And this is a construction site.'

'And I happen to be overseeing it,' she said curtly. 'Which means you won't be here very long.'

He leaned over and stroked her cheek, his finger making a direct connection to her pussy. 'That's not a very friendly attitude, Miss Quinton.'

'Don't touch me,' she said, recoiling.

Hank shook his deeply tanned head in mock distress. If possible, he looked more masculine, more dangerous and wicked than ever. 'Baby, why are you fighting this? You know what's going to happen as well as I do. Hell, you ought to be thanking your lucky stars you're going to get it this good again.'

Out of any other man's mouth that would be a complete turnoff and a barefaced lie. Unfortunately, this man had the balls, and the cock to back it up.

'I have to go home for something, Hank. We'll talk about this later.'

'I'll go with you,' he said, and hopped into the passenger seat. 'Might as well get the lay of the land, seeing as how I'll be crashing with you.'

Maggie's heart slammed in her chest. 'You'll be doing no such thing. How can you even think that after running out on me like you did?'

Hank took her face in his hand, answering her objection with a kiss. It was a hot, tongue-probing affair, with its own unique taste and a memory that made her body ache with need.

'I forgot how sexy you were,' he murmured, unbuttoning her blouse. 'I gotta get me a look at those prize tits.'

'Hank, not here. Someone could see.'

Maggie loathed her weakness for him. With a man like this, faint little protests were like waving a red flag in front of a bull.

'Get us to a bed, then. You're the one behind the wheel.'

Maggie nearly lost traction in the sand. The wheels spun noisily, wasting valuable seconds. By the time they were out of view of the construction site, Maggie's blouse was wide open. Without waiting to undo her bra, he buried his head in her cleavage.

'Hank, I'm trying to drive.'

'And I'm trying to suck your nipple.' He made her whimper.

'Please, just wait till we get somewhere . . .'

But where? There'd be one or both cops at her house and maybe Ketch too.

He took one of her hands and put it on the crotch of his jeans. 'Feel what you do to me, sweetheart?'

Her legs went to rubber. 'I – I have to pull over.'

'Your call.' He thrust his finger between her sopping wet thighs as she jerked the car over to the shoulder and down into a shallow culvert. 'As long as you end up horizontal you're fine in my book.'

Maggie reclined her seat and lifted her ass to pull down her panties. 'Don't make me wait,' she panted, reaching for him.

'Hey, let's not forget who calls the shots here,' he reminded her, grabbing her wrist to deprive her of a shot at his zipper.

Maggie felt a stab of hot weakness as he held her wrist in the air; she was little more than a rag doll to him and they both knew it.

'I want to see you play with yourself. Spread it real wide and tell me how much you missed me.'

'May I have my hand back?' she asked pliantly.

'No, one's good enough.'

Maggie licked her lips in anticipation. They were hot and dry and slack. She had no strength in her bones at this point, except when it came to obeying the man's commands.

It was a challenge to pull up her skirt to her waist with just the one hand, but she managed it. Her hot pussy awaited the inevitable touch. He wanted her legs wide, and she did her best to brace them on either side of the seat.

'I – I missed you bad,' she shuddered, slipping her fingers down between her swollen pink lips.

'You went with other men, didn't you?'

'Yes,' she hissed, penetrating herself.

'But in your heart you knew I'd be back.'

She thought of the sleepless nights, the times she'd worn those foolish pyjamas. 'I did, Hank.'

'Do you have a boyfriend?'

He picked up on the split-second hesitation as she denied it.

'You're lying. Lean forwards.'

Maggie obeyed, blown away by the man's staggering self-confidence. If he'd been a master lover before, now he was just plain master, taking total control of her body.

'I've learned a thing or two since I saw you last, Maggie.' He pulled the shirt and jacket over her shoulders. 'Let's get these off. The bra, too.'

Her hands trembled as she bared her torso. Meekly, she handed over her clothes, everything she had left but her skirt. He tossed the outer clothes in the back seat, keeping the bra.

'Hands behind your back, turn away from me.'

'What are you doing, Hank?'

'What does it feel like I'm doing, Maggie?'

It felt as if he was putting her in bondage, using her own brassiere to render her helpless.

'Give it a try. See if you can free yourself.'

Maggie pulled at her wrists with all her might.

'Well?' he demanded.

'I – I can't,' she whispered, the confession causing little spasms all the way down to her pussy.

'Louder, Maggie, I can't hear you.'

'I can't free myself,' she declared, giving her captor exactly the kind of formal confirmation he wanted.

'No,' he agreed, taking her breasts from behind. 'You can't.'

Maggie fell against him, begging with her body for more of the man's attention.

'Like I said,' he continued, massaging her, rolling her nipples casually between his fingers, 'I've learned some things since last time. Things about women. Did you know, Maggie, that there are women, some of them right under your nose, who choose to be slaves, and

that there are men who keep them exactly that way –
naked and chained, on their knees, collared and
leashed?'

She shook her head, denying what she knew well
from books and magazines, as well as from a few of her
own late-night masturbation sessions. It wasn't something she'd ever contemplated in real life, but it was
one hell of a sexy fantasy. Mostly it was the idea of the
power, one lover surrendering completely to another.
And maybe the next night reversing things completely,
master to slave, slave to master.

For Hank, though, it seemed pretty real. And, for the
moment, his passion was more than enough to get her
off.

'You're lying again.' His fingers squeezed, just a little
tighter, bringing a throbbing to her nipples, a tiny ache,
right on the verge of pain. This, she was quite sure, was
punishment – or at the very least a warning.

'I have heard of it,' she corrected herself. 'Sometimes
I play with myself, looking at pictures.'

'Good girl,' he praised, rewarding her with gentle,
feather-like touches.

Maggie gave a little moan in response, something he
clearly liked.

'You see,' he chortled. 'You're being trained. Reward
and punishment. Girls aren't much different from dogs,
Maggie. They can be taught to sit, roll over, beg. Is that
something you'd like? A collar on your throat. My collar.
Your naked body at my feet.'

'Yes,' she egged him on, feeling dirty and hot and
shameful for so easily succumbing – and forgetting her
deep desire to go and find Ketch. 'Master.'

'I've had a lot of slaves, Maggie. It's not a game.'

'I know.' She bobbed her head. 'And I beg to please
you, master.'

Following her suggestion perfectly, Hank grabbed her by the hair in one hand, unzipping his pants with the other. He was licking his lips in sheer anticipation. Contrary to what he was saying, at least from what she was seeing so far, it was the slave who called the shots and not the so-called master. Without her playing along, he'd have nothing.

Going with that thought, she proceeded with the blowjob. Greedily she fell on his naked cock, sucking it deep and hard for no other reason than because she wanted to. Doing this in a car, seemingly against her will, tied up, was one hell of a rush. He might not get off, she decided, rubbing her thighs together, but she sure as hell would.

'I told you,' he croaked. 'You'll never have enough of me and you know it.'

Funny, she'd never realised before how much this man's sexual mystique was a product of her own imagination. He had the power only because she gave it to him. Without her energy, her feeding his ego, he really was just another dick on a string.

Maggie bit down on him, just a little.

The invincible Hank yelped. 'What are you doing, you crazy bitch?'

She popped her head up, greeting him with a long, wicked smile. 'Did master's slave do something naughty? Please let the slave make it up to master.'

Scrambling astride him, she reached down for his seat release with her bound hands, plopping him back to the horizontal, just the way she was supposed to have been. The look of astonishment was priceless. Talk about having the wind taken out of your sails.

'The little slavie-poo wants to serve her big strong master,' she said in her best cutesy voice.

Hank was eminently mountable, and in one smooth

manoeuvre she had him. She was quite proud of herself, especially as she was managing all this in an automobile, with her hands nearly unusable.

All there was left to do now was to fuck the shit out of the man, using him as she pleased and dumping him as soon as she got off. Provided she could outlast him and keep him hard.

'Oh, baby, yeah,' he was chanting, as if he still had something to say in the matter. Maggie could care less herself. This man had disappeared from her life already and he wasn't coming back. He'd realise that, too, as soon as she was done with him. And then she'd go and find Ketch and have a talk with the boy. A real talk.

The tiny lizard scampering along the window-sill had just changed his life.

Ketch was running down the road, as if all the weight had been taken off his shoulders. It was a miracle, a revelation and now, at long last, everything was perfectly clear. He was going to find Maggie at her worksite and he was going to apologise to her and tell her he loved her. Then he was going to turn himself in. It might all sound crazy, but it made perfect sense in his own mind. The apology was obviously owed. As for being in love with the woman, what else would explain his bizarre behaviour with her, his schoolboy antics? And handing himself over to the police, well, that was just the right thing to do. He saw that clearly, now that he knew he was in love. He should never have tried to right Heeter's wrong with one of his own. Besides, who needed an amulet when one had the real thing – a living, red-haired charm?

No, he would never truly possess her, but that was the lesson he had learned. Seeing the gecko on the windowsill on his way out of the house, that's what had done it. The window frame was painted yellow, and the lizard was trying to adapt. It was not a colour in its repertoire, though it had come close with a pale brown. Lizards did this all the time, but he'd never realised the symbolism. A creature must be itself, and there are times it cannot hide. The very attempt is foolish and, unlike a lizard, a man must know his true appearance.

Ketch Walker must be a man today and not a lizard.

Seeing Maggie's car on the side of the road had seemed, at first, a confirmation of destiny. She was waiting here for him, instinctively knowing he would come, knowing she must hear what it was he had to say. Then it occurred to him that she might be in trouble. Approaching at a steady clip, he heard her crying out and then he was really terrified.

Why were the windows all steamed up? Crouching behind some bushes, he made a surreptitious examination. At first he refused to believe what he was seeing through the fogged glass. How much clearer could it be, though? There she was, bare-breasted, having sex with a man – riding him, in fact, like a possessed cowgirl, her hands tied behind her back.

For a moment he felt the pain, but then it passed, leaving behind a clear, meditative peace. Clearly steps one and two of his plan were no longer necessary. Maggie would have no need of an apology or any profession of love on his part. Obviously she had another. That left only step number three, surrendering to the authorities.

He straightened himself with as much dignity as he could muster under the circumstances and returned to the road, walking slowly and deliberately towards the island's police station.

* * *

Star was standing in the clearing behind her house, gazing out at the three tiny markers. He knew from the look of her and where she was standing that they would not be having sex today. It was a remembering day, a mourning day. Tiny flowers were woven in her cornsilk hair. The homemade purple dress hung deliciously about her slender frame. One bare foot was turned out. In her fingers she twirled a single lily.

Griff stood behind her, head bowed, maintaining a respectful distance. Her children had been three and five at the time of the fire. Jimmy Jack, their father, was supposed to be watching them. Instead he was at Muldoon's, drunk as a skunk. Lisa May couldn't have been expected to keep tabs on him every minute, not with her having to work two jobs, one as a cocktail waitress in Marston and the other as a cleaning person in the Continental hotel. Everybody said it should have been her staying home instead of him, but Jimmy Jack never could seem to hold down a regular job.

Lisa May had tried to run in after them. It had taken two grown men to hold her back and even so she tore them up pretty bad. Any firefighter will tell you a trailer burns like paper. After the first two minutes, the whole thing is liable to come down. They'd sent men in, but it was too late. More than one person had reported hearing her screams all the way to Muldoon's. Jimmy Jack came stumbling in just after they brought the bodies out. It had taken every ounce of restraint for Griff not to shoot the man on the spot.

'What do you want me to do with him?' Griff had asked Lisa May.

She took one look at Jimmy Jack and spat in his face. The chief had personally and promptly escorted him off the island, making it very, very clear that if he ever returned there'd be a place for him in the ground next to his children.

Lisa May's screams were the last sounds she'd uttered. From that moment on, she fell into total silence. The fire department report indicated the blaze had started on the stove. One of the children must have lit a burner and left it. No one would ever know if it was the three-year-old or the five-year-old. Both were boys, cute as buttons.

Everybody chipped in to provide Lisa May with a decent living for a while. She used the money to build out here, where she'd lived alone ever since, with no one for company but the ashes of Jason and Jordan buried in her back yard and her occasional visits from Griff. Most folks thought she'd gone crazy, but Griff knew her heart had just been too pure to take that kind of blow.

It was the third cross that really got Griff. That one was for Jimmy Jack. She'd put it up shortly after they got the report from the Georgia State Patrol that he'd been found shot to death at a truck stop on I-75. Apparently it was a drug deal gone bad.

Now that was a woman who knew how to love.

Griff felt a little tinge of guilt, the way he always did, thinking about why it was he kept coming out here. Maybe this wasn't working any more. Maybe he ought to look at a change. Maybe his whole life was missing something. Up to yesterday it had all seemed fine, and then he'd met Diane, and now nothing made sense any more.

'Star?'

She made no acknowledgement.

'Lisa May?'

Still nothing.

'I've been thinking –' he cleared his throat '– about us.'

Now she turned, her eyes dotted with tears, a sad smile on her face. Raising herself on tiptoe, she gave him a kiss, gentle as a butterfly.

'What's that for?'

Star waved a finger, indicating she wanted something to write with. This was rare, indeed. Printed messages were for very special occasions, like the time just a few weeks after the fire when he'd come to check on her and she'd written down her new name. He never did ask where she got it from, and the woman hadn't volunteered it either.

Griff pulled a small notepad from his pocket, along with a pencil, cop-short and eraserless. With adept fingers, making the instrument look almost graceful, she wrote out three words.

'Not your fault.'

'*My* fault?' He held it out to her. 'What's not my fault?'

She took it back.

'Jimmy Jack,' she wrote this time.

Jeezus, she was absolving him for any guilt in her husband's death because he'd been the one to beat him within an inch of his life and exile him from the only place he'd ever called home.

'This isn't necessary, Lisa May. I sleep good every night, trust me.'

She took his hands, holding them to her heart, as if she was pleading. Her eyes went up to the sky and this time he knew what she meant without her writing it down. Star wanted him to ask forgiveness from God, the way she had herself.

He put her off as gently as possible. 'You know I'm not religious.'

One more time she asked for the pad. 'Find her.'

'Her who? Jeezus, woman, you know I can't stand riddles either.'

Unless . . .

No – there was no way she could know about Diane. Could she?

Star gave him a final kiss, warm but chaste. So it was true. Their sexual relationship was coming to an end.

'I'll come back,' he promised. 'You know it was never just about getting my rocks off.' Even if it was, he really did care. She had to know that.

'Her name's Diane. I'm not sure how you know, or if you knew at all. Maybe it's in my eyes. But it doesn't matter, Lisa May. She's gone. Back to a world you and I only dream of. Which means we're going to be a couple of cranky old folks together, like brother and sister.'

Where was all this coming from? Was he the same Griff for whom life was about scoring the best tail and catching the most fish? Since when had he become a downhome philosopher?

'I better get going, kiddo, before I lose my resolve.'

One last look at that body he knew so well and he was on his way back to the Jeep, feeling as young as a teenager and nearly as scared. As far as he could tell, he was walking off the edge of a cliff with a smile on his face.

And he hadn't even gotten to the really hard part of handing in his resignation.

Diane turned her cell phone on to call Maggie and discovered Maggie had already called her. There was no message, but there was only one thing it could be about. Diane had an apology of her own, too. Magdalene hadn't deserved to be unloaded upon. It wasn't her baby sister's fault that Diane's life was one disaster after another. Chalking it all up to helping everyone else was all well and good, but when it came right down to it, the only one responsible for her life was herself.

What had brought about this change of viewpoint? It was the birds. Enormous ones, with huge white wings, soaring through the pure blue sky. On the ground they looked awkward and gangly, but once aloft they were pure poetry in motion. And they were so alive, too. Just seizing hold of life. All of this place, this island, seemed full of new life. Sunsets bleeding a hundred shades of yellow, orange and purple, shimmering blue-green water, teeming with life, life everywhere, year-round, indestructible creation. No snow, no shovels, no grey and grungy sludge. How could you not look at things a new way? It wasn't too late. Not even on one's way to the airport.

Which is why she'd turned around. Things were happening for her here. In under a hundred hours on Osprey she'd unloaded more baggage than in a dozen years of therapy. Hell, she'd told her sister to fuck off and had sex with a wickedly sexy and delightfully poor police chief. What would she do in a month? A year? The possibilities staggered the mind – and warmed the libido. Not that she'd see Griff again – that was a big no-no in her game plan – but she might try to find others like him. Quirky, hunky, exasperating men, domineering but soft as putty underneath, paradoxical, impossible to read, impossible to love, impossible not to love, and, of course, built like happily aging Greek gods.

Someone like Griff, yes. Very much like him, in fact. But not the man himself. Not in a million years.

* * *

Ketch reacted to seeing the van much like a sailor encountering some terrible ghost ship he'd thought he evaded, only to have it reappear suddenly and dramatically off his bow. He was filled with utter exasperation and dread.

'It's no use,' he told Stella as the VW microbus came to a stop directly in front of him, dead centre of the yellow line. 'I'm not getting in there with you of my own volition and I don't intend to drink any more of your wine, so you might as well keep right on driving.'

'Baby, you're just no fun at all any more,' she lamented, looking incredibly fetching in her low-cut purple spandex top and white leather collar.

'I'm sorry if I wasn't sent into the world to be your primary source of amusement. As it happens, I am on my way to the police to turn myself in.'

'For what?'

'Robbery. Rape. Kidnapping. You name it.'

'My, my,' she clucked. 'You have been a naughty boy. Still, we can't have the police messing up my own punishment plans for you with their cold, nasty prison, can we now?'

'Stella, I don't find this very amusing,' he told her as she hopped out of the driver's seat in her short Spandex shorts and high white boots, aiming the rifle at him.

'I do.' She squeezed the trigger of the dart gun. 'I find it immensely amusing.'

The tranquilliser dart hit him in the thigh. He pulled it out, but he knew it was already too late.

'You can run if you like,' she told him. 'But that will only make the drug work faster. Personally, I'd advise getting in the van before you pass out. That road is an awfully hard surface to fall on.'

'You, Stella,' he informed her, 'are the most devious and evil woman on the planet, bar none.'

She laughed. He was fucked again.

'Come on,' she said as she opened the passenger door. 'I have a surprise for you.'

He was already feeling light-headed. Stumbling to the open door he threw himself on the seat. 'What is this stuff?' he slurred. 'Elephant tranquilliser?'

'It's for rhinos, actually, but I'm pretty sure I converted the dose right for your weight. What do you weigh again?'

He thought he caught himself laughing at the irony of it all just before the dart sent him to rhino heaven. He wanted the simple peace of a jail cell and instead he'd just been sentenced to a living hell, Stella Sawgrass style.

The police truck was just in front of Diane as she pulled over the bridge. It was Griff all right, signalling to turn into the police station and town office. Would he give chase? she wondered. It was a wicked thought, without a lick of common sense behind it. Hadn't she just said she didn't want anything to do with John Grifford ever again?

Then again, there was the sport of it. Maybe this time she could try and outrun him. Pushing down on the accelerator, she blew past him, leaving the unwitting police chief to choke on her dust.

For a minute he just watched her and she thought maybe he wasn't going to bother with her. Then the lights came on, and the siren too, and she felt a familiar tingle between her thighs. She was going up against him again, head to head. The trouble was, she didn't know this road all that well and she sure didn't want anyone getting hurt.

In her rear-view mirror she saw the look on his face as he closed the gap: expressionless, full of stony resolve. Unable to help herself, she opened her jeans and dug her hands between her legs. The speedometer was topping ninety and she was dripping wet, her pussy yearning for attention. Would he call for backup or handle her all by himself? Or would she yield first, pulling the car over to be apprehended? Diane found her clit. She was going to come, right here with the police chief on her tail.

Griff was gaining steadily. He was only a car's length from her bumper. Shivers raced through her overstimulated body as she thought how mad he would be and what he might do to her. Oh, God, he was pulling alongside her, pointing for her to stop. She shook her head, determined to see the game through to the end. The chief gave her a slight frown and returned his hands to the wheel. Just like that, the Jeep speeded up, passed her and pulled back into her lane. Now he was slowing down, forcing her to do the same. Wilfully, she tried to pass him, but he kept blocking her path. No matter which way she moved, he was right in front of her. He had her now for sure.

Diane's entire body ached with anticipation; her every nerve fibre was alive. She had no choice now but to pull over. The Jeep stayed just in front of her, waiting for her to come to a halt. As soon as she did, Griff backed around behind her. How small her sports car was in comparison. Just like her, next to its driver. Not wanting him to know what she'd been up to, she zipped up quick.

Griff took his time getting out of the Jeep. Her pussy spasmed of its own accord as she watched him slip the nightstick into the ring on his belt. Obviously this was for her benefit. So was the little swagger he assumed on the way to the driver's window.

'Licence,' he said crisply. 'And registration.'

Diane handed over the documentation. 'I know I did wrong, officer. I expect to pay the penalty for my action.'

He made a show of comparing her licence picture with her face. 'Get out of the car,' he told her.

'I'm in big trouble, aren't I?'

'Against the car,' he ordered. 'Spread your legs.'

Diane leaned against the hood, palms on the hot metal. Griff treated her just like a man, patting her down from neck to ankle. Except that he seemed to linger just a little longer on her T-shirt-clad breasts and shapely hips.

'You have the right to remain silent,' he said, running his hands over her denim-clad ass.

'I think you'd have to gag me for that.'

Griff pushed her feet further apart with the sides of his shoes. 'You have the right to an attorney. If you do not have one of your own, one will be provided for you. Do you have anything sharp in your pockets I should know about?'

'I have a wet pussy,' she purred. 'Is that dangerous?'

'Do you understand your rights as I've explained them?' he asked as he slapped the handcuffs on her wrists.

'Will I be abused?' she asked huskily. 'While in police custody?'

He steered her towards the passenger side of the Jeep. 'As long as you cooperate, you'll be just fine.'

'I'll try very hard to be a good girl,' she promised as he helped her up into the seat.

Griff looked at his lovely, mischievous prisoner. 'Somehow I doubt that,' he said, reaching under her shirt to cup her full, ripe breast. 'But you're nothing I can't handle.'

Diane's lips parted to relase a tiny mew – a brand new sound, one she'd developed just for this man. 'That's good,' she whispered intensely, 'because I want to be handled ... in the worst way.

Griff closed the door and went around to the driver's side. 'You're a repeat offender,' he informed her, putting the truck in gear. 'I'm going to be taking you into the jailhouse.'

'Will I be strip searched?' She leaned across to kiss his neck.

'Full cavity search,' he promised, making no effort to dislodge her. 'Followed by solitary confinement, in close chains.'

'Will I stay naked?' she wanted to know.

'Maybe if you ask real nice.'

Diane fell hungrily to his lap, trying in vain to chew at his erect dick through the khaki shorts. She'd never been hungrier for a man in all her life. Or more helpless in his presence.

'Are you trying to bribe an officer?' He pulled her up gently but firmly by her hair.

'No, sir,' she insisted. 'I just can't help myself around authority figures.'

'I can see you're going to need a lot of correction. You know, there was a time on this island when an unruly woman was dealt with on a more intimate basis.'

'How intimate?' she wanted to know. She was now trying to pull the buttons off his shirt with her teeth.

Griff took instant control, taking one of her swollen nipples between his fingers for leverage. 'I think you already know the answer to that question,' he said as he placed her in an upright position, still and ladylike.

Di nearly fainted from the sensation, the sheer power of the man. 'You mean spankings?'

'Bare-assed, to be precise.'

'I'd have to get used to that,' she said, 'if I were going to stay around here.'

'Among other things, yes.'

Her breasts rose and fell with her heavy breathing. He still hadn't let go of the tiny nub, so perfectly captured through the material of her T-shirt. 'Other things, Griff?'

'That's right. Other things. Because, if you stayed around here, you'd be mine, and I can be a pretty possessive son of a bitch.'

'I'd know I was yours,' she said, spinning out the fantasy that had been germinating in her heart since the moment she'd first laid eyes on the man.

'I'm a one-woman man, Diane. I don't share well. And I'm goddamn tough to live with. I've got opinions about everything under the sun and if you live to be a million you'll never please me.'

'Seems to me I've held my own so far.'

'Maybe,' he acknowledged. 'Just maybe.'

'All right, then. Are we going to jail, or what?'

Griff took a cigarette from a pack on the visor. 'Smoke?' He put one in her willing mouth. After lighting it, he waited for her to get a good drag before answering her question. 'How about the clerk's office instead? We could pick up a marriage licence and be hitched in seventy-two hours by a notary public under state law.'

'John Grifford, are you crazy?'

'No crazier than you.'

He did have a point.

'I want a wedding gown, and a reception.'

'You're a prisoner, you'll take what I give you and like it.'

'Is that right? Well, if you ever want to see this unholy little union of yours consummated, you'll see your way clear to doing what I say.'

Griff got a good look at the bound body in front of him. His fiancée, lover and soon-to-be mate for life. 'I think we can negotiate,' he announced.

Diane grinned. 'Good boy. Now how about we let Little Griff out for some air and see if we can't give him a nice treat.'

'He's not really all that little.' Grifford unzipped his pants. 'Maybe I ought to rename him.'

Diane suppressed her laughter and swallowed him whole. She could hardly believe how good he tasted, or how comfortable it felt to be doing this. She really had found herself, not only on this island, but in the arms and heart of this man. Diane intended to tell him that. As soon as she was done swallowing his lovely cop's spunk.

Stella waited for the young woman to pull up to the house. She was standing next to the trusty old VW, Ketch sound asleep in the back in a drugged stupor. Hopefully it wouldn't last too long, because the man was about to have a job to do. A big one.

'You're Maggie Quinton,' Stella told her as soon as the woman got out of her car.

'I am.' She looked at her curiously. 'But who are you?'

Stella shook her dark curls, contained, but just barely, under a paisley kerchief tied tight, gypsy style. 'That isn't important. What matters is that I have something for you to hold. For a friend of mine.'

'A friend?'

Rather than try to explain any more, Stella took Maggie's hand, palm up and placed the necklace in it.

The young woman examined it, stunned. It was obvious Ketch had told her all about it, down to the last detail.

'This is Ketch's amulet.' She fingered the jade elephant as if verifying its reality.

'Yes, now you know it really exists.'

'But Heeter is supposed to have it.'

'He did. I bought it back from him.'

'Ketch thought he'd never part with it.'

Stella laughed. 'Everything has a price. You should know that.'

'Yes,' she agreed. 'I should. But what's yours? I mean, why do you want to help Ketch?'

'Because I'm the one who stole it from him in the first place.'

Maggie's eyes widened. 'You're ...'

'The bitch goddess,' she said, completing the thought. 'In the flesh.'

The redhead blushed slightly. 'I'm afraid Ketch is given to hyperbole at times.'

'You love him,' said Stella, 'don't you?'

'Yes,' she replied with less hesitation than Stella might have expected. 'I do.'

'Good. Then what you need to do is go back inside and wait.'

Maggie blinked. She was obviously a very intelligent as well as a pretty girl. 'You're going to send him in, aren't you?'

'Anything's possible.'

She lowered her eyes. 'I'm not sure ... that is to say ...'

'You're not sure he feels the same for you? Trust me, it's written all over his face like a billboard. If the two of you don't connect soon, I'm going to have to do it for you.'

Maggie's lower lip was trembling. 'Thank you,' she said, embracing Stella, the makings of tears in her eyes.

'I'm the one who should thank you. For getting him

off my hands. Frankly, he's no good to me any more, now that's he's all sappy and lovey-dovey. Now go.'

Maggie didn't need to be told twice. Clutching the necklace, she ran straight to the door.

Now to awaken sleeping beauty in the back of the van, along with his new friend and temporary bedmate, the equally unconscious Officer Cosgrove. Drugging the spying cop had been one of the prerequisites to making her little plan work. He'd be somewhat miffed when he woke up, but she intended to reward him for his trouble. A witch's work was never done, Stella thought with a sigh.

Ketch had to be the biggest idiot in the world for trusting her yet again. After all that woman had put him through, all the times she'd lied to him, double-crossed him and left him in the lurch, how could he possibly think that she meant any good for him by sending him into the Heeter house for yet another go at reclaiming the amulet? If he weren't already hell-bent on his own destruction, he would probably be running full throttle in the opposite direction. As it was, though, he no longer cared who did him in or how: the police, Stella or Maggie herself, shooting him with Heeter's gun if she happened to catch him in there red-handed.

The front door had been left open, just as Stella had said. Supposedly he would find Maggie gone and the amulet close at hand. She was up to something, he just didn't know what.

'What you seek will pop right out at you this time, guaranteed.'

Naturally, he'd asked why she was helping him. According to Stella it was in order to appease her guilt and also to balance the moral scales of the universe. As if that could ever mean anything to her. Ketch took his usual route: kitchen, living room, den. The place might be his, he knew it so well. One small joy in all this was imagining the look on Calvin Heeter's face if he knew Ketch had taken such liberties in using his property. Not to mention his architect.

The search turned up dry. The last place to look was the master bedroom. Maggie's bedroom. Bittersweet memories there, to be sure. One quick eyeball sweep and he'd be gone, deflated and dejected. It was obvious this was just Stella's sick idea of a joke. Ketch turned the knob, opened the door and froze.

'It's about time,' said the red-haired dryad, happily reclining on the bed, buck naked save for the amulet around her neck. 'What's a girl have to do to get robbed around here anyway?'

He blinked hard, just to see if she'd disappear into the sunlight streaming through the window, like some apparition sent to torment ancient mariners.

'Well,' she asked impatiently, 'are you going to plunder me, or not?'

He licked his lips. The woman was far and away the most delectable sight he'd ever laid eyes on. It was difficult to decide where to look first – at her wild mane of hair, arrayed about her on the pillow, her sleek curves and full breasts or the other red thatch between her slightly parted thighs. His dick rose in response. The fact that she was wearing the jade elephant between her wondrous breasts only confirmed what his heart was already telling him. This was the woman he loved, lusted after, desired and craved more than food, water or even air.

Peeling off his clothes, not depriving his eyes of even a second of watching her, he bared his bronzed skin. Every inch of it burned with the need to touch, to belong to this woman. If he was a man at all, if he'd made it this far in life, it was only for her, in readiness for this act that was to come. He was going to take her. He was going to come inside her, not for the first time, but in a way that would open a dam, release a torrent of emotions. Delaying the gratification, just for a second, he crawled onto the bed, waiting, holding his dick in his hand. With her arms and legs she was reaching up to him, drawing him in. Ketch clenched his buttocks, feeling the fullness of his balls. His cock hung heavily, the blood pumping along its length. It was a pleasure stick, designed for this woman, made to fit her pussy.

Placing his palms alongside her upper arms, he arched his back. In one smooth motion, his eyes locked on hers, he found his way home, sinking himself to the hilt. Maggie drew in some air, her eyes widening to signal that this was exactly what she wanted. More than anything in the world. No other man, no other cock.

Ketch raised his head and took several long breaths. He hadn't expected her to lean forwards to lick at his nipples. She took them in her mouth in turn, delicately, lovingly, like a female animal honouring her mate. Ketch's nostrils flared, and he took a few tentative thrusts. Maggie moved to grasp him, her crossed ankles gripping his ass.

Ketch was thankful for the soft bed, the give in the springs. It wasn't just lovemaking, it was fucking, and were they on something hard, he'd be afraid of crushing her slender body. As it was, she moaned in pleasure each time he pushed her down. Not wanting to let him go, she clung with each withdrawal. It was a battle of wills, a fight to be in control of the having, the taking. His body was as much at stake as hers. This wasn't a casual encounter. Bones might not be broken, but souls could.

Maggie's teeth clamped into his shoulder, muffling her screams. His own cries disappeared into the hollow of her neck. Ketch could feel his cock expanding, the way it always did just before the final thrust. At the same time, he felt her muscles tighten for the inevitable counterthrust. In nature this was reproduction, the making of new creatures through the melding of the flesh of the old.

Speech was unnecessary, even the calling of each other's name. There was only the quick-time of breath, the mutual convulsions, a rhythm, in, out, back, forth, till the rest of the world washed away, past and future gone in the moment, as if they'd always known each other and always would. On and on, riding the crest and then back down together, the joy and pleasure doubled by union and trust and burgeoning friendship. This time there was no outwaiting each other, no one wondering who'd get the rope first. Unless, of course, it would be done for fun.

'I suppose,' she sighed dreamily, 'that you'll be wanting the necklace now.'

'Are you surrendering it?' he murmured, rolling onto his back.

Maggie put her head on his chest, kissing his golden, glistening skin. 'No,' she decided. 'Not yet.'

His hand went to the back of her head, stroking. 'In that case, you'll have to remain as my hostage.'

'Is that right?' She looked up impishly. 'And what if I never take it off?'

'Then I'd have no choice,' he said solemnly, 'but to marry you.'

'Oh. I was hoping you were going to torture me instead.'

Ketch lifted her onto his cock, which was already hard again. 'That can be arranged.'

'Promise?' she sighed, putting her hands behind her neck, thrusting out her breasts.

'Promise,' he agreed, taking the hint to suck at a nipple while moving her up and down on top of him.

'I love you, Mister Burglar,' she said softly, her voice suffused with pleasure.

'I love you, too, my darling dryad.'

Epilogue

Chief Cosgrove fished in the brown paper bag to see what Rayleen had made him for lunch. There was egg salad, cookies, applesauce and a note. He read the note first, which made him so hard he didn't care about the food any more. Adjusting himself in the seat of the big Jeep, the department's coveted Unit One, he kept an eye out for speeders. There weren't too many nowadays, what with the spring breakers gone and the resort project having fallen through. Most folks were shocked when Cal Heeter pulled the plug on the whole thing after just one weekend with Stella Sawgrass, but, from the little time Cos had spent in her clutches, nothing would surprise him. The last anyone had heard from the pair, they were sailing the world in a junk, both stark naked as the day they were born.

The Quinton sisters sure hadn't gone anywhere, though they weren't single any more. Maggie was a Walker, hard at work with her new husband designing a nature reserve on the far end of the island. Diane had married the retired chief and bought out Diamond Pete, turning the establishment into a somewhat classier club for both ladies and gentlemen. There were male strippers, too, now – something Diane had insisted upon, for equality's sake. Katy Sue was no longer among the dancers, having finally left Jake and moved to the big city to follow her dreams. Last they'd heard, she was working in off-Broadway shows.

It seemed everyone's life had changed, except maybe

for Star, who hadn't changed a bit, although there were a few reports of Katy Sue's ex, Jake, wandering over to her corner of the woods every now and again. In one way, if you thought about it, it was all the doing of that necklace. And one man's fierce determination to get back something he thought rightfully his.

Cos tried to adjust his dick again. This wasn't working at all. Especially with images of Rayleen popping constantly into his mind, bent over the stove in her short shorts, or breastfeeding the new baby, the little tyke latching on to those full, firm titties. It might make him a male chauvinist, but that was what got him off: thinking of having a wife like that to go home and fuck. It was what Rayleen wanted too, though he was pretty sure she'd have other things in mind when the kids got a little older, what with all the time she was spending with the forward-thinking northern sisters and their big ideas of college and such.

Meanwhile, she was all his, and, since he was the chief, he saw no reason not to head home for a little emergency relief. Turning the engine over, he drove the vehicle out of his favourite hiding spot and back onto the asphalt roadway.

'It's good to be the chief,' he said to no one in particular as he flipped on the lights and siren for no special reason.

Very good, he thought, taking out his penis in anticipation of his wife's warm and willing mouth upon the silky shaft. Seeing his gold badge always did it for the woman, making her fall right to her knees for her chief. And the best part was, he'd have the job for life. Or at least until the next young buck came along to replace him. That, or another necklace showed up.

Visit the Black Lace website at
www.blacklace-books.co.uk

**FIND OUT THE LATEST INFORMATION AND TAKE
ADVANTAGE OF OUR FANTASTIC FREE BOOK OFFER!
ALSO VISIT THE SITE FOR . . .**

- All Black Lace titles currently available
  and how to order online
- Great new offers
- Writers' guidelines
- Author interviews
- An erotica newsletter
- Features
- Cool links

**BLACK LACE – THE LEADING IMPRINT
OF WOMEN'S SEXY FICTION**

**TAKING YOUR EROTIC READING
PLEASURE TO NEW HORIZONS**

LOOK OUT FOR THE ALL-NEW BLACK LACE BOOKS – AVAILABLE NOW!

All books priced £6.99 in the UK. Please note publication dates apply to the UK only. For other territories, please contact your retailer.

MIXED DOUBLES
Zoe le Verdier
ISBN O 352 33312 X

When Natalie Crawford is offered the job as manager of a tennis club in a wealthy English suburb, she jumps at the chance. There's an extra perk, too: Paul, the club's coach, is handsome and charming, and she wastes no time in making him her lover. Then she hires Chris, a coach from a rival club, whose confidence and sexual prowess swiftly put Paul in the shade. When Chris embroils Natalie into kinky sex games, will she be able to keep control of her business aims, or will her lust for the arrogant sportsman get out of control? **The gloves – and knickers – are off in this story of unsporting behaviour on court!**

Published in November 2004

WILD BY NATURE
Monica Belle
ISBN O 352 33915 2

Talented chef Juliet Eden imagines she has the perfect marraige to Toby
– a titled aristocrat – and no need to stray from her vows of fidelity. Yet
when temptation comes in the form of rough sex with the barely
civilised gamekeeper, Ian Marsh, she finds it surprisingly easy to give in.
Naughty Juliet persuades her husband to accept an invitation to a
boating holiday, only to discover that the hosts are also offering the lure
of saucy delights. Neither Juliet nor Toby is able to resist. But once on
board, there's a clash of sexual personalities. There's a foxy minx called
Annabelle in the crew and she's got her eye on Toby. However, everyone
is determined to get to grips with the notorious rogue who calls himself
the spanking Major. **Full steam ahead for an orgasm-packed excursion!**

UP TO NO GOOD
Karen S. Smith
ISBN O 352 33589 O

When Emma attends her sister's wedding she expects the usual polite
conversation and bad dancing. Instead, it is the scene of a horny
encounter that encourages her to behave more scandalously than usual.
It is lust at first sight for motorbike fanatic, Kit, and the pair waste no
time getting off with each other behind the marquee. When they get
separated without the chance to say goodbye, Emma despairs that she
will never see her lover again. But a chance encounter at another
wedding reunites Kit and Emma – and so begins a year of outrageous
sex, wild behaviour and lots of getting up to no good. *Like Four Weddings
and a Funeral* – but with more sex and without the funeral.

Also available

THE BLACK LACE SEXY QUIZ BOOK
Maddie Saxon
ISBN 0 352 33884 9

- What sexual personality type are you?
- Have you ever faked it because that was easier than explaining what you wanted?
- What kind of fantasy figures turn you on – and does your partner know?
- What sexual signals are you giving out right now?

Today's image-conscious dating scene is a tough call. Our sexual expectations are cranked up to the max, and the sexes seem to have become highly critical of each other in terms of appearance and performance in the bedroom. But, even though guys have ditched their nasty Y-fronts and girls are more babe-licious than ever, a huge number of us are still being let down sexually. Sex therapist Maddie Saxon thinks this is because we are finding it harder to relax and let our true sexual selves shine through.

The Black Lace Sexy Quiz Book will help you negotiate the minefield of modern relationships. Through a series of fun, revealing quizzes, you will be able to rate your sexual needs honestly and get what you really want from your partner. The quizzes will get you thinking about and discussing your desires in ways you haven't previously considered. Unlock the mysteries of your sexual psyche in this fun, revealing quiz book designed with today's sex-savvy girl in mind.

Black Lace Booklist

Information is correct at time of printing. To avoid disappointment check availability before ordering. Go to www.blacklace-books.co.uk. All books are priced £6.99 unless another price is given.

BLACK LACE BOOKS WITH A CONTEMPORARY SETTING

☐ SHAMELESS Stella Black	ISBN 0 352 33485 1 £5.99
☐ INTENSE BLUE Lyn Wood	ISBN 0 352 33496 7 £5.99
☐ A SPORTING CHANCE Susie Raymond	ISBN 0 352 33501 7 £5.99
☐ TAKING LIBERTIES Susie Raymond	ISBN 0 352 33357 X £5.99
☐ ON THE EDGE Laura Hamilton	ISBN 0 352 33534 3 £5.99
☐ LURED BY LUST Tania Picarda	ISBN 0 352 33533 5 £5.99
☐ THE NINETY DAYS OF GENEVIEVE Lucinda Carrington	ISBN 0 352 33070 8 £5.99
☐ DREAMING SPIRES Juliet Hastings	ISBN 0 352 33584 X
☐ THE TRANSFORMATION Natasha Rostova	ISBN 0 352 33311 1
☐ SIN.NET Helena Ravenscroft	ISBN 0 352 33598 X
☐ TWO WEEKS IN TANGIER Annabel Lee	ISBN 0 352 33599 8
☐ PLAYING HARD Tina Troy	ISBN 0 352 33617 X
☐ SYMPHONY X Jasmine Stone	ISBN 0 352 33629 3
☐ SUMMER FEVER Anna Ricci	ISBN 0 352 33625 0
☐ CONTINUUM Portia Da Costa	ISBN 0 352 33120 8
☐ FULL STEAM AHEAD Tabitha Flyte	ISBN 0 352 33637 4
☐ A SECRET PLACE Ella Broussard	ISBN 0 352 33307 3
☐ GAME FOR ANYTHING Lyn Wood	ISBN 0 352 33639 0
☐ CHEAP TRICK Astrid Fox	ISBN 0 352 33640 4
☐ THE GIFT OF SHAME Sara Hope-Walker	ISBN 0 352 32935 1
☐ COMING UP ROSES Crystalle Valentino	ISBN 0 352 33658 7
☐ GOING TOO FAR Laura Hamilton	ISBN 0 352 33657 9
☐ THE STALLION Georgina Brown	ISBN 0 352 33005 8
☐ DOWN UNDER Juliet Hastings	ISBN 0 352 33663 3
☐ ODALISQUE Fleur Reynolds	ISBN 0 352 32887 8
☐ SWEET THING Alison Tyler	ISBN 0 352 33682 X
☐ TIGER LILY Kimberly Dean	ISBN 0 352 33685 4

BLACK LACE BOOKS WITH AN HISTORICAL SETTING

BLACK LACE ANTHOLOGIES

BLACK LACE NON-FICTION

To find out the latest information about Black Lace titles, check out the website: www.blacklace-books.co.uk or send for a booklist with complete synopses by writing to:

Black Lace Booklist, Virgin Books Ltd
Thames Wharf Studios
Rainville Road
London W6 9HA

Please include an SAE of decent size. Please note only British stamps are valid.

Our privacy policy
We will not disclose information you supply us to any other parties. We will not disclose any information which identifies you personally to any person without your express consent.

From time to time we may send out information about Black Lace books and special offers. Please tick here if you do not wish to receive Black Lace information. ❏

Please send me the books I have ticked above.

Name ....

Address ....

....

....

....

Post Code ....

Send to: Virgin Books Cash Sales, Thames Wharf Studios, Rainville Road, London W6 9HA.

US customers: for prices and details of how to order books for delivery by mail, call 1-800-343-4499.

Please enclose a cheque or postal order, made payable to Virgin Books Ltd, to the value of the books you have ordered plus postage and packing costs as follows:

UK and BFPO – £1.00 for the first book, 50p for each subsequent book.

Overseas (including Republic of Ireland) – £2.00 for the first book, £1.00 for each subsequent book.

If you would prefer to pay by VISA, ACCESS/MASTERCARD, DINERS CLUB, AMEX or SWITCH, please write your card number and expiry date here:

....

Signature ....

Please allow up to 28 days for delivery.